E-MURDERER

A JENNA SCALI MYSTERY

Joan C. Curtis

MuseItUp Publishing
CANADA

MuseItUp Publishing
https://museituppublishing.com

Cover Art © 2015 MuseItUp Publishing
Print ISBN: 978-1-77127-915-4
eBook ISBN: 978-1-77127-744-0
First eBook Edition *September 2015

"It was a bad idea to read this book three nights in a row before trying to go to bed. I 'might' have stayed up way too late because I couldn't put it down, which coming from me (I like my sleep) is a huge endorsement of any book." Sunshine Summerville, author, Koya series.

"This book grabbed my attention from the beginning and held me captive until the last page." RO G'ma, reader

"If you want a preview of just how eerie this book can be, take a look at the book trailer on Joan's website. An excellent book that brings thrilling suspense and mystery into the digital age." Linda Thompson, Host The Author's Show

"Holy crap this was an amazing book! I had to read it twice back to back cause I didn't want it to end...lol." Peggy Salkill, book blogger

"To the author: What an amazing journey that you created for Jenna. I must say going into this book you had already floored me and it is safe to safe I am still on the floor." Dawn Marie Carpintero, Blogger for Goodreads

"The story that unfolds is exciting, intense and will leave you on the edge of your seat." The Ordinary Housewife blog.

"I would recommend anyone who loves a good suspense/thriller to pick up a copy of e-Murderer, you will not be sorry you did." Jody Joy, blogger Jody's Book Reviews.

To John and to all my felines…

This story loosely describes an anonymous server similar to the one developed by Johan (Julf) Helsingius called anon.penet.fi. That server was closed down in the mid 1990's. Since then, other anonymous servers exist with the sole purpose of protecting the identity of persons sending e-mails. The server described in this book is fictitious.

My thanks to all my Beta readers, particularly Peggy Kreshel and Terri Valentine.

Chapter 1

ALL I WANTED IN LIFE was a good man and a million bucks. With my lucky penny I rubbed off a lottery ticket, hoping to reach one of those goals. I tossed the losing numbers in the trash, sipped my skinny latte, and turned on the desktop. Halfway down my Inbox, this jumped out at me.

I stabbed her to death last night. The life flowed from her body and her flesh turned sallow. Oh, the sheer pleasure of it. It's the first time I've killed anyone, BUT IT WON'T BE THE LAST.

I blinked twice and reread the message. Good grief, what a way to start the week.

"Mornin', Jenna," said Starr, tossing her purse on the desk adjacent to mine.

"Look at this," I said.

Starr peered at the screen. Her large blue eyes widened as the words registered.

"What do you make of it?"

"Not much, considering where we work. Probably just a message from some sick weirdo. What's *fi* mean?" she said, referring to the return address--anon@anon.signet.fi.

"I've no idea. It was probably meant for Dr. B—"

My words were cut short when another e-mail flashed on the screen.

The smell of blood really turned me on. I had no idea it would excite me like this. Can't wait to do it again.

Silence

Starr asked, "What are you gonna do with them?"

"Given a choice I'd flush them down the proverbial commode, but I guess I'm gonna show them to Dr. B, and then I'm gonna hit that delete button and hope to never see anything like this again."

"Good plan. I'm sure Dr. B will know what to do."

Starr's short dishwater-blond hair stuck up like a Mohawk on the back of her head as if she'd just woken up. She took out her compact to straighten her mop-top.

"The appointment charts are on the file ledge," I said, stretching high over Starr's head and adding one more folder to the stack in front of her.

I squeezed behind Starr's desk to open the blinds and let in a beam of sunlight in the hopes of giving a smidgen of life to the pitiful philodendron that drooped next to the file cabinet in our tight quarters.

"You okay?" I asked.

"Yeah, just a bit of a row this morning. Steve can be such a louse."

Yeah, right, more like a class A-number one jerk if you ask me.

"God, it's hot already. My face is redder than my Cousin Wallie's ripest tomato. This has gotta be the worst August yet." She dabbed some powder on her nose and let out a long sigh.

"Come on, surely you're used to summers like this."

She snapped her compact shut. "Nobody gets used to this. When it got this hot down home, Mama used to strip us naked and plop us in a tub of icy water smack dab on the front lawn, facing the main street in Americus. Once, we spent the whole darn summer in that tub." She sighed. "I'm sweating clean through my undies already and it's not even nine o'clock."

"I'll find you a tub if you like."

Another anonymous e-mail binged onto my screen. Starr flew to my desk to take a look.

I thought killing her would make me feel better. The little jitters inside me didn't go away, they grew worse. I'm more excited than ever. I guess that's what people mean when they talk about runner's highs and all that kind of stuff. I don't get a high running; I get a high killing. Ha!

I cleared my throat. "Do you think this might be some sort of virus?"

"Could be, but you'd better talk to our friendly shrink about it as soon as he gets in."

Starr returned to her desk and commenced digging around inside her purse.

"Changing the subject, sweet pea, you should wear a bright red lipstick. Something like this *Sizzling Flame*." She smoothed a smear of gloss across her shiny red mouth. "With your dark skin and those green eyes, red would suit you like a hog to sunshine."

I shut down my computer, not wanting to see another one of those ugly messages and began sorting through the mountain of insurance forms covering my desk. "I've never worn much lipstick."

"That's what I'm saying, honey. I'm not believing how little your mama taught you. Put on a little of this and some blush on your cheeks. For real, you gotta think about these things. You're young now, but in two years you'll face the big 3-0."

"Hey, thanks for the news bulletin and by the way, I'm not the one with a birthday. Isn't yours this weekend?"

"Touché," she said with a grin.

I took the tube of lipstick she offered and smeared some across my lips. One glance in the mirror made me shudder. I looked like a circus clown who'd eaten too much cherry pie.

"So who's on for this morning?" She picked through the files. Her long fingernails matched her sizzling red lips. "Oh boy, Mrs. Lehman is coming. She's a real trip. Who will she think she is today?"

I rubbed off the lipstick. "Last week she was an angel working on behalf of God. Maybe by now she's been promoted to the Virgin Mary."

"Jenna, you shouldn't joke about those things," Dr. Bingham's deep voice boomed behind me. "Only last week Mrs. Lehman told me she was exhausted. It's not easy being an angel."

Starr giggled. "I'd never know."

"Your first appointment is in ten minutes, Dr. B." I trotted down the hall after him with the day's folders in hand. "But, can we talk first?"

"Mr. Porter is usually late," Starr hollered after us. "I sure hope he doesn't bring his wife again this week. Last time she flat out drove me crazy with all her chatter. She ran her mouth the entire time y'all were in session. No wonder that poor man needs a psychiatrist."

I kept pace behind Dr. Bingham's long strides. When he reached his desk, he lifted a pipe and loaded it with tobacco.

"Better not light that if Mrs. Porter comes. She had a fit the last time you smoked while her husband was with you."

He shrugged and lit it anyway. Puff, puff, puff. "I'll put it out before he comes. So, what's up?"

Dr. Bingham took the files for the day and a pile of insurance forms. He put the folders on the corner of his desk, scrawled his name on the insurance forms, and puffed on his pipe, never looking up.

"We got a couple of creepy e-mails this morning. Not the usual stuff, you know, love letters or nasty words for the shrink who couldn't pull off a miracle cure. These were different." I settled across from him, smoothed out the wrinkles in my skirt, and watched his face.

His thick, dark hair flopped in his eyes, making him look more like twenty-three instead of forty-three. "Oh?"

"They talked about murder. It's probably a patient trying to get attention or something, but could you take a look? We might need to alert the authorities."

"These things are rather common, aren't they? I mean, cyber viruses and such."

"Well, yeah, and that's a possibility, but I've never heard of a virus quite like this."

"What did the e-mails say exactly?"

I shifted in my seat, not wanting to repeat the gruesome words. "Stuff about killing someone and wanting to kill someone else. How 'bout I forward them to you so you can take a look."

He nodded. "Okay, but it's probably just a prank of some kind." Puff, puff, puff.

"So, how's school?" asked my boss.

"Pretty busy right now with lots of reading and two papers due by the end of the week. I've been knee deep in research about the criminal mind."

"Could be that's why you're a bit jumpy about those e-mails. You probably need to get away from the books awhile."

I laughed. "Not much chance when you're a doctoral student."

"I thought you had a couple of suitors."

Suitors?

"Are you still dating Tim?"

I looked away and cleared my throat, hating the way he asked these personal questions, but recognizing, he just couldn't help himself. "Timothy. He doesn't like to be called Tim. And Frank. I've been going out with the two of them for about six months."

"Can't make up your mind?"

Dr. Bingham's buzzer interrupted us.

Starr's deep Southern voice said, "Your first appointment has arrived. Better put out the pipe and tell Jenna to get her tail out here. He brought you-know-who with him."

Back at my desk, when I rebooted my computer, another message flashed on the screen, making me take a deep fortifying breath before opening it.

She fought me, but I managed to slit her throat. My knife went in as smooth as butter. So neat and cool.

My God. This has to be a patient trying to push our buttons. *Or maybe someone crying for help,* my psych professor would say. Whatever. I wasn't the least bit interested in the gory details.

"That surely is a pretty red shirt," Mrs. Porter said. She stood at the reception window, opting not to sit quietly in the waiting room. "It goes good with your black hair."

"Thanks. My mother gave it to me last year." I typed, *Why are you sending these messages to Dr. Niles Bingham's office?* Then forwarding the e-mails to Dr. B, I prayed he'd have time to look at them between patients.

"You don't come from these parts, do you?" Mrs. Porter continued.

Usually I dreaded these conversations with Mrs. Porter, but today her chatter kept my mind off the disturbing e-mails.

"I could tell you weren't from these parts," she went on.

Ping went my inbox. *Message undeliverable.* Darn. I should have known. The word *Finland* appeared among all the garbled words letters and numbers.

"You hadn't done that, have you, honey?"

I looked up from the computer. "Hadn't done what?" I'd completely lost track of what Mrs. Porter was rattling on about.

"Had surgery to look prettier."

"Good heavens, no. But, if my lottery numbers would just come through, I'd let them make me a new nose, real small and dainty like Starr's." I wrinkled up my nose.

Finland? Who in the world could be e-mailing us from Finland? I clicked on our registry to do a quick nationality search for our current patients.

"Your snout is fine, my dear, Miss Scali," Starr said, emerging from the copy room with a stack of insurance forms. "My Steve already pants like a horny hound whenever he sees you." She let out a trickle of giggles.

Mrs. Porter shot me a toothy grin. "My babies put lots of weight on me. You wait, deary. You'll be round like the rest of us after you have a few younguns."

Younguns? The thought sent chills down my spine.

Mrs. Porter droned on while I continued to watch my computer screen. *No results for Finland.*

When my telephone rang, I grabbed it, grateful to get away from Mrs. Porter's chatter and those weird messages and back to more mundane things, like arguing with an insurance provider.

Ten minutes later Dr. B shot out of his office with briefcase in hand. "You'll need to reschedule today's patients," he said, heading for the door. "I've got an emergency at the hospital, a potential suicide attempt."

I raced after him. "Did you have a chance to look at those e-mails?"

"No time, Jenna. I'll have to get back to you later."

Starr and I spent the rest of the day reshuffling appointments and before I knew what hit me, it was 2:30 p.m. and almost time to leave for a meeting with my major professor. My inbox showed no more creepy messages.

Maybe the e-mailer had gone on to terrorize someone else. Time to think about school. I gathered my books.

"If Dr. B calls about those e-mails, text me right away."

She saluted. "Sure thing, hon-bun. That nut won't torment me this afternoon. You can count on that. Not gonna go near your e-mails, if I can help it. Have you deleted the others yet?"

"Nope, they're still in the inbox, but I answered one, just to see what might happen. Unfortunately it bounced."

"If you ask me, it's some bored kid wanting to stir up a little trouble." Starr shrugged as if we were discussing the latest sale at Macy's.

"What if he—or she, for that matter—really murdered someone?"

"What can we do about it?" She handed me half a Hershey bar.

I broke off a piece of chocolate—Starr's cure for everything. "I could go to the police. They'd track down the server. By the way, *fi* stands for Finland."

Starr perked up. "My lord! A person from Finland e-mailed us?"

"I'd have to find out more about sending anonymous messages, but right now it looks like it."

"This is too wild. I've heard of people writing e-books online. Maybe you got tangled up with some writer. Gosh, maybe even Stephen King."

I laughed at Starr's zany imagination.

"By the way, Jen, that V.I. Warshawski mystery you gave me was great."

"I'll bring you another one. I've read them all."

She finished munching on the chocolate before saying, "Listen, honey, whatever is going on, you need to keep your little self out of it. People get in heaps of trouble for sticking their noses where they shouldn't."

"Starr, these messages came to us."

"Yeah, by accident maybe. My mama used to tell me, 'Starr if it ain't none of your business, it ain't none of your business.' Keep out of this, Jenna."

I tossed my backpack over my shoulder. *Keep out of this, Jenna.* How many times had those same words driven me to do just the opposite?

Chapter 2

After my appointment with my advisor, I headed for the post office/drug store on the way to my one-bedroom house located in the old part of Athens. A woman in a big straw hat was weeding the flowerbeds while her husband pushed a wheelbarrow full of branches to the curb, a miniature terrier yapped at their heels. The small neighborhoods and houses with yards full of pink and purple crepe myrtles reminded me of why Georgia was my home of choice. Too bad everything I planted died. An image of Michael, bent over weeding our tiny tomato plants, flashed in my mind, and a wave of regret settled over me.

I reached the stoplight at the point where five streets joined. A mom and a toddler meandered along the sidewalk outside the deli and in front of the specialty health food grocery. Planters overflowing with bright yellow mums and deep purple irises stood next to the old-fashioned lampposts where a large bulldog stood tethered, his owner undoubtedly inside one of the shops.

I snagged the only available parking space in front of the Five Points Drug Store, which also served as a post office.

The door opened with a loud swish. Our neighborhood druggist hollered at me from the other side of the counter.

"Hiya, Jenna. Whatcha been up to?"

"School, work. You know, Artie, the usual exciting stuff."

I headed for the greeting cards to purchase one for Starr. After opening several, I selected one that read: *At your age, calories no longer count*. Inside was a picture of a gray-haired grandma, smeared from head to toe in birthday cake.

"This heat is awful. Hopefully we'll get more rain this week," Artie said.

I put the card on the counter along with the mail from the office. "I had enough rain last night to keep me a month,"

He wiped his glasses. "Yeah, that was quite a gully-washer, but what we need is a slow steady rain or my grass is gonna dry up and disappear. How's the neighborhood shrink? Still treating you right?"

"The best."

"Mrs. Bingham was in here yesterday. She's quite a busy lady. My wife says the Binghams never eat supper together anymore, what with her working at night and all. People say her PR business is doing real well even though—"

"Dr. Bingham never complains," I cut in, and put a few bills on the counter next to the mail.

"Nope, you'd not catch me complaining about eating overcooked meatloaf night after night if my wife looked like Mrs. Bingham. That'd make it worth the trouble." He posted the mail and handed me my change with a leer he quickly changed to a half-smile. "She's quite a lovely little thing, eh?"

Jealousy rose inside me. I bit my lip. My dislike for Dr. Bingham's wife probably had everything to do with the fact that she was as Artie put it, "a lovely little thing." At no more than five-two, Beth Bingham looked more like a child than a forty-year-old woman. When I'd first met her, my petty self decided her luscious blond hair had to be dyed. No one had hair that yellow unless they were two years old.

"You're a dirty old man, Artie." I pocketed my change, clutched the card to my chest, and left.

Once home, meows of all levels from growls to chirps greeted me before I got one foot inside the door.

Churchill sat atop the white side chair under the fake Ficus tree, imperceptible except for his anxious mouth. Stalin stalked along the edge of the couch with his tail high and his back arched like an upside-down question mark.

"Okay, okay." I went toward the kitchen with the cats right under my feet, and once they dug into their tasty buffet, switched on the answering machine to listen to the messages.

"Where have you been?" rang my mother's voice. "I've been calling and calling."

"It's me," Frank said. "I miss you. Call when you get home."

I dialed Mom's cell number.

"You're not there much, are you? How can you call yourself the mother of two cats when you're never home?"

I bit my tongue. "I was at work till early afternoon and then meetings at school afterwards. Today's Monday, remember?"

"It's not easy keeping up with your schedule. And what about last night?"

"You phoned last night?"

"I didn't leave a message because, well, you know me and voicemail."

"Why didn't you call my cell?"

"I did."

Oops, I hadn't checked my missed calls. "If you don't leave a message, there's no way for me to know you called." Mea culpa, it was always mea culpa with my mom.

"I left a message today, didn't I? Where were you last night?"

"I had practice. We're getting ready for the Athens Community Dance Festival next week."

"Why you'd want to take belly dancing is beyond me, and with that…"—sniff—"…teacher of yours."

"What do you mean? Quentin is a well-respected history professor at the university, not just a belly dance instructor." *Be calm, Jenna. Take a deep breath and be calm.* "And you shouldn't talk about him that way. Gay men make wonderful friends. They're not competitive and jealous like women friends." I sucked in another deep breath and willed myself to silence.

"I didn't call to talk about the merits of gay men. Lou's coming home in a month, Don't you wanna see your little sister?"

Silence.

"You could show some excitement, Jenna. She hasn't been home in three years."

"I know. It's just I never hear from her."

"What do you expect? Daily phone calls? Remember she's been in Africa and on a Peace Corps budget, no less."

"Annie Lynn Scali," someone announced in the background.

"Right here," my mother said, presumably not to me.

"Where are you?"

"I'm getting my driver's license renewed at Kroger. They're open till seven, and there's a line a mile long. Don't want to lose my place. So, can you come home when Lou's here?" she asked me as she spelled her name out to some driver's license bureaucrat.

"Mom, I'd love to see Lou. How long'll she be home?" I started to point out to my mother I'd e-mailed Lou a number of times without the ghost of a response. And I'd even suggested we Skype. I'm sure the Peace Corps could afford Skype. But in the last second, I stopped myself.

"I'm not sure. She's scheduled to arrive on August fifteenth, but that could change. Maybe you could come for the weekend...My address is Twenty-Twenty Rockhill Drive," she told the bureaucrat.

The fifteenth was the week after my classes ended. "I'll plan to do that. Incidentally, have you got that recipe for the chocolate peanut butter delight? It'd make a nice dessert for Starr's birthday on Sunday."

"I've got it somewhere. I'll e-mail it to you."

After my odd conversation with my mother, I tried Frank, but his phone rang and rang. I let out a long sigh and kicked off my shoes. When the newspaper thumped down on the front step, I raced out the door and grabbed it and the mail while texting Frank. *Why isn't your voicemail working?*

A small handwritten envelope addressed to *Resident* fell from the stack of catalogues and junk mail in my mailbox. Not recognizing the writing, but curious, I tore it open and read the typed note: *Look at today's headlines.*

My mouth grew dry. In big, bold letters the headline read: *Young Woman Attacked in Five Points Near UGA Track*. With my heart thumping with dread, I began reading, but my cell beeped, stopping me in mid sentence.

"Hiya, beautiful. Did you get my message?" It was Frank.

"Yeah, did you get my text?"

"The damn storm blew out my microcell. I'm not getting any calls. AT&T promised to get it hooked up this evening. Hey, let's go out real soon, like tonight maybe? By the way, be kind. Three boards went to the competition today, and I'm depressed as hell."

I bit my lower lip, wanting to read the newspaper, trying to make sense out of today's events. I didn't want to deal with Frank's lost billboards, but such was life. "I'm sorry about the boards, Frank."

"I'm feeling better hearing your voice. Can I come over for some special Jenna T.L.C.?"

"Sorry, sweetie, tonight is impossible. I'm working on two papers, both due this week, and I've got to get going on my prospectus. Mason gave me the go-ahead today. Maybe tomorrow, but that's stretching it," I said, omitting the fact that belly-dancing practice was tonight because Frank didn't quite approve of me swiveling my hips in public and irritating him wasn't a good plan at the moment.

"You always study. Mama would have loved you. Why can't you lighten up just this once for good ol' Frank? C'mon, Jenna. How 'bout it, please, pretty please? There's something I want to talk to you about."

"Yeah, Frank the devil, trying to lure me away from my work, right? Seriously, I can't—not before tomorrow and just to eat."

"Tomorrow's great then. I'll pick you up at seven."

"No, to save you and my cats trauma, let's meet at DePalmas."

I hung up and returned to the newspaper, which by now lay under Churchill's fluffy white body. It read:

A twenty-year-old coed was stabbed to death in her backyard on West Rutherford Street, one block from the UGA track. She had apparently been out for a jog. The article said the police had few leads. The ghastly details from the e-mails flashed in my head.

I put the paper aside. The track was a couple of blocks from my house. I walked to my front door and bolted the lock. Returning, I picked up the envelope that had contained the typewritten note.

It had no postmark.

With hands trembling, I lifted the phone to call the police. Before I got halfway through the number, I stopped. If those e-mails were from a patient, Dr. B would kill me if I contacted the police without talking to him.

I dialed his cell and got the answering service. "Is this an emergency?" the woman asked. I had no idea how to answer that question. "No, but tell him Jenna called and to call me back as soon as he can."

I paced the house for fifteen minutes. *Why the devil isn't he calling me back?*

With my head screaming stop and my heart screaming go, I dialed the police.

Chapter 3

"IMAGINE YOUR ARMS ARE SNAKES," Quentin told the three of us women dressed in leotards and tights later that night.

"To be graceful, you must pretend your arms are not attached to your body. They float." He undulated his long hairless arms like an octopus.

"I simply can't get mine a'going," Lucille complained with her arms flailing in the wrong direction. In her red leotard and black tights she looked like a fiery-haired lioness poured into a trapeze artist's costume.

"Try harder, love. Like this." Quentin demonstrated with enviable grace.

Although my eyes focused on Quentin's movements, my mind wandered. I'd gotten nowhere with the police. They didn't take too kindly to an anonymous tip, wanting to know more about me than what I had to say. Fearing retribution from Dr. B as well as the police tracing my call and ending up on my doorstep like on *CSI*, I hung up in frustration. I mopped the sweat off my brow and released a tired moan. Stopping by the office on the way to practice and finding another e-mail threw me into a tailspin. How could someone e-mailing from Finland deliver a letter to my front door? Was it the same person? A conspiracy? And what about the murdered girl? None of it made sense. I wanted to jump on a plane, head for a Caribbean island, and hide under a beach umbrella with an Agatha Christie mystery.

"Jenna," Quentin called. "Wake up. You're not driving a lorry. You're dancing, sweetheart." His strident Manchester accent struck me to attention like a slap on the face. "Sorry."

"But, Quen," panted Doreen, her tall, slender black body glistening with sweat, "My arms and feet won't cooperate today." She bent over backwards, stretching her muscles.

"Take ten," he said, and rubbed his hand over his buzz cut.

I made my way to the water cooler with Quentin hot on my heels.

"What's with you, love? When you're off, it throws everybody else. Are you pining over one of those boyfriends of yours?"

"No, it's not that. Let's go for a drink after class. There's something I need to talk about."

"Love to, but you know the others will want to come, too."

"I know, and that's fine."

After thirty more minutes of arduous hip thrusts, Quentin released us, and I headed for the heart of downtown Athens. On my way I almost ran over two undergraduates, walking and texting without a single care. By the time I pulled into a parking place in front of an early-twentieth century tavern clogged with college students and buzzing with music, regret hit me. What was I going to say to my friends? I lifted my phone to text Quen and begged off.

"No way love," he shot back.

Entering the City Bar, I spotted my friends already seated around a dark wooden table surrounded by upholstered seats. The place hummed with muffled conversations and the odor of tobacco wafted from the outside. A young man at the bar loosened his tie and winked at me. I pulled in my stomach and straightened my shoulders, a natural response when men stared at me.

"I'm sweating clean through to my undies," Doreen said, lifting her heavy mop-top from her neck. Even in her exercise garb, Doreen looked ready to pose for a *Shape Magazine* layout.

"You're wearing undies?" Lucille asked with a grin. She waved to the waiter and pointed to her empty glass. She must have inhaled the first Diet Coke.

"Ladies, don't talk about your knickers around me. Have some respect." Quentin swallowed his beer and smacked his lips. "That's the best stuff when you're hot, isn't it?" He turned to me. "What's cooking, love? You're quieter than my poor students at exam time."

I glanced at my friends. Lucille's usually overly made-up blue eyes still held a touch of mascara on the lashes, but the rest covered her lower lids. Doreen was texting on her iPhone. Quentin fidgeted with his earring and watched me.

"Some really weird things happened today at work."

Doreen's eyes widened. She clicked her phone off and returned it to her purse. "Do you mean a shrink's office kind of weird or do you mean spooky?"

"Weirder than our usual stuff and yeah, a bit spooky. Things I can't explain."

"Tell us, and you'll feel better," Lucille said, placing her hand on mine.

The waiter put another Coke in front of her while I ordered a glass of Cabernet and proceeded to tell them about the e-mail messages.

"Are you saying someone from Finland sent you those messages on your computer at work?" Lucille asked with a scowl.

"The only information I have about the person is the originating place, which happens to be Finland. All the messages I've gotten have been anonymous. I tried to respond but my message bounced."

Lucille pushed her frizzy hair off her face. "Why would a person in Finland send you e-mails, Jen? Do you know folks there?"

"No, and I don't understand why we're getting these messages. This one came while I was out this afternoon." I pulled a slip of paper from my purse with the latest message I'd printed out right before I'd come to practice.

She tried to fight me and boy did she scream. But I stabbed her in the neck to shut her up. Blood poured from her like a pig. Poor Marty. She shouldn't have fought like she did.

Quentin's scowl deepened. "I've told you a hundred times never to open a message from someone you don't know, and you should never respond to them."

"But I have to open all the messages at work, unless they're selling Viagra, of course. I don't know everyone who might be e-mailing us."

"Maybe, but once you saw this rubbish, you should've never opened another. You've probably got a whopping bad virus on your computer now."

"Whoa," Doreen said, rising. "Wish I could stick around to hear more, but I've got a hot date with the cutest buns this side of Atlanta." She reached for her purse. "See y'all tomorrow same time, same place. By the way, Quen, we've got a big sale on tomorrow at the shop. My guess all of Athens's soccer moms will be there rifling through my clothes. Bargain hunters. God, I hate them! So, I might be a tad late." She turned to me. "You be careful now, Jenna. Hear me, girl? I don't like the sound of this. Don't you get tangled up with one of Dr. B's crazy people. Okay now?"

A group of men at the bar broke out in a roar of laughter.

After Doreen left and the noise quieted, I said, "Something else happened. When I got home this afternoon, I had a note in my mailbox, telling me to look in the newspaper. Did y'all read about the murder in the paper?"

"I never read the paper," Lucille said. "It's too depressing."

"A young woman was killed near the track."

"And you think that murder might be connected with those anonymous messages and the note in your mailbox?" Quentin asked.

I nodded and drank more wine. The fruity liquid settled my jumpy heart.

"But how? The messages are coming from Finland," he said.

"I have no idea how it's happening, but it's too much of a coincidence. First the strange e-mails, then a girl is stabbed half a block from my front door and a note appears in my mailbox."

"Was the murdered girl named Marty?" Lucille asked in a near whisper.

"Don't know. The paper didn't say."

"Do you know any Martys?" Lucille persisted.

I shook my head.

Quentin leaned in closer. "Have you gone to the coppers?"

"Big help they are. I called them right before practice, and they acted like I was some sort of lunatic."

"I don't like this one bit," Quentin said. "If the bugger who killed that girl knows where you live, you might be in danger. Did you tell the police that?"

"Well, not in so many words."

Lucille touched my hand. "What did you say to them, hon?"

I shrugged. "I told them what happened with the e-mails and the note and all, but I didn't leave my name. I didn't want them contacting the office."

"Why in bloody hell not?" Quentin asked. "I'd think that's the first place they should look."

"If it's one of our patients, I'd like to talk to Dr. B first."

"Why?" Lucille asked.

The noise in the bar had picked up again, and I could barely hear.

"I would hate for the cops to come snooping around our office without first warning Dr. B. Y'all know how adamant he is about confidentiality and protecting our patients' privacy. He'd fire me for sure, and I can't afford to lose my job. Those messages on the computer came through our e-mail. I can't go to the police without the doctor's okay. Besides, if the killer is a patient, Dr. B might know who the person is. Maybe someone said something in therapy. Some threat." I was babbling, but there was no way I'd put the police on Dr. B's trail without first talking to him.

"But your life might be in danger, and it was your mailbox where this bugger decided to drop off that note," Quentin cut in, his voice shrill.

"You want me to spend the night with you, honey?" Lucille asked.

"You're sweet, but you've got Ralph to worry about." The image of Lucille curled up on my couch with two fat cats on her stomach while I dreamed about a killer who liked to watch people die, popped into my head.

"I can handle Ralph," she said, sitting up straighter and glancing at her watch. "Speaking of the devil, I'd better hightail it home. He'll be looking for a snack before the Braves game ends. Sure you're gonna be okay?"

"Really, I'll be fine, but thanks for listening."

Lucille rose. Her orange burlap purse clashed with her red leotard. "Call me anytime, sweetie." She tucked her bag under her arm. "Ralph or no Ralph, I'll come."

Her smile didn't convince me. Lucille was as dedicated to Ralph as I was to my cats, and that's pretty darn dedicated. "Thanks, Lucille."

"Seriously, love," Quentin said, "I think you should march straightaway to the coppers and tell all. Make them listen. I know how much you respect Dr. B and I know how hard-headed you can be—like all the time—but you can't sit back while some lunatic goes around killing people."

"We don't know the messages and that note are related. Starr thinks it's some practical joke, somebody testing the limits of the Web or maybe someone writing an e-book. Who knows?" I finished my wine. Talking to my friends had convinced me of one thing. I had to make Dr. B see how serious all this was.

"The Web is full of crazies. More and more people are abusing the system for the fun of it. Maybe you ought to talk to that computer geek at the university. There might be some way to block these anonymous messages."

"Michael might know something too," I said, thinking aloud.

"You don't need to be asking Michael. He's your ex remember, not your BFF."

I gave Quentin a slight shove and expelled a long sigh. "I'm more worried about the note in my mailbox. Someone had to put it there. That really freaks me out."

He took the last swallow of beer as we rose to leave. "I wish you had a dog with huge fangs instead of two fat, happy felines."

"My neighbors are close by. I'm sure I'll be fine." My voice wasn't convincing even to me.

"And you refuse to go to the police?"

I shook my head. "You should have heard them on the phone today, Quen. They asked all kinds of questions about me—who I was, did I know the girl, what did I know about the murder. Stuff like that."

"But, Jen, they had to find out if you were legit."

"I'll call that guy at the university tomorrow." I managed a half smile. "It was good talking about all this. Starr, much as I love her, turns everything into a lesson from her granny."

When we reached my car, Quentin said, "You've got a shrink under your nose every day, and you talk to me? I should send you a bill."

I retrieved my keys. "See you tomorrow."

"Oh, no you won't. I'm going to escort you home."

"You don't need to do that," I said, but nearly hugged him on the spot. Right now I sure didn't relish the idea of walking into my dark house alone.

"Hey, it's nothing. Just wait till I get to my car."

Under the dim streetlights Quentin snaked through the mob of students to his 1970 Dodge Dart station wagon with one headlight.

When we turned onto West Rutherford, my stomach lurched. I crawled along the road, glancing from side to side, searching for where the dead girl lived. Quentin's one-eyed car moved closer to mine. I came to a dark one-story house where yellow crime-scene tape gleamed like a bright-colored ribbon, completely surrounding the yard. Realizing how close the murdered girl had lived to my house caused my stomach to do another quick somersault. Who could have killed her? The faces of several patients ran through my mind. I squeezed the steering wheel and drove on.

Quentin parked at the curb in front of my house and hopped from his car. "Want me to pop in and case the joint?"

"No, Sherlock, you go on. The cats will protect me. Thanks, Quen. You're the best." I hugged him and turned to go inside.

He shifted from foot to foot, waiting until I unlocked and opened the door.

"Let's just have a little look about," he said, pushing past me.

Once inside, the first thing I noticed was the absence of cats. My heartbeat quickened.

"Churchill, Stalin?"

A light shone from the kitchen. I hadn't turned on a light before I left this evening. We tiptoed toward the faint glow. Everything looked as I'd left it. Even my juice glass remained on the edge of the sink. I nearly jumped out of my skin when Stalin rubbed against my leg.

"My gosh, I'm getting paranoid." I lifted the squawking cat and scratched him behind the ears.

"Maybe so. But that's better than being daft." He opened the backdoor and peered outside. "Looks clear to me, love."

He followed me into my bedroom where I found Churchill curled on my pillow. As a precaution and to ease the tightness in my gut, we looked under the bed, in my closets, and in my bathroom. All proved empty.

"Are you satisfied?"

He headed for the front door. "For now, but if you hear the slightest sound tonight, call me, you hear?"

I hugged him goodnight. How lucky was I to have such a friend? Returning to my bedroom, I snuggled up close to Churchill and closed my eyes. Clearly the threatening e-mails caused me to accidentally turn on that light. My cats were smart but not smart enough to turn lights on and off. I did it and that was all there was to it.

My tired body sank into a deep, fitful slumber.

Chapter 4

THE SUN WOKE ME ON Tuesday morning before my alarm buzzed in my ear. I stretched my aching limbs, knocking Stalin off the bed with a thud. Any killer who wanted to do me harm could've been in and out and all about, and I'd have never even opened my eyes. I leapt out from under the sheets, quickly dressed, and drove to West Rutherford Street, determined to find out if the dead girl was indeed named Marty.

In the daylight, the house didn't seem as spooky as it had the night before. In fact, the little one-story, wood-frame structure with green shutters looked as if it belonged to somebody's grandmother. A few weeds grew in the flowerbeds, but at least discernible beds existed. That was more than I could say for my yard.

Two patrol cars stood in the small driveway. Next door, a gray-haired lady sat in a rocker on her porch, apparently enjoying the excitement of the murder as well as a chance to sit outside before the oppressive afternoon sun hit.

I parked in front of the old woman's house, reached into my glove compartment for a notepad, and mounted the steps.

"If you're selling something, I got no money," the woman's gruff voice called out.

"I'm not selling anything, ma'am. I only want to talk to you for a few minutes."

"Are you from the newspaper?"

When I reached the front porch, I could see the woman's crinkly face, soft like an overripe apple. Thick glasses pinched the end of her nose. Her stockings were rolled down to her ankles, and she wore a thin short-sleeved dress.

"My name's Jenna," I said, deciding not to share my last name. "Did you know the girl who lived next door?"

"Knowed 'er all 'er life," the woman said. "This was 'er granddaddy's house. He passed on come three years now, I expect."

The woman's light brown eyes looked huge behind those thick lenses. Sweat trickled down her face. "Marty moved in several years ago. She was studying at the university. She'd bring me cookies now and again, poor dear."

My heart froze and my throat tightened at the mention of the dead girl's name. "And you're Mrs.—"

"You say you're from the paper?" The woman eyed me.

"Yeah, the *Flagpole*," I said, looking away so she wouldn't notice the lie in my eyes. "We're thinking about doing a feature on the girl." I settled on the front step.

"My name's Arlene Sosbee. That's S-o-s-b-e-e."

"Thanks." I jotted the name on my pad. "Tell me about Marty. Did she have many friends?"

Mrs. Sosbee wiped her forehead with a ratty-looking handkerchief. "Quite a few as I recollect. She was a nice girl. People liked 'er. I guess she'd be about nineteen or twenty by now. Every evening when it cooled down, she'd go out to jog. Ran from here and up at the track. I worried about 'er going out after dark. I knowed something like this would happen. I tolt 'er often enough. There are too many dangerous sorts lurking out there, not like it used to be. Used to we could walk the streets anywhere in town without a single thought. When my younguns were little, they walked clean to downtown from here, and did I worry? Not a once. But Marty fretted about 'er weight even though she was as skinny as a polecat. I reckon it was too hot to run before nighttime, tho'."

"Did Marty live alone?"

"She had a boyfriend—some long-haired fella who played a guitar and smelled like paint. But that didn't last long. He moved out some months ago, I reckon. Thank the Lord if you ask me. Since then she's been alone. I watched out for 'er. I knowed Sam'd want me to. Sam was her granddaddy. We was in grade school together, over there at Barrow. He passed on right 'fore Marty moved back."

"The night she was killed, did you hear or see anything unusual?"

"The police asked me that, and I've been racking my brain. I went to bed early, so I reckon it happened after I was sleeping. They say she was kilt about nine-thirty or ten. I heard the Williams' dog bark and keep barking. The Williams live up the road, the other side of Marty. He's a dentist. Hadn't lived there long. That dog'll bark at everything, so I never pay it no mind. Must've been some fool kid on drugs that did it. That's what I figure. I seen that big shiny car again. But it's been here before." She slapped her arm. "The bugs have been awful this year. I guess it's 'cause of all the rain we been having, don't you reckon?"

"Probably," I said, biting my tongue to keep from smiling. "Do you remember what kind of car it was?"

"Lordy, child, I couldn't tell you one car from another. It was real big and shiny and black."

"When did you see it?"

"Now let me think." Arlene Sosbee looked off in the distance, as if the answer lay across the street in the neighbor's hedges. "Maybe a few weeks back," she said. "It used to be here a lot, but I hadn't seen it for a spell till yesterday."

I supposed Mrs. Sosbee told the police about the car, and I wondered if it had any significance. Of course, if she had told the police, who knows if they'd take her seriously. They probably treated her—an old busy-body lady—with as little interest as they did me. "Who found Marty?"

"I think it was one of 'er friends done found 'er. She used to jog with them college girls. A couple of 'em came by with Marty whenever she brung me cookies. Nice girls. I guess when she didn't show up, they came 'round looking for 'er."

"What's her full name?" I continued to write notes on the small pad like a dutiful little newspaper girl.

"Martha Meeks. But everybody knowed 'er as Marty. Poor dear. I still can't believe it. Oh, yeah. One of 'er friends was Courtney Jenkins. I remember 'er 'cause 'er mama used to go out with my Ronnie back when they was at Athens High. Always thought they'd hook up. But, they never——"

"Do you know where I might find Courtney?"

"Dunno. Her mama lived on Boulevard, but that was twenty years back.

"That policeman told me they'd be out today," she continued. "I hope so. They're making all kinds of noise. You should've seen this place yesterday. There must've been twenty cars here."

And you loved every minute of it.

I rose. "Thanks, Mrs. Sosbree."

"You're sure welcome, honey. I don't take your paper, so you send me a copy, hear?"

"Yes, ma'am." I waved to her.

By the time I closed my car door a trickle of sweat ran down my back, both from the heat and from the uncomfortable feeling settling over me. The person sending those deadly e-mails knew Martha Meeks well enough to refer to her as Marty.

I entered the office at about 8:15 a.m. and found Starr on the telephone. She rolled her eyes to signal she was involved with a chatty patient. Because no one was waiting to see Dr. B, I waltzed directly to his office.

I found him hunched over his desk, puffing on his pipe, and studying a chart.

"Do you have a minute?"

"Sure. My first patient isn't due till eight-thirty."

"Did you read those e-mails I forwarded to you?"

Dr. Bingham's eyebrows lifted. "Sure did. Pretty eerie, I'd say. But nothing to——"

His buzzer sounded and Starr said, "Tell Jenna Frank's been calling. Said he'd texted her, and she didn't answer. Told me he'd pay me big bucks if I could track her down." It was my turn to roll my eyes.

"Hadn't you better take care of that?" Dr. Bingham asked and bumped out his pipe tobacco into an ashtray.

"He can wait a few minutes. This is more important." I told him about the mysterious note in my mailbox and my visit with Mrs. Sosbee. A frown creased his brow while I spoke.

"Have you gone to the police?"

"I called anonymously yesterday afternoon, but because I didn't give them my name, they weren't much help nor could I be of much help either, for that matter."

He refilled his pipe and took his time lighting it. Puff, puff, puff. Finally he asked, "So you think the person who wrote those e-mails had something to do with that girl's death."

"I'm not sure, but the last message was pretty detailed. He even mentioned the girl's name."

"The messages came from Finland, right? That's a rather long commute for murder. Wouldn't you say?"

"I haven't figured that out yet." I squirmed. Another trickle of sweat meandered down my back. A wave of anger passed over me. *This nut had been to my house*, a voice in the back of my head said. I took a deep, calming breath, and focused on Dr. B's words.

"Perhaps the e-mail messages and the note in your mailbox are from different people and are totally unrelated."

"I suppose it's possible. But is it likely?" said my naughty, rebellious self.

He rubbed the edge of his chin. "Have there been other messages?"

"I haven't checked today. Starr stays off my computer if she can help it. By the way, I'm going to call a computer guy at the university to see if we can get some sort of block against anonymous messages. My guess is we can at least filter them somehow."

He leaned back in his chair and glanced out the window. Pipe smoke filled the air. Then he faced me. "I understand your concern, Jenna, especially after that note appeared in your mailbox." He cleared his throat. "Let's try to ferret this out rationally. I'll take another look at those messages in view of what's happened to that coed. We need to discover why the messages are being directed to us. If it's a patient, maybe he or she is trying to get attention or calling for help."

"So you think it could be a patient?"

He shrugged. "Let's not speculate that far yet. I need to study those messages more carefully. Can you forward them to me again, including the one you got last evening?"

"Sure, I'll do that right now."

"Good. But I have to warn you, you can't let your healthy, young imagination run away with you. This isn't one of your class projects. There may be a simple and logical explanation to all this, and it could be totally unrelated to the murder. We wouldn't want to get in the way of a police investigation, you know. Clog up their work with irrelevant information. As I see it, some hacker sent these messages across the Internet to get attention, someone from Finland. From what I understand, this kind of thing is quite common. The note in your mailbox could've been from anyone. Maybe someone heard about those e-mails we got yesterday, who knows? I don't mean to be too relaxed about this, but I don't want to overreact either. And I sure don't want the police snooping around here and asking questions about my patients. You know how I feel about confidentiality."

"But do you think one of our patients could've killed someone?" My voice squeaked, sounding nervous and high pitched.

"Who's to say? But I really doubt it. None stand out in my mind as homicidal. Try and relax. We'll sort this out. I'll take a long look at those e-mails. That might be a place to begin."

His buzzer announced the arrival of his appointment.

"Are you feeling any better?" he asked, walking out the door with me.

"A little," I said with about as much conviction as a student walking into finals unprepared.

Back at my desk I turned on the computer. Messages filled my screen, including one from my long-lost sister, Lou.

Mom tells me she called you. Would love to see you while I'm home. Planning to hit the outlets in South Carolina. Wanna go? I'm sick to death of my clothes and the food here. OMG! BAD! Can't wait for some good ol' Southern fried chicken. Let me know. Love, Lou

Hiya Lou
You're on. I could eat a barrel of fried food but am always watching my waist. I'll save up for you so we can pig out. Text me when you get home. It's been too long. LOL Jen

Images of my sister climbing Stone Mountain in the seventh grade popped in my mind. She'd tried to get me to join her while she hung from a rope, daring me with everything from quarts of butterscotch ice cream to free little-sister slave services for a week. I passed on both, preferring to keep my feet squarely on the earth. God knows what kinds of risks she'd taken since she'd been in the Peace Corps. I smiled thinking about fried food and the outlets, two temptations Lou knew would jingle my bell.

Lou's surprise message brought me back to myself. How would Lou respond to these e-mails? I could hear my little sister's voice: *Jen, give it a rest. You don't know fear till you face a mamba snake or stumble on a herd of elephants. You need to toughen up, girl.* I relaxed, smiled inside, and worked my way through a stack of insurance forms.

When a new message from Finland popped up in my inbox, I blinked twice and steadied my heart.

Glaring at me as if written in blood were the words: *Jenna, you're ignoring me and that makes me unhappy.*

Chapter 5

I PACED OUTSIDE OF DR. B's office until his patient left, determined to catch him before the next appointment arrived.

"Look at what I just received."

He glanced at the e-mail. "How do you think this person learned your name? We don't mention staff names on the website, do we?"

"No, we don't. But, look, it came from Finland as well. Obviously someone wants us to think they're in Finland when they're not."

He glanced at the clock on his desk. "Look, Jenna, I'll call my attorney after this next patient and see what he recommends. Don't panic yet. I still want to hold off going to the police if we can. There might be a logical explanation for all this, like I said. Maybe someone heard about these anonymous e-mails and is trying to scare you. Did you copy the others?"

I handed him the stack before leaving his office. My thoughts were more muddled than before.

* * * *

Later that night, I rolled into the DePalma's parking lot at 7:05 p.m. to meet Frank. Cars lined the curb next to the edge of the building and filled the huge lot. More piled in behind me, forcing me to snag a parking place next to the dumpsters.

I snaked between people like a Zombie, my mind running through the events of the previous two days. I couldn't shake the sight of the e-mail with my name on it. Fortunately I'd heard nothing more from the anonymous e-mailer for the rest of the day. A reprieve or silence before the storm? A chill ran up my back at that thought.

Frank sat outside in the sweltering heat, puffing on a Marlboro. Spotting me, he smashed out the cigarette.

"Boy, I've missed you." He rose and gave me a kiss on the cheek.

I settled across from him. "You saw me Sunday. It's only been two days."

"Two long, lonely days," he answered with a lopsided grin.

I raised my voice above the noise. "Sure hope you put our name on the list. This place is nuts."

Frank reached over and took my hand. "We're good. No worries." He paused. "I've been under a hell of a lot of pressure lately. Why didn't you answer my texts and calls?" His voice held a touch of anxiety.

The hostess called Frank's name. We walked inside.

"Didn't check my messages. Guilty as charged," I said once we settled in the booth. "You're not the only one under pressure."

He leaned back and grinned. When Frank smiled, he looked like a little boy. My heart fluttered. "I know. School and work. It's tough," he said and then asked, "Hey, how about a drink? I'd say we both could use one."

Frank wore a plaid shirt I hadn't seen before. A few pens and a package of cigarettes protruded from the pocket. His round baby face contrasted with the sharpness of his eyes—"They're ice blue," he'd told me when we first met.

"The usual, please," I said.

The chatter of people nearly drowned out the nasal-sounding country song playing in the background.

Frank motioned to a waitress wearing blue jeans and an apron splattered with grease. She had huge floppy breasts and long reddish-permed hair.

"Bring me a Bud Light, and the lady will have a glass of Merlot."

"Sure, cowboy." She smiled a yellow-toothed grin and disappeared.

"So what's going on, Frank?" I hadn't told him about my crazy life at work, but he seemed too jumpy to lay that on him quite yet.

"It's been unbelievable. Business is booming. Of course the damn City Commission keeps putting restrictions on outdoor advertising." He glanced around the restaurant and leaned closer to me. "I'm calling in my chips every time I turn around. I must've been on the phone two hours today with the mayor, trying to make her see how important our business is to visitors. These politicians have such a narrow view of the world. Everything's all about green. They call outdoor ads eye pollution. Ridiculous." He reached for the cigarettes, but stopped himself. "To make matters worse, Larry is riding herd on me to sell, sell, sell."

"Here ya go," the waitress said, and put the drinks down. "Y'all ready to order?"

"We'll let you know," Frank said. Floppy breasts stuffed her pad in her apron and moved away.

I reached for Frank's hand. "Gee, Frank. There must be some weird karma going around."

"What do you mean?"

"I've been getting these strange e-mails and, well, at first we ignored them, but then they persisted and other things started happening."

Frank downed his beer and motioned to the waitress for another. "Well, whatever the karma is, I hope it stops." He rubbed his arms as if a chill ran up them.

"Frank, what else is bothering you? I mean, you seem so edgy, like you're about to jump out of your skin."

He looked away and clenched his fist. "You read me so well." He sighed. "My mom used to get these stupid sweepstakes things. You know, *Reader's Digest* and Publisher's Clearinghouse crap."

"Get rich quick as long as you buy our magazines, right?"

"Yeah, she spent hours filling out the damn entry forms. She always ordered magazines even though they said it didn't matter. I'm still getting these ads and some other stupid stuff." He blinked several times before continuing. "This week another notice came. Usually I trash them, but her name was in big bold letters at the top—VALERIE SUTTER—with a gold seal announcing she'd won a million bucks. Of course it was a gimmick, but I stared at that name, and I lost it." He tossed his head sideways to avoid my seeing his tears.

I drew his hand to my lips. "Oh, Frank, I'm so sorry." I kissed the top of his knuckles.

He sniffed. "I haven't told anyone about this. Everybody looks at me like I should be over it by now. After all, she's been gone since last December."

"I don't think you ever get over losing someone close to you."

Frank lifted his face to mine, blinked and stared at me, his eyes dry now. "It's been six months, hasn't it?"

"What?"

"Our first date. You know at Starr and Steve's party on the Saturday after Valentine's."

"Of course, but what's that got to do with your mom?"

"I guess I'm feeling sentimental, that's all."

I sipped my wine, recalling Starr's words when Frank and I started dating—*Frank is the best catch in town. Wear a little makeup for a change, Jen.*

"You were a bit uncomfortable on that first date, weren't you?" he said.

"Me? What about you? All you did was talk about your work. You told me virtually nothing about yourself. You didn't even tell me about your mom till we'd been going out a month."

He bit his lower lip. "Give me a break. I hadn't dated much. Besides, it wasn't easy talking about her to anyone, especially someone I didn't really know."

"Maybe, but you were like a man hiding behind a wall."

"No more." He rubbed the back of my hand with his thumb. Something was definitely up. "You blasted through that wall. Knocked it clean to the ground. That's what I'm getting at, Jenna. You've been great for me. I don't tell many people these things. You know how I am, but, well, you're special. I want you to understand me and support me. You mean so much." He lowered his voice. "When we're together, geez, it's heaven. You know, really together."

Heat rose up my neck. "Thanks, Frank." I sipped more wine and looked away from his intense eyes.

"Anyway, we've been together long enough for me to know you're the best thing that's ever happened to me. We're both single, and I'm not getting any younger."

"Good gosh. Don't be stupid. You're just a baby."

The waitress slipped a fresh beer mug in front of him. He released my hand and winked at her with a half grin—the same grin that made me tingle inside. The poor girl almost tripped when she backed away.

"But look." He pushed his long golden hair back to show the early stages of a receding hairline. "I'm losing my hair. Every day one more falls out. I need to think about my future. I want to get married and have a coupla kids before I'm too old to play touch football. I need someone to share my life with. Someone like you."

So that was it.

"You know where I stand on that count." I turned away from his razor-sharp stare.

He pulled my hand back toward him. "Listen. I've never felt this way about anyone. I think about you all the time. I'm making a decent salary. I wanna buy a house over near Green Acres. One of those nice two-story jobs with a backyard. We could fence it in, even have a dog."

"Frank, you're really sweet, and I appreciate what you're saying. But you know how uptight the subject of marriage makes me. I'm not ready for that, not after what happened between me and Michael—"

"I'm not Michael," he cut in.

Silence.

"I'll think about what you've said. That's all I can promise." *Furthermore, what about Timothy?* Before my face gave away my wanton thought, I added, "Right now I'm starving."

"That's all I want. Think about it, okay?" He looked down at his hands holding mine. "I can't express very well what you mean to me. I didn't date much while my mom was alive. After my dad died, she depended on me a lot. She didn't like me going out."

"How old were you when your dad died?"

"Fifteen. I was in high school. I dated some before she got sick, but the girls were so immature and maddeningly stupid. You know the type. I never really found anyone I could hang with. But then you came into my life. I don't want to lose you. Try to understand."

Maybe I hadn't been fair to Frank.

We ordered dinner and spent the rest of the evening talking about school and work. Frank asked no more questions about my mysterious e-mails, and I shared no more information.

He had a business trip coming up at the end of the month and wanted me to go. I begged off, telling him about my sister's homecoming.

When he walked me to my car, he said, "Want to come over for a little while?"

I laughed and gave him a kiss on the cheek. "You never give up, do you?"

He pulled me close enough to feel his heart beating against my chest. "You're driving me crazy. But I can wait."

I reached home just before 9:30 p.m. The cats greeted me with meows that said, "I'm hungry." I fed them their nighttime snack and then dialed Michael's number.

"Am I disturbing anything?" I asked.

"Nope, just getting ready to crash. It's been a long day."

"Tough day at work?"

"A total circus. I nearly completed a million-dollar contract, but it fell through at the last minute this morning. I've been trying to recover ever since." From his slurred speech I'd bet my life's savings a bottle of whiskey was easing his disappointment.

"Sorry, Michael. But the world is full of live wires anxious for your financial smart tips." Someone once told me he could sell fifty cents for a dollar, and indeed his winning personality first attracted me to him.

"They're not beating down my door. And you, did your major professor give you the go ahead on your research?"

"Sure did. Now he expects a proposal by the end of next semester. Speaking of proposals, I got one tonight."

"Ah, so that's why you called. You want me to tell you what to do."

"Don't be a jerk. I just wanted to talk." Men could be maddening. Did he really believe I wanted him to tell me what to do? Give me a break.

"Is this one of the guys you've been dating a lot lately?"

"Yeah, how do you know about them?"

"I have my sources. Do you love the guy?"

"I'm not sure. He can be wonderfully sweet, and he does seem to care a lot for me. What's more, as he pointed out, he's a good catch."

"Either you love him or you don't. 'A good catch' doesn't sound like a reason to get married to me."

"You're not prejudiced, are you?"

"Of course. I'd be happy to see you die an old maid. But I also have to be realistic."

"Me, too. Starr never stops reminding me of my advancing age. Nobody will want me once thirty hits me." I was rubbing the top of Churchill's head with my foot.

"Don't be an idiot. You're more beautiful now than you were at seventeen when we met. And Starr knows it. If you hadn't been such a goodie two-shoes, we'd still be married."

"You mean if I hadn't insisted that you quit drinking and sleeping around?"

"Come on, Jenna."

"I'm sorry. That's past history."

"You know what I think?" Michael asked.

"I can't wait to hear."

"I think you're in love with that shrink you work for and no one else is gonna suit you."

Anger boiled up inside me. "Who's being the idiot now? Dr. B is happily married. I respect him, but I sure don't love him, for God sakes. There's a huge difference between love and respect, in case you hadn't notice. You've got a lot of nerve bringing Dr. B into this. After what you did, I'd never, I repeat, *never* consider getting involved with a married man."

"Hold on, sweetie. I didn't mean to upset you."

Hearing the tinkle of the ice cubes against his glass, I bit back a sarcastic comeback. We fell silent.

Finally I said, "Michael, have you thought about trying to give the stuff up?"

"Don't start on me again. I've been there, done that, and it didn't work. I don't need any more lectures."

"But you didn't give it enough time."

"I was miserable. I won't put myself through that kind of shit again. Listen, weren't we talking about you? Tell me about this dude. What's he do?"

"He's a talented business executive. Pretty ambitious. He's got zillions of connections because he's lived around here all his life and knows most everybody. He's also a real looker according to Quentin—light blond hair, blue eyes, tall, a body to die for. He brings me flowers and opens the car door for me."

"Sounds perfect to me. Too good to be true. Better grab while the grabbing's good."

"Maybe so."

"Seriously, how does he treat you?"

"He's very affectionate, but he's also a bit demanding. Wants me with him all the time. I think he's even jealous of the cats, if you can believe that."

"Be careful."

"I'm not sure I've given him a chance, Michael. I mean..." Putting into words the battle fighting inside me wasn't easy. "I push him away whenever he gets close. I'm still afraid."

"Gosh, Jen. I don't know what to say."

"Sorry might be a start."

Silence.

"I hurt you a lot, didn't I? It kills me to think about it, but I couldn't help myself. If my mother hadn't been such a bitch. And you know how my dad drank. Of course, I've got problems. Who wouldn't with a childhood like mine? If I could erase what happened to us, believe me, I'd do it in a minute, but—"

"Yeah. Well, that's over. Now it's my chance to put my life back together, and for some reason I'm pulling away."

"Come on. All this couldn't be my fault."

"It's nobody's fault, only the way things are."

I propped the phone under my chin and began tugging off my jeans.

"Listen, Michael, I didn't actually call you to talk about this. Some strange things happened at work yesterday. I got these disgusting e-mails on the computer at work. What do you know about sending anonymous mail?"

"That was a quick subject change."

"Maybe, but that's really why I called, and I thought you might have some ideas."

"There's a guy in Finland who specializes in anonymity. He'd give up his life before he'd divulge a client. At least that's what I read in *Wired*."

"God, did you say Finland?"

"That's the place. He has a site that guarantees anonymity. As far as I know it's the only one. So, if you want to send an e-mail and you don't want it traced, he's your man."

"You don't have to generate the message from Finland?"

"The article explains how it works, and I don't remember everything. But, more than likely his clients can initiate their e-mails from anywhere."

"Do you have the article?"

"Someplace. I'm sure I can dig it up. I'll send you the link. What are these messages? Some type of obscene stuff?"

"Weird's more like it. I'd appreciate the article."

"No problem."

Turning off the phone didn't erase Michael's face from my mind. Clearly, I kept in touch with him because breaking away hurt too much. Okay, so it wasn't healthy, but what can I say? Starr told me on more than one occasion, "You ought to put a contract out on that slime ball." The problem was I partially blamed myself for our failed marriage. When we'd married seven years earlier, it was no secret he drank a lot, but I thought he'd change once we were together. Ha! What a joke that was. Then came the other women. That was a shock. And what a blow to the ego.

I turned out the light and curled up next to Stalin, who was sleeping on my pillow. Unable to keep Marty Meeks and anonymous messages from Finland out of my subconscious, snow-filled landscapes drenched in blood filled my dreams, and I woke up every hour on the hour till my alarm sounded.

Chapter 6

"**Y**OU LOOK PALER THAN MY Aunt Tillie after she had her hip replaced," Starr said when she walked into the office on Wednesday morning. "Another message?"

"Nothing yet, but whoever this person is, he's getting to me, and I don't like it. I'm starting to get mad."

"That's the spirit." Starr came to my desk and gave me a hug.

I told her about my bad dreams and waking up every hour, thinking someone was about to pounce on me.

"Come on, honey. Take it easy." She tossed a *Glamour* magazine on the table in the lobby. "It'll all sort itself out."

She'd barely finished consoling me when the bing alerted me to a new message. I glanced at Starr's anxious face before retrieving it.

You're not paying attention to me and that causes me to get angry, and when I get angry, there's no telling what I'll do next. You have to understand or else…

Starr stood behind me and read the words as I scrolled down. "What are you gonna do?"

"First of all, I'm going to show this message to Dr. B."

"Oh, I forgot to tell you. That computer guy from the university called —don't remember his name—but he said he couldn't find anything that might work to block these messages, but he's gonna keep searching."

I thanked Starr and went down the hall to the doctor's office. He sat at his computer, his hands poised over the keyboard. "What is it? My eleven o'clock here?"

"Not yet. I thought you'd like to see this." I handed him the printed copy of the latest e-mail.

I stood with my hands on my hips. "I'm going to take all this to the police today." My voice was sharp.

His eyes widened, but before he could respond, Starr buzzed. "Dr. B, your patient is here."

"Let's talk more about this later." He rose.

My heart was thundering. I couldn't spend another night tossing and turning. "When? I'll be leaving before you're out of session."

He patted my shoulder. "I've talked to my attorney and I've been in touch with a colleague who had a problem similar to this one. I know you think I'm not doing anything, but I am. Let's talk later. How 'bout I call you tonight or else we'll talk tomorrow, depending on what I find out. Right now the thing for you to do is try and calm down. Okay?"

Easy for him to say. He wasn't the one being threatened by some lunatic. *Three deep breaths, Jenna. Three slow, deep breaths.*

When I reached my desk, I found Starr working on a new filing system. She'd piled a mountain of charts on the desks and chairs, and others lay on the floor.

"What'd he say?"

I sucked in more air to control my anger. "Not a dad-blasted thing. He's been in touch with a shrink friend of his who is giving him helpful advice and his attorney who is probably telling him to do nothing. That's all I know. Sometimes his cool, calm composure drives me nuts. I wonder how Mrs. B stands it."

Starr laughed. "Hey, you'd better get a-going, it's almost noon. Call me anytime if you need me." She sat back down in her nest of files. "By the way, how long do you think we should keep these files?"

I removed a scrap of paper caught in one of Starr's permed curls and flipped it into the trash. "Seven years. Isn't that the requirement?"

"Beats me. What if the patient is dead?"

I grabbed my backpack. "I believe seven years is the rule regardless. Put the dead ones in a separate stack. I'll sort through them later. The invoices and the insurance claims are finished and on my desk and ready to be mailed."

Starr saluted me. "I've got a great idea, sweet pea. Why don't you get a pedicure this evening?"

I grinned. Starr's cure-all. "I'm afraid pedicures are out of the question on my budget."

"But they're so relaxing. I'll give you one for free."

I moved toward the door, curling my toes at the thought of someone touching my feet. "Maybe when the semester ends. See you tomorrow."

"Steve's Aunt Mabel and Uncle Horace are coming from Americus on Friday. I'd rather be here, buried in files, than home with those two."

She ran her hand through her hair and messed it up even worse.

"Wanna take tomorrow off as well as Friday? That way you'd have one day of rest before they come."

"I just might. Maybe I'll hide out under your desk until they leave. Promise never to tell where I am? Oh, Jen, come a little early for the party on Sunday, will you?"

"No problem."

Mrs. Bingham was sitting in her silver Mercedes convertible sports car in the parking lot, talking on her cell. As I neared, she pounded her fist on the steering wheel. Problems in PR land?

"But you don't understand," she said in a raised voice. "I'm in this up to my eyeballs." She leapt out of the car and slammed the door.

I fumbled with my keys, trying to appear as if I hadn't overheard.

"Good afternoon, Jenna," she said in a voice as sweet and controlled as ever.

"Hello, Mrs. Bingham. I believe Dr. Bingham is with a patient now."

"We've got a lunch date. I'll just read in the waiting room till he's finished. You look mighty pretty in that yellow."

I glanced down at the yellow seersucker dress I'd thrown on this morning and mumbled thanks.

Backing my Honda away from the office, I watched the boss's wife march up the stairs. She had the steady strides of a woman who felt good about herself. And why not? She had looks, brains, a successful doctor husband, and a cool car. She'd have made my mother so proud.

I parked my un-cool car near the UGA campus, gathered my backpack, and began a brisk pace to my seminar.

Walking under the wrought-iron arch, which symbolized the oldest chartered university in the country, I let the stress of the last two days fall from me. I climbed the embankment toward Baldwin Hall. Old Campus welcomed me like a distant grandparent. Ancient oaks and amazing fifty-foot magnolias shaded the wide quadrangle bordered by nineteenth century buildings. The University of Georgia, although chartered in 1785, didn't open its doors to students until 1801—hence the long-standing feud with the University of North Carolina, which received its charter in 1789 but began classes soon thereafter. Students lolled all over the grass with their faces to the sun, anxious to keep their golden tans. No worries about a murdered coed among this lot.

After a three hour seminar and a short bout in the library to research one of my papers due this week, I returned home. Churchill greeted me, certain my early arrival was designed to feed him an early supper. I picked him up and held him close to my face. The rumble of his purr reminded me of a cheap motel-bed vibration but was a lot more soothing. That pedicure Starr mentioned sounded awfully good right now. My toes curled in protest again.

Carrying the cat, I walked into the bedroom and switched on my laptop, determined to find Marty's friend, the one Mrs. Sosbee told me about. Twenty-eight Jenkins popped up in the online directory, but only one on Boulevard. Maybe Courtney's parents still lived there. I scribbled the address on a scrap of paper—gotta start somewhere—and then sent Quentin a text. By the time I'd changed clothes, the doorbell rang.

Quentin stood at the door, wearing a baseball hat, tennis shoes, a T-shirt, and jeans. He shifted from foot to foot. "You rang, love."

"Come in."

While I explained my plan to Quentin, his steel-gray eyes turned to slits, but he didn't interrupt me.

"Let's go," he said.

We drove to Boulevard in Quentin's Dodge. The sun penetrated the car as if it were a tin can, and sweat inched down my neck. My Honda had air conditioning, but Quentin insisted on driving.

As we passed West Rutherford, I glanced toward Mrs. Sosbee's porch, but no one was in sight. A dog barked at the neighbor's house on the other side. To an unknowing eye, this looked like a sleepy Southern neighborhood, not the site of a ghastly murder.

Quentin broke the silence. "Maybe it was some psycho who did her in."

"Yeah, having a psycho on my tail is very comforting."

"You still don't know if your freaky e-mail chap is connected to the murder."

"He used Marty's name, remember? By the way, Michael is sending me some information about anonymous messages. Maybe I can trace them."

"You called him? Didn't I tell you not to?" He shook his head and sighed. "By the way, did you know Michael was in town last week?" We turned onto Boulevard.

"What? He never said."

"I saw him Saturday night at the Georgia Theatre. He was up to his usual stuff. You know, drinking himself into la-la land. Pity such a good-looking chap has to act that way."

"I've told myself that a million times."

"Well, I'm glad you're finally rid of the bugger."

Michael had been such a disappointment. I thought I could change him. That was one mistake I was determined never to make again. Frank's proposal loomed in front of me larger than one of his mighty billboards.

"There's the place. Slow down," I told Quentin.

We faced a small brick house. A beat-up Chevy blocked the driveway. The yard was covered in tiny blades of grass intermingling with the weeds and dandelions.

"I hope we find this girl, and she helps me figure out why the devil I'm getting these disgusting e-mails. Get ready. I'm going to tell her I work for the *Flagpole*."

"Whatever you say. You're in charge," Quentin said, emerging from the car.

We walked up the broken sidewalk to the front door and rapped on the screen. After a few minutes, the door cracked.

"Courtney Jenkins?" I asked.

"Yeah," the girl answered.

"I'm Jenna Scali, a freelancer for the *Flagpole*, and this is my assistant, Mr. Pearson." I nodded toward Quentin who smiled at Courtney but kept quiet. "We have some questions about Marty Meeks. Can I come in?"

Courtney's small blue eyes filled with tears. She sniffed but moved aside.

"I've already told the police everything I know."

The small living room was filled with early 1930s furniture with the worn look of never having been refurbished. The chair Quentin chose had a tennis ball-size hole in the arm with stuffing popping out. I plunked down opposite him on a dingy couch. Papers were neatly stacked on the bookcase and the books evenly lined. An old-fashioned window-unit air conditioner worked overtime in the far corner. The place smelled of Lemon Pledge.

"We won't take long." I glanced at the expensive-looking Oriental lamp on the table next to the couch. It seemed as out of place as a glamorous woman in a Waffle House.

"I understand you were one of Marty's good friends," I began.

Courtney plopped down next to me, causing my seat to rise like a see-saw. From the indention on the couch, she must've sat here often. "Yeah. We went to high school together until her parents moved to Michigan. She wrote me all the time, tho', till she moved back."

"Do you know anyone who might have wished her harm?"

"No. The police think some kind of druggie killed her, not someone she knew." Her bloodshot eyes searched my face as if she might find an answer there.

"But wouldn't the person need to know her habits to have attacked her before she went out to jog?"

"The police didn't think so. They said anyone could have seen her leave the house because it wasn't dark yet—if someone had been what they called loitering, that is. Anyway, that's what they said. I still can't believe it." She sniffled, and blew her nose into a nasty-looking Kleenex. "I haven't been able to go back to school. Every time I think about not seeing Marty there, I feel sick."

I reached for her sweaty hand and patted it. The girl didn't look at me.

"Tell me about Marty."

"She was my best friend. You could tell her anything, and she'd keep it secret. We went camping together last weekend and stayed up all night talking."

"Talking about what?"

"Oh, girl stuff, mostly. I don't even remember now. Probably boys and movies. Marty loved movies. Her favorite actor was Kevin Costner. We saw *Dances with Wolves* five times. Marty loved to eat too, but never gained an ounce. We'd go to Angelo's and get an extra large pizza with all the trimmings. Marty'd eat nearly the entire thing by herself. Me, I'd eat a few bites that'd go straight to my hips." She massaged her ample thighs. "Of course, Marty exercised all the time. She ran every day, even in this heat. I never jogged with her. Couldn't get up the energy." She stopped talking, the implication hanging in the air like a sick scent. "Lot of good it did her. I can't believe she's dead. She'd planned to do so much. People our age don't die like that, do they?" Her voice cracked.

"What was her major?"

"Biology. It used to be Spanish, but she changed or was going to."

"Was she happy?" I asked. Depressed people saw psychiatrists, like Dr. B.

"I think so. She joked around all the time. She wasn't upset about stuff or anything like that. Not like Fran."

"Fran?"

"She was Marty's friend, not mine. Marty met Fran after she came back here. They ran together. Fran dropped out of school last semester. She's a real troublemaker if you ask me. Into drugs and stuff."

"Did Fran hang out with Marty a lot?"

"Yeah. But Marty knew I didn't like her. Marty never used drugs. Don't put that in your article. And I'm not sure you should mention Fran either." She glanced from me to Quentin.

"Sure, don't worry. I'm trying to find a connection. Anything that might have led to Marty's death." *Anything that might lead to me.* "Where can I find this Fran?"

"Her name's Fran Knotter. I think she lives on the eastside somewhere, but I'm not sure. I've never been to her place." Courtney opened her mouth as if to say more, but stopped herself.

"Is that Knotter with a K?"

She nodded but said no more.

I squeezed her hand. "Maybe when you feel better you'll call me if you think of anything else. This is my home telephone number." I handed her a slip of paper.

In the car I asked Quentin, "So what'd you make of it?"

Quentin scowled. "She's definitely not telling all."

"Nope, she's not."

I pulled out my smart phonebook app and entered the information Courtney had given me. "Frances Knotter with a K, 141 Cedar Street. Let's go."

He put his hand on mine without starting the car. "Listen, I don't see how this is leading to your mysterious e-murderer. What if Courtney decides to call the *Flagpole* to check you out?"

"Does that girl look like she might check me out? She doesn't have a suspicious bone in her body, and besides, I think she trusts us. Don't be so pessimistic. My curiosity is piqued now. I couldn't stop if I wanted to. Come on. It's too hot to sit here. Let's go."

"But where's it leading, love?"

"I don't have any idea. But sitting at home and twiddling my thumbs is not exactly my style. I've got to do something or I'll go crazy." I caught my breath. "One of Marty's friends might lead me to a name, something I recognize."

"And going to see this Fran Knotter chick might do that?"

"Yeah. Are you game?"

He clicked his tongue. "I've got about another forty-five minutes before Alan kills me for missing his pre-dinner cocktail hour."

"His what?"

Quentin glanced at me sideways. I loved the way he exaggerated. No doubt Alan would pout, but I suspected Quentin would survive his lover's wrath.

"Alan insists on a drink before dinner. Not simply a drink, but a cocktail and quiet conversation—a reviver, so to speak. He says it's the best part of his day. When I miss it, good Lord, it's the devil to pay. Usually between jogging, the gym, researching, grading papers, and belly dancing, I rarely get home in time. Tonight's the test. Just can't miss it or else…"

"I'll get you home for your reviver, ol' boy," I said, mimicking his accent and patting him on the head. "Wouldn't want you to disappoint a looker like Alan." I grinned at him.

"Seriously, Jen, Alan doesn't ask much from me. He's really a good sort about most things—unlike the others."

"Hey, you don't have to explain." I gave his hand a quick squeeze.

We pulled off the bypass circling Athens and headed for Cedar Street. I scanned the road signs. Finally, we turned down a narrow thoroughfare off Barnett Shoals Road. A policeman stood in the center of the street. More police cars flanked both sides.

"What's going on?" Quentin asked the officer.

"You live here?"

"No, sir."

"Then you'd better turn around and go on home," he said with a huff. Clearly he hadn't taken advantage of the public relations training at the Police Academy.

"But my sister lives down here." My voice caught on the last word.

"Whereabouts, miss?"

"At the end on the corner."

"Well, you can't go through now but tell your sister to lock her doors. A girl was found murdered in this neighborhood this afternoon."

Chapter 7

"**D**RIVE, QUEN."

"Calm down. I'm going as fast as I can. This car isn't a bloody race horse, you know."

When Quentin stopped for a yellow light, a loud, exasperated sigh escaped my lips. My heart pounded right out of my chest. Could he drive any slower?

"What's the god-awful rush, anyway?"

"I've got to find out if I have a message from the killer."

"Surely you don't believe this one is connected to your computer bloke, do you?" He glanced at me.

The light finally changed.

"Of course I think they're connected. I've thought so all along. If I have a message, I'll know for sure the other murder wasn't one gigantic coincidence as some people seem to think." My own favorite shrink, I didn't add.

A jogger ran down the street. The muscles in the young man's legs were as tight as ropes. Sweat poured off him, and his face looked grim. Running in the summer took extreme dedication. Marty was one of those dedicated runners and look what happened to her.

"So you think Fran Knotter was murdered?" Quentin asked.

"It was her street, and the police were everywhere. I couldn't tell which house the murder took place in. But if I had to hazard a guess, I'd bet Fran was the latest victim of this maniac." My stomach lurched and my breath lodged inside me like a bomb about to explode.

When we turned into the office parking lot, I jumped out of the car before it stopped.

"Whoa, Jenna. You're going to get yourself killed."

Fishing in my purse for the keys, I flew inside.

Without even turning on the lights, I raced to the computer and switched it on. My heart thundered during the endless boot-up. I scanned down the usual e-mails until my eye caught the one I wanted. It had come in at three forty-five today.

I stabbed another one last night. She fought hard, but I managed to cut her throat before she screamed. Sometimes I feel such pain. My head feels like it might explode. I get jittery inside, like when I was little. Scared, sort of. Someday I'll explain all this to you, and I know you'll understand because you always do.

I stared at the message. Once again it originated from Finland. But now I was certain the killer lived right here in good ol' Athens, Georgia, the Classic City, home of the Georgia Bulldogs. My hands trembled and a tear rolled down my cheek as I typed a response knowing it would go nowhere.

Who are you? Why are you doing this? You're wrong about me. I don't understand, and you must stop killing people. It's WRONG. Please stop.

I pounded on the computer keyboard.

Quentin came up behind me, put his hands on my shoulders, and massaged gently.

"I honestly don't expect him to get this, but what else can I do?" My voice shook with frustration..

"You can go to the police, can't you? Come on, love. Let's leave now, shall we?"

I searched for answers on his concerned face. The fine lines around his mouth that usually broke so quickly into a laugh appeared deeper. For the first time since I'd known Quentin, fear showed on his face, making him look ten years older than his thirty-four years.

"No, it's not fair for you to get mixed up in all this. Go home to Alan. It's almost your witching hour." I logged off the computer just as the undeliverable message binged.

"Bugger Alan, he'll understand. I'm already mixed up in it. I'm not leaving you alone."

"I'll be all right. Really. I don't want to jump to any conclusions. The message didn't threaten me. Surely I'll be okay." Even though those words fell from my lips, my mind was as fuzzy as Starr's disorderly desk.

"What other bloody conclusions are there? You got the first message, and a girl was killed. You got another message, and a girl was killed. I was doubtful before, but I'm convinced now. You said yourself this proves it's not a bloody coincidence." He moved away from me.

"I want to check through the patient files before I notify the police. Whoever is writing these messages has to have some connection to me at this office. It must be a patient or a family member. All I have to do is find a person crazy enough to kill. That should narrow the field and satisfy Dr. B."

"You're talking nonsense. The police can do that. Don't you think they've collected anything from the murder scenes? They've got fingerprints and murder weapons, all that kind of CSI rubbish. If you tell them what you know, they'll nail this bloke. Come on, Jenna. Think." He was pacing from one end of the office to the other, dodging the files Starr had left on the floor.

I grabbed his hands and stared into his face. "Settle down, for heaven sakes. I *am* thinking. Look. We don't even know for sure Fran was killed. Can't we wait and go to the police tomorrow morning? Please, Quen, give me some time."

"You mean give Dr. B some time to protect his murdering patients," Quentin countered with an angry slur to his voice.

"Look, the police blew me off, acted like I was some kind of weirdo. Let me tell you, that's something I don't intend to go through again. What can I tell them, anyway? They know these girls were murdered, and they'll discover, if they haven't already, that they were friends. How can the fact that weird e-mails are coming to me make any difference? If I can give them a name, some lead—now that would make more sense."

He placed his hands on my shoulders. "Okay. But you must go tomorrow, regardless of what you find out about the patients, and you must go there personally. No more anonymous phone calls. Promise me."

"I promise."

"And promise you won't do any snooping around without me. This person has killed twice. A third time won't bother him one bit."

"Okay, Quen." But I wasn't sure I could keep that promise. Things were happening too fast. It wasn't my style to sit home and wait until the murderer knocked on my door.

Quentin dropped me at my house and walked me to the door.

"I'll call tomorrow." He shot me a lingering look before turning to go home and face the wrath of Alan.

Earlier, I'd texted Frank and asked to see him even though I'd just seen him last night. He was thrilled. "*Let's plan to go see "No Strings Attached" with Kevin Kline, playing at the dollar theater,*" he'd shot back. Kline was one of my favorite actors, and tonight I wanted to lose myself in his shenanigans. I fed the cats and called Frank.

"I'm gonna be a bit late. Let's meet at the theatre, and we can get a bite afterwards, okay?"

"Hey, babe, where have you been all day? Starr said you left early."

I clenched my jaw and closed my eyes. "I went to my seminar. Then to the library. For heaven's sakes, Frank, must I report my every move?"

"Sorry but you didn't answer your cell, and. . . It's just that sometimes you're not an easy person to catch up with. I called this afternoon to invite you to an early dinner before the movie. But now it's too late. The movie starts at seven-fifteen. I'll see you there."

Petulant. That's the word. He sounded petulant. After I hung up with my petulant boyfriend, I took a quick shower and returned to Dr. Bingham's office where I began searching through the files without any real sense of what I was looking for.

It didn't take me long to discover that Fran Knotter had been a patient of Dr. Bingham's. A new thought hit me. Maybe I was barking up the wrong tree. Maybe it wasn't a patient sending those messages but someone who wanted to kill patients, someone who had access to our files.

My mind fiddled with this idea for a time, but came up with few possibilities. No one had access to our files except Dr. B, Starr, and me. Furthermore, as far as I could tell Martha Meeks had never been a patient.

I sorted through the dead files Starr stacked for me. Halfway through dating, labeling, and boxing them, I caught sight of a familiar name.

Much as my curious nature wanted to peek inside the folder, the little voice in my head stopped me. The patient had died the previous year and was none of my business. I fiddled with the edge of the folder, debating. Maybe she was an itsy-bitsy bit my business, the devil inside me said. I sighed and put the file aside. Athens was a town small enough that nearly everyone who lived here eventually saw Dr. B or had a relative who did.

I bit my lower lip, looked around as if someone might see me, flipped open the file, and began reading the cryptic notes about my boyfriend's mother, Valerie Sutter.

When my watch read seven. I boxed the file with the others and took off to meet Frank.

* * * *

While I sat next to Frank in the movie, my mind replayed what I'd learned about the murders. Marty and Fran had been friends. Perhaps the killer knew both women. But why was someone sending messages to me —a person who didn't know either woman? Maybe I had met them but didn't realize it. Fran had been a patient, but nothing about her jogged my memory. So many people came through the office. How could I possibly remember all of them?

What kind of person would kill another and then seek understanding for his dastardly deeds? Several psychological studies flashed in my mind. One demonstrated how researchers could program perfectly normal people to do horrible things, but in those instances the perpetrator had been detached from the victim or under group pressure. Maybe this killer struck at random and didn't know the victims.

Frank reached over and took my hand, causing me to nearly jump out of my skin.

"You okay, babe?"

"Shh. Watch the movie."

After the film, which I barely noticed, I agreed to go to his place on Dearing Street, a few blocks from downtown in an old part of the city. These condos were constructed ten years ago to revitalize that part of Athens. Frank said he bought it to demonstrate his civic concern, but I suspected he liked the quaint, highly desirable location. His condo faced some of the oldest Victorian homes in town and sat adjacent to an historic cobblestone street.

Entering Frank's abode always startled me with its starkness. A small leather couch sat in the center of the shiny, new-looking hardwood floors. A TV tray with an art deco-style lamp stood in a corner. A fancy entertainment center, complete with a flat screen and an upscale sound system occupied the built-in shelves. No papers, books, doodads or cat hairs anywhere.

"One of these days you'll need to buy some furniture," I said, entering and throwing my purse on the floor.

He shrugged. "Maybe. I'm happy enough as it is. I'm a simple man with few wants." He winked at me. "You like Wyton Marsalis, don't you?"

"Perfect," I said, rubbing my arms and wrinkling my nose to deaden the lingering odor of cigarettes.

Soft-sounding music bounced off the empty walls.

I gazed at a family photograph that stood next to a speaker. A younger version of Frank in a cap and gown stood next to a tall, stately woman, presumably his mom. I stared at his mother with a new curiosity.

Frank fixed the drinks, leaving me to wander into the study where his desk—an old-fashioned roll top with polished brass drawer handles that he'd told me belonged to his grandmother— sat like a beacon from the past. On it, Frank's fancy-looking Mac, scanner, and laser printer looked out of place.

At least he owns one piece of decent furniture.

Frank entered with a dishtowel over his shoulder. I never realized how sexy a man looked sporting a dishtowel.

"I'm baking some lasagna that'll be ready in about thirty minutes," he said.

"You fixed lasagna?" This man continued to surprise me.

He shot me a sideways grin. "I whipped it up last night, hoping I could entice you over. It's one of my mom's recipes. That's why I was trying to call you earlier."

The rich odors of cheese and spicy meat wafting my way rumbled my stomach. "Thirty minutes you say?"

He raised his brows. "Now what can we do for thirty minutes?"

As we headed down the narrow hallway to the bedroom, Frank pawed me with a strange new roughness, but I didn't stop him. He seemed eager for my attention, and I was all too happy to oblige.

Later, in the kitchen and after he'd dished up the cheesy-smelling lasagna, he said, "So have you had time to think about my proposal?"

"No fair asking me in a weak moment." I washed the smooth pasta down with a swig of rich-tasting Chianti. "First lovemaking and now a delicious dinner. What girl could refuse?"

I broke off a piece of crusty bread and dipped it in a small dish of peppery, extra-virgin olive oil.

"That's the point."

"I believe I've shown you how much I like you. My reluctance to make a commitment has nothing to do with you. It's more about me."

He rubbed my thigh. A thrill ran up my leg like a charge from a live outlet. My breath quickened.

"Do my needs matter at all?"

"Of course."

He pulled me onto his lap. "I need to feel you close to me and know you're there for me and only me."

Like his mother hadn't been.

We held each other for several minutes. His deep breaths tickled my ear.

"I'm not sure you'd like the way I'd clutter up your house," I said with a grin. Not to mention the contribution my two felines would make.

He nuzzled my hair. "I'd love your clutter."

Right. That'll last all of one week, if I'm lucky.

I returned to my seat and resumed eating. "Maybe we should consider moving in together first. That way we could get to know each other better. There's so much I still don't know about you." *So much you haven't told me.*

His jaw locked, and he knotted his fist. "Call me old-fashioned, but I believe in commitment."

I put my hand on his arm. "Sorry, I didn't mean to upset you."

Frank poured himself more wine. "I'm not the moving-in sort of guy. You either love me or you don't. I don't play games. That's how I operate at work and how I live. If we love each other, we should get married. Plain and simple. No fuss."

"Michael said almost the same thing before we married. I wasn't ready then, and I'm not ready now. Please try to see things from my point of view."

"So, you're saying no?"

I leaned toward him, lifted his chin, and stared into his eyes, misty with emotion. "For now, but not forever. Can you live with that?"

He shrugged. "I suppose I have to."

I munched on the lasagna. "Frank, I've been meaning to tell you why I've been a bit distracted lately."

"Talk about an understatement."

"You know I told you about those strange e-mails I've been getting at work."

His head shot up. "What kind of e-mails?"

"I mentioned them last night, just odd e-mails. Anyway, I've gotten more of them and there've been other things going on, including the deaths of two young women. I don't know how I'm involved in this, but I'm gonna go to the police tomorrow."

"Forget the cops. Just forward all the e-mails to me and I'll find out who this jerk is and take care of him. It's probably nothing more than a hacker." He pulled me to him again and fondled my hair. "I'll take care of you, Jenna. You don't need cops as long as you've got me."

"Sure, thanks, Frank. Between you and Quentin, I'm well covered."

I returned to my seat and changed the subject.

* * * *

Thursday morning Starr texted me to say she decided to stay home. Since Dr. Bingham would be at the hospital all morning and seeing patients only in the afternoon, I told her that was fine and to enjoy some respite while she could. Just after entering the office, my phone rang.

"Jenna." It was Dr. Bingham. "Have you gone to the police?"

"Not yet, but I'm planning to this afternoon. Quentin is going with me."

Silence.

"Can you wait a bit longer? I've got to see the patients here at the hospital, but after that I'll have some time to talk. Have you had any more e-mails?"

"No. Not since yesterday when—"

"Good. If you get another one before I get in, let me know."

"Wait, Dr. B., another girl was killed yesterday. But, I really don't know if her death was related to Marty's."

Silence.

Finally, he said, "Don't go jumping to conclusions, Jenna. We'll talk later," and hung up.

Thursday proved uneventful in many ways. No e-mails from Finland, —or wherever, and Dr. Bingham never returned to the office. He had another emergency causing me to cancel all his afternoon patients. I called Quentin and left a message to postpone going to the police quite yet. Afterward, I took off for the library, glad to get away from creepy e-mails and cloistered among old, stuffy books until my eyes burned.

When I arrived home, both cats were asleep on the couch, curled up together like pillows. Stalin lifted his head and Churchill opened one eye, but, otherwise, they remained in their peaceful positions, stomachs full of the dry Friskies I'd put in their dishes that morning. The kitchen clock read 9:30 p.m., and I hadn't eaten, but eating was the furthest thing from my mind.

My mother's recipe for the chocolate peanut butter delight lay on the kitchen counter. To make it I needed six Hershey bars and real whipping cream.

I grabbed my car keys, kissed both cats, and headed out the door to purchase the missing ingredients at Kroger.

On my way, I passed the scene of the first murder. Two streetlights illuminated one end of Lumpkin Street, but the light faded to black by the time Marty's house appeared on the left. Tonight the moon was nearly full and bright enough for me to distinguish a car sitting in her driveway, suggesting the arrival of someone in her family.

I parked across the street, looked at the house, and tried to conjure up the girl who had lived under that peaceful-looking roof. Her life had probably been as uneventful as mine, full of work and school. Had the killer e-mailed her before he struck? Had she been afraid each night when she locked her door and closed her eyes? I put my head down on the steering wheel and cried, for myself and for Marty.

Drying my eyes, blowing my nose, and starting the engine, I caught sight of a shadow inside Marty's house. My heart froze. I turned off the car and stared in the direction of the movement.

I glimpsed a beam, like a flashlight. Moments later, a figure appeared at the side of Marty's house. I locked my car doors, rolled up my window, and scrunched low in my seat. Sweat seeped through my T-shirt. If he found me, what would I say? Just out for a late night snooze in my car. Sorry if I interrupted your breaking and entering.

Maybe this intruder was the proverbial murderer returning to the scene of the crime. Quentin's words of caution floated in my head—*This person has killed twice. A third time won't bother him one bit.*

I scrunched a little lower, peeked over the edge of my door, and tried to make out if the figure was a man or a woman. Couldn't tell. He carried something the size of a shoebox. A purse? Looting tools?

The shadow turned. He surveyed the terrain. The way the person walked struck a familiar note. Where had I seen that walk—a slight limp, the left leg slightly shorter than the right? Starr's husband, Steve, flashed in my mind. He had fallen off a bicycle as a kid and walked with a limp. But darn, was it his left or right leg? Sweat dampened my neck. Why would Steve break into Marty Meeks' house? Impossible thought.

The car engine started. Brake lights broke the darkness. I ducked too far down to see any more and held my breath. When no more car noise rumbled, I peeked out. The car's taillights disappeared around the corner. It was too far and too dark to read a license plate number.

Frustrated, I drove to Kroger.

The next morning I called Starr.

"So how's everything?" I asked with as casual a tone as I could muster.

"It's crazier over here than a Saturday-night watermelon festival in downtown Americus," Starr whispered into the telephone. "Steve's aunt and uncle came this morning, bursting with energy like two old maids on a mission. They've been nagging me to change around the living room furniture. Aunt Mabel thinks we need to rearrange the room so we can squeeze in two more chairs—old faded Lazy-boys they want to give us. Thanks but no thanks. She said we've got too much wasted space. But their house looks like a sardine tin, full of junk. Uncle Horace up and moved all he could, lickety-split before I could turn around. God, Jen, what am I gonna do?"

"Grit your teeth, nod, and smile pretty-like. When they leave, you can move everything back."

"Yeah, easy for you to say. They're not badgering you like a couple of hungry piglets."

"Where's Steve during all this commotion?"

"Are you kidding? That's the sixty-four-thousand-dollar question. He ups and disappears every chance he gets. I hope he'll stay good and gone so Uncle Horace won't be able to move the couch, which weighs more than he and Aunt Mabel together."

"I made your birthday dessert last night. It's begging me to gobble it down in one fell swoop."

"Don't you lay one grimy paw on it."

"Will the aunt and uncle be here for the party?"

"No, they're leaving Sunday morning, if I don't murder them first."

"What time do you want me to come?"

"Five o'clock."

I hung up with no more information than before the call. If Steve had been snooping around the dead girl's house, Starr probably wouldn't know. She'd likely been daydreaming about killing her relatives-in-law. It made no sense for Steve to be at Marty's place anyway. It must have been someone else.

Plenty of people had limps.

Chapter 8

AT WORK ON FRIDAY MORNING, I spent more time than any human being might want to hitting annoying telephone menu choices and listening to elevator music, trying to persuade the insurance companies to give me information so patients could get the help they needed. I could forget about catching up on the billing today. No wonder no one wanted my job.

I gobbled down a soggy turkey sandwich before calling Dr. Bingham. This morning he called again and told me he had talked to his colleague, and he wanted to talk to me before I went to the police. We agreed to meet sometime today.

"I'm afraid he's already left for the golf course," Mrs. Bingham told me. "But he should be home by three o'clock."

"He promised he'd call. Please tell him to phone me. It's kind of important. He'll know why."

"Glad to, Jenna."

When I returned home from my afternoon slugfest in the library, I decided to lose myself in housework. While down on my hands and knees, waxing the kitchen floor, I played Pavarotti's *Greatest Hits* and let the murders drift from my mind and "Vesti la Giubba" fill my soul.

At 3:05 p.m. my telephone rang.

"You're finally home," said Timothy, my long-lost, so-called boyfriend. "I've been trying to reach you."

"Have you now? I guess my phone must not be picking up missed calls."

"Well, I've been thinking about it anyway. Wanna go out?" he asked.

"That depends on what you have in mind."

"There's a new group at the 40 Watt. I've heard they're pretty hot. Called the 'Demons' or something equally ominous. Thought we might hang out there awhile tonight."

I hadn't made definite plans with Frank, but knowing him, he expected us to do something. Even though I had made it clear to him on Wednesday night I wasn't ready for marriage, in his mind we were practically engaged. I hesitated. I liked Timothy as a friend. Maybe that's just what I needed right now—a friend—someone who'd put no pressure on me.

"What time?" I asked.

"Why don't we meet at ten o'clock?"

I agreed, deciding to have an early supper with Frank and then tell him I needed to work on my research.

Dr. Bingham called at three-thirty.

"I thought you were going to phone me earlier," I said.

"Sorry. Yesterday turned into a circus, as you know. I didn't get away from the hospital until nearly ten o'clock. What are you doing now?"

"Not much. Do you want to come over?" For once my house sparkled after my therapeutic scrubbing.

"Can you come to the club? I'll spring for a drink."

"I'll meet you in the lobby in ten minutes."

The hallway table at the Athens Country Club held a brass bowl full of purple and white hydrangeas. The green and gray marble floor glistened. Soft, comfortable maroon chairs surrounded the edge of the room. Although I'd brushed and re-braided my hair and put on some burgundy lip gloss that tasted like grapes, I still wore my comfy housework jeans and T-shirt. The people milling about were decked out in flowery summer dresses or bright green or yellow sports coats. I stood out like the imposter I was.

Plopping down in one of the maroon chairs, I hoped to disappear into the woodwork.

Dr. Bingham arrived, resembling a snapshot from a Land's End catalogue. He wore navy shorts and a stripped Polo shirt with the collar upturned. His hair had the windblown look of an athlete, and his face was flushed.

He smiled when he spotted me. "Hope I haven't kept you waiting too long. One of my golfing buddies is getting a divorce and needed to talk."

"No problem."

He glanced around. "Have you eaten?"

"Yeah."

"Well, I need a snack. How 'bout we go down to the Grill?"

We moved through the hallway and down the stairs to a carpeted lounge with neat clusters of tables and chairs, empty except for one other couple sitting on the far side of the room. Big windows faced a luscious green golf course. The other couple looked as if they had just finished a tennis match. The man, in polished tennis whites, had an enviable suntan. The woman wore a short, white tennis outfit and was sipping a lemon colored drink.

Once we sat down, Dr. Bingham ordered nachos and a beer. I ordered a Diet Coke.

"Now, let's try to figure out what's going on," he said.

"As I told you on the phone, I talked to one of Marty Meeks's friends."

He frowned as if he didn't understand.

"She's the first girl who was murdered."

Dr. Bingham nodded.

The waiter placed our drinks before us in the same moment my cell vibrated. It was Frank. I switched it off.

"Go on," he coaxed.

I explained about Courtney and what she said about Fran Knotter. Then I described how Quentin and I had driven to Fran's house.

"When we got to the street where Fran lived, it was crawling with cops. They told us a woman had been murdered. This morning the paper said that Fran Knotter had been killed. This is the latest message I got." I pulled out the printed page from my purse.

He studied the killer's words. "It's all very puzzling."

"Michael e-mailed me a link to an article about an anonymous server from Finland. It confirms that the person sending these messages could be from anywhere. I think it's time I take everything I know to the police."

Silence.

Finally he asked, "Have you gotten any more notes hand delivered to your mailbox?"

"No. Maybe that wasn't related. I don't know. Too many questions are unanswered."

"Tell me what you were doing talking to this dead girl's friend."

My cheeks tingled in what had to be a royal blush. "Well, I thought if I could find out more about Marty, maybe I could figure out if there's a connection between me and her. I don't understand why I'm getting these messages. The second victim, by the way, was one of your patients."

He raised his eyebrows. "Oh? What did you say her name was?"

When I repeated Fran's name, Dr. Bingham stared at me as if I had said something wrong. He blinked. "Are you certain?"

"Do you remember her?"

He looked away just as his nachos arrived. A deep frown creased his brow. I sipped the Coke and waited.

"I remember some things about the case. But it's been some time since I've seen Fran." He lifted one of the tasty Mexican treats covered in a thick coating of cheddar cheese. His eyes avoided mine.

"Can you think of any of Fran's friends, patients or otherwise, who'd be capable of killing her?"

"I can't think of anyone off the top of my head." He munched on a second nacho. "I'll need to study her chart, and I'd need to know more about the murders. There's no way to identify a killer with so little information." He pushed the nachos toward me. "Have one."

I shook my head. "We do know the killer stabbed one and possibly two young women and that he writes me afterwards with the gory details and begs me to quote 'understand' him, as if I could empathize with what he's doing. Doesn't that tell you anything?"

"Very little. Did the perpetrator know the women? Was it a random murder? Did the killer break into the houses? Was anything stolen? Did he rape them or otherwise abuse them physically? And why is he e-mailing you? What's the connection there? You can't expect me to identify a killer with such sketchy information. I can't even give you a psychological profile on what you've got."

"I see." I fiddled with the rim of my glass and bit back a snide remark. He seemed more concerned about his patients than he was about me. What did I have to do to get this man's attention? Get myself killed?

Dr. Bingham drank some beer. "Jenna, I don't want to put you in any danger, and I do appreciate your waiting to go to the police."

Yeah, right. "Well, I don't think I'm in danger." *Not yet anyway* "But I have to tell you, it's been scary. The e-mails don't exactly threaten me, but how can I not *feel* threatened. He knows who I am, and he's murdered twice. I don't know who he is or what he wants me to do. Is he going to kill me tomorrow? Maybe not. But, who's to say? And who's to say he won't murder someone else?" I paused and drank some Coke before continuing. "This second murder has the campus like a cemetery. Usually people are all over the place cramming or finishing last-minute papers before exams. This afternoon even the library looked dead. Everybody's scared. Not just me."

He reached over and patted my wrist. I focused on his neatly manicured fingers and wondered how long we could put off going to the authorities. Quentin thought we'd waited too long.

"Let me tell you what will happen as soon as you notify the police. First, they'll disrupt the office in ways you can't even imagine. Second, I'm not sure how much we can actually tell them. For one thing, we cannot divulge a patient's name. That includes Fran Knotter. Do you understand?"

"Yes, sir." I couldn't look at his face because if I did I'd scream at him and probably lose my job.

"Look. It's Friday. Can't you wait until Monday? I've already talked to my attorney to see how to handle privileged information. But, I want to clarify a few more things with him, particularly after having talked to Dave Pittman. He had a similar situation. The police suspected one of his patients was involved in some criminal activity—drugs, I think. Anyway, they asked for his help in the investigation. Dave agreed. He was later sued for defamation of character. This is what I have to avoid. You see, Jenna, simply because someone has a mental problem doesn't make that individual a killer. Of course, many killers are psychopaths or narcissistic, but some people, who have no apparent mental pathology, kill for one reason or another. I'm afraid the police will assume all my patients are potential murderers. I don't want to go through what Dave did. Please try and understand my position."

I looked away and said nothing. How could I wait until Monday? This nut had killed two women in four days. I couldn't risk waiting because Dr. B worried about a little office chaos.

When I got home, I had a message from Quentin. "Have you gone to the police? Ring me *now*, Jenna."

"I'm going in the morning," I told him. "It's too late now."

Quentin sighed. "Bugger, Jenna. You've got to go. I'll go with you if you want, but you must do it, love."

"I'm going. I promise. First thing tomorrow morning."

That evening, Frank pouted when I asked him to take me home after dinner. I mumbled something about being tired and needing to study, but perhaps he read the guilt on my face. I have never been a good liar.

A few minutes after 10 p.m., I walked into the 40 Watt Club and spotted Timothy sprawled at a table adjacent to the bar. He was talking to a young blue-jean-clad girl with long, wavy blond hair.

"Hello, Jen. This is Mel. She's in my ecology seminar," he said as I reached his table.

I nodded to the girl and took a seat next to Timothy.

"See ya around, Tim," Mel said in a slow smoker's voice.

"I thought you didn't like to be called Tim."

"I don't. But some people can't get used to Timothy, and I've given up. Want something to drink?"

"How about a Diet Coke with lemon."

Timothy raised an eyebrow.

"I reached my limit before I got here," I explained.

While Timothy went to the bar, I thought about the article I'd just read in the online Athens newspaper where a lead story linked the deaths of Marty and Fran, and the police assured the public that they didn't believe they had a serial killer. The final words of the article stuck in my mind: *So far the police have few leads.*

I rested my head in my hands. My temples throbbed. I really dreaded going to the police, but at the same time, I wanted to get all this over with and in the hands of the authorities.

Sauntering over with my Diet Coke and a longneck beer for himself, Timothy lowered his six-foot-three frame onto the chair like an accordion.

"So what's going on in your world?" he asked, and took a slug of beer.

I squeezed the lemon into my drink. "Lots. I've been playing amateur sleuth, trying to get a handle on a couple of murders."

"Gosh, Jen," he jumped in. "You're not talking about those two coeds, are you?"

"I sure am. Did you know either of them?"

"I don't think so. I just saw it in the paper. But people on campus are freaked. What're their names?"

"Fran Knotter and Marty Meeks."

"Fran Knotter. Hmm, her name sounds vaguely familiar. But I'm sure I don't know her." He drank from his bottle. His Adam's apple bobbed as he guzzled the beer.

"Are you certain?"

Timothy rubbed the top of his head. "Yep. Never heard of her. But girls are scared to walk out at night—that's about all I know. I overhead a few of them talking."

Timothy kept turning toward the door. His eyes followed each woman who walked in. My frustration mounted.

"This is serious stuff, Timothy. It's real-life murder. I think I'm getting e-mails from the killer because one of Dr. B's patients might be involved. Maybe you've seen one of the girls around town. If you know anything, tell me."

He took my hand. "Hey. You need to chill."

I let out a long sigh.

"So how 'bout we dance and forget the monsters hovering in the shadows?" he said.

By now the club was beginning to buzz. A couple of musicians had arrived on stage and the music had begun.

"Yeah. Let's," I said.

We danced the remainder of the evening, losing ourselves to the rhythm of the music and the murmur of voices filling the room.

Timothy made everything seem so simple.

Chapter 9

THE NEXT MORNING THE BLINK, blink of my message light reminded me that I hadn't checked the machine when I'd come in the previous night. I pressed the button

"I'm calling Jenna Scali?" a shaky voice said. "This is Courtney Jenkins. We spoke about Marty, my friend." Pause, the telephone clicked.

I looked up Courtney's number. Her phone rang ten times before she answered.

"Courtney, this it Jenna. You called me."

Silence.

"Courtney," I repeated.

"Yes," she answered in almost a whisper. Clearing her throat and raising her voice she said, "When I heard about Fran, I got scared."

"I could come over, if you want but not before nine-thirty. I've got something I've gotta do first."

"Okay," Courtney said, and hung up.

At 8:03 a.m. I drove to the police station. I'd never been to the police station before. When the city and county merged, the main seat of police operations moved from its cozy downtown location, near City Hall, to this building in what some might consider the country. In fact, the parking lot faced a small wood-frame house surrounded by sycamore trees and a pond. On the bank of the pond, a flock of geese grazed—not a scene one would expect so near the police station and certainly not consistent with my *Law and Order* image.

Once inside, I spotted a dirty-looking man in mud-caked jeans sitting in the waiting area. I approached the information window.

"I'd like to talk to the detective investigating the murdered coeds." My voice shook.

Seemingly oblivious to my condition, the policeman peered up from the form he was filling in. His shirt gaped at each button, giving me a peek at his white undershirt. "Are you a family member?"

"No. But I might have some information." I prayed he wouldn't cross-examine me like the time I'd telephoned. What did one have to do to give the cops a lead?

The man slurped coffee from a hole in the plastic lid of a McDonald's cup. "What's your name?"

"Jenna Scali."

"Have a seat over there," he said, and pointed to the black vinyl two-seater in the waiting area. "I'll tell the detectives you're here."

I sat next to the mud-caked man and reached inside my backpack for a book. Instead of reading, however, my mind re-played what I was going to tell the police. A sense of dread and foolishness shot through me. I suppressed an urge to dash away when a young man in a light-blue, short-sleeved shirt with a navy tie came into the waiting area. One of the first things I noticed about him was his thick, straight hair, the color of oatmeal.

"Jenna Scali." His voice was deep and rich. A singer's voice.

"That's me." I stood. With heart racing I replaced my book in the backpack and flipped it over my shoulder.

"I'm Detective Richard Watring. Let's go to my office where we can talk."

I followed the detective along a brightly-lit hallway with walls painted a deep shade of blue. He led me into a small cubical-type office. Pink telephone slips filled a message pick near his phone. Who still used message pads? His computer reflected the city seal on the screen saver.

Detective Richard Watring measured a few inches taller than me and his smooth, clear face suggested he was no older than I was.

I perched across from him on a rather uncomfortable straight-back chair.

"So, you might have some information about the murdered college girls?"

"Well, yes." I hesitated. "Are you in charge of the investigation?"

He blinked and bit his lower lip. "I'm one of the investigating officers. Sergeant Pete Lewis and I are working on the cases. Sergeant Lewis is off today, but I beeped him about your visit. He may stick his head in if he should come by before you leave. Hope that suits you." He smiled and so did his light blue eyes.

I swallowed and caught my breath. The muscles in his upper arms tensed when he linked his hands together. He waited for me to begin.

"That's fine," I stammered. "It's just, well, umm, my story is a little strange." I pushed a strand of hair off my face.

Just then, the detective's phone buzzed. "Excuse me."

After a few words, he replaced the phone. "It seems a friend of yours is here. He's coming back."

When Quentin waltzed in, my face burned with embarrassment.

"I wanted to make sure you got yourself over here, love," he said with a wink. He introduced himself to Detective Watring with one of his more radiant smiles.

"Quentin's like a big brother," I explained.

"I see," the detective said, with a bemused expression. "Now what can I do for you two?"

I told Detective Watring about the events that had happened since the first e-mail appeared in my inbox on Monday morning.

"At first she didn't want to come to the police because she didn't think these events were connected," Quentin explained in my defense.

"Well, they may or may not be," the policeman answered.

"I did call once," I said. "But when I explained things, nothing made much sense even to me, and the policeman on the line seemed only interested in who I was and my relationship to the victim, which, of course, there wasn't any relationship, at least, as far as I knew. Anyway, when the e-mail appeared after the second murder, I decided it was time to come here in person. The note in my mailbox might have been some stupid prank. Besides, it could've been directed to someone else. My name wasn't used."

The detective studied me, causing me to feel warm and fuzzy inside. "I'm glad you came. Now tell me about these anonymous computer messages."

I reached into my backpack and handed him a printout of the article Michael had sent. "My ex-husband is a computer expert." The detective's eyebrows rose at the mention of an ex-husband. "He used to work for a computer security firm here in Athens. Now he's in Nashville. I asked him about anonymous servers. He said there used to be several, but most went out of business because they couldn't guarantee anonymity. This guy in Finland assures his clients they'll remain anonymous. Here's the article. I doubt y'all will get much out of him. He sounds pretty dedicated." I was talking faster than a NASCAR driver nearing the finish line, and my heart was pounding like crazy.

"We'll see." The detective took the article with his left hand where my naughty brain registered the absence of a wedding ring.

Had I put on lipstick this morning? Probably not.

"Now you say the first messages were directed to you?"

"Well, yes, all of them came to our office e-mail."

"So, clearly, the sender had to know of your business."

I nodded. "That's what's so confusing. Why me? I'd hoped it was some mistake. Maybe the sender got a letter out of place and meant to send the messages to someone else. Who knows? It might have been some game." Or an e-book as Starr suggested, I didn't say. "But when he used my name...I paused. "Jenna isn't that common a name."

"No, it isn't."

I squirmed and wondered if the man across from me was lightly admonishing me for not coming sooner.

"Do you think the killer is someone Jenna knows?" Quentin asked.

"That's hard to say. But this gives us something to go on. Miss Scali, did you keep copies of the messages?"

"Yes, sir." I handed him the pages from my backpack. "As for the note in my mailbox, I'm afraid I tossed it away."

"That's too bad. We might have picked up something."

I glanced nervously at Quentin. He was staring at the young detective like a lovesick puppy.

"Did you know Martha Meeks or Fran Knotter?"

"No. But Mrs. Sosbee told me they were friends." Actually, it had been Courtney who told me that, but I wasn't ready to pull her into this.

"Miss Scali, I don't want to sound harsh, but you really shouldn't have talked to the dead girl's neighbor under false pretenses."

"I know. It was stupid. But, you see, I wasn't sure any of this was related. And I couldn't see why I was getting the e-mails. I didn't know what to do, but I had to do something. I hated to muddle up your investigation with something so vague. I'm sure you're swamped as it is trying to solve these murders." I sounded like a babbling idiot, but I couldn't stop myself.

"Most of the leads we follow are dead ends, but we follow them all and hope one will produce something. The police must make that decision."

"I kept telling her to come to you," Quentin piped in as if he wanted a pat on the head.

"Let me get your contact information. I'm sure Sergeant Lewis will want to follow up. Now, where did you say you worked?"

Hesitating, I turned to Quentin who nodded. "I work for Dr. Niles Bingham, a psychiatrist."

Detective Watring's eyebrows shot up. "Is he the doctor on Milledge Avenue?"

"Yes, sir. The office is on the corner of Milledge and Dearing Street. It's an old Victorian house Dr. Bingham restored." I changed gears. "Do you think the same person committed both these murders?"

"We don't know." He looked away, clearly not going to tell me much.

"Surely you've found some clues. Didn't y'all find any fingerprints or anything that might point to the killer?"

"We don't have much to go on right now, Miss Scali. You might be the break we've been waiting for." He frowned. "There is one thing you might be able to help us with. Wait one minute." He lifted the telephone. "Sam, this is Rich. Have you got that printout we looked at yesterday? Could you forward it my way?"

A few minutes later, the detective's printer spit out a couple of pages.

"Do you recognize anyone here?" Watring asked.

I peered at the printout. All women. Marty and Fran appeared halfway down the first column. I recognized no one and told him so.

"What is this list?" I asked.

The detective cleared his throat. "I'm really not at liberty to tell you that now." He stood. "Thank you for coming in, Miss Scali. You made the right decision. If you could get me copies of any other suspicious e-mails you might get, I'd appreciate it."

"Could I have a copy of that list?"

Detective Watring blinked.

I glanced at Quentin who gaped at me as if I'd totally lost it. "There might be some former patients on there. I could check for you," I added.

"The police can do that, Jen," Quentin said, and tugged gently on my arm.

I shook my head. "I doubt Dr. B will allow them free access."

A frown creased the young detective's clear brow. "Okay. But you must promise not to contact anyone on this list and not to show it to anyone else."

"Agreed." I put the list into my backpack.

Outside, I asked Quentin, "What in the world possessed you to come here this morning?"

He grinned. "I thought you might need some moral support. When I called your cell and got your voicemail, I decided to pop in. I'm glad I did. That was one yummy-looking copper. Jenna, you make me so mad. I'd give anything if he'd look at me all starry-eyed. Pity it is."

"Don't be crazy. He wasn't looking at me in any particular way. I had to use all my persuasive charms to get that computer list."

"Sometimes, love, you're as thick as a London fog. He was doing his job. He can't go around telling every chap who walks into his office all about his investigation. But I'll tell you one thing, that copper couldn't take his eyes off you."

I stopped walking and stared at Quentin. Something inside me did a little flip. Then I gave him a light kiss on the cheek. "Thanks for coming. It did help having you with me. I was a nervous wreck."

He opened my car door. "I'll see you tonight at practice," he said.

A slight twinge of guilt ran through me as I drove directly to Courtney's—doing exactly what that handsome cop told me not to do.

When I arrived, I found the girl freaking out over Fran's death.

"Who could have done this?" she kept repeating like a broken record.

"That's what everyone is trying to find out. Now, is there anything you can tell me that might help?"

She glanced from side to side. "You can't put this in your article. You have to promise."

That was easy enough since there wasn't any article. I gave her my assurances and took hold of her fleshy, nail-bitten hand.

"I don't really know much about this. Really, I don't. And it may not mean anything, but one time I heard Marty and Fran talking about a problem with the ring."

I scowled. "The ring?"

"That's what they said. I asked Marty what the ring was, and she laughed and said every unmarried girl knows what the ring is. So I asked if she was engaged. I couldn't believe she would be since she hadn't told me about it. That made her laugh harder. It was like she was laughing at me, and it made me mad. After that, I never heard anymore about any rings."

"Was Marty engaged?"

"Like I said, she never said she was. I'm sure she was joking about that. It was some other kind of ring."

"Courtney, what are you suggesting?"

She looked away from me. "I think Fran got Marty into some kind of trouble."

"You said before you thought Fran was mixed up with drugs. Do you think it was a drug ring she was talking about?"

"I'm totally clueless. All I know is what happened. Marty never told me what the ring was. Then she died. Now Fran is dead. I'm scared."

I squeezed tighter on her trembling hand. "You've got to tell the police about this ring."

"No!" She pulled away and crossed her arms over her chest.

I gave her Detective Watring's number. "Call him. He's really nice. He can help."

A tear rolled down her cheek, but she nodded and finally agreed to call before I left.

After practice I texted Frank to cancel our date for tonight. We'd been out three nights, and he was coming to Starr's party tomorrow. Enough was enough as far as I was concerned, and I didn't like his possessiveness. Instead, Quentin arrived at 6:00 p.m., and we grilled hamburgers.

By 10:00 p.m. I was nestled in bed with two cats and a stack of scholarly papers—great tonic to put even a restless mind to sleep.

And sure enough, for the first time in nearly a week, I slept like a baby until a noise sounded near my window. I awoke and froze. Stalin jumped onto my bed and rubbed against my face. Cats! They wandered around all night long.

I turned over and put the pillow over my head. The problem was now in the hands of the police. They'd take care of everything, wouldn't they?

Chapter 10

Rising late on Sunday was one of my special treats to myself. As a good Catholic girl, I had gone to Mass every Sunday for the first eighteen years of my life. Grownup, however, my politics moved me further from the church, leaving Sunday mornings open to browse through the newspaper and sip tea.

Churchill rubbed against my legs as I puttered around the kitchen. When his meows persisted, I picked him up and hugged him close. He pushed me away, letting me know I wasn't getting his attention until I filled his stomach. When it came to a battle of wills, Churchill always won. I refilled his dish.

Feeling restless, I moved from room to room. My mind wandered to Steve. I kept seeing that limp and wondered if he'd been in the dead girl's house—another minor detail I'd neglected to tell the good detective. Also, I wanted to explore Dr. Bingham's files some more before the police came knocking. When the teakettle whistled, I returned to the kitchen and poured the steamy water over an Earl Gray tea bag. As soon as I sat down, Stalin scratched at the back screen door. I let him in and Churchill out. Life with cats meant responding to their endless demands.

After having spent an hour collecting and sorting my recyclables into tidy bundles, I called Quentin. He answered on the second ring.

"Did you see the funeral notice in today's paper?" I asked without preamble.

"Whatever happened to good morning?" he complained. His voice sounded deep as if I'd awakened him.

"Sorry, but I'm a bit edgy. I'm thinking about going to Fran's memorial service this afternoon and wondered—"

"Sure, why not? I've nothing better to do than go to some strange chick's funeral."

"Quentin, are you and Alan having a tiff?"

"He's pouting because I'm never here, according to him. 'Between that damn practice and Jenna's demands,'—as he puts it, I'm always gone. He's annoyed because he planned for us to go on a picnic yesterday. Who the devil goes on a picnic in August? It's daft. Anyway, by the time I got home after escorting you to the coppers, it was too late and too hot, mind you. Burgers at your house last night fueled a major row."

"I'm sorry. If you can't go today, it's okay. I've got to go. I feel connected to those girls. Fran's death really shook me up. I should've done something."

"But what could you have done? We didn't even know she existed till she was dead."

"I know. But that doesn't change the way I feel, now does it?" I said, picking at a blister on my foot.

Silence.

"Bugger Alan. Where do you want to meet?" he finally said.

"How many times have I heard bugger Alan? You'd better watch out or you'll lose this one, too."

"Don't worry about Alan. I'll handle him."

"In that case, come here at one-thirty. The memorial service is at Bridgestone Funeral Home. Oh, and, Quen, don't wear jeans."

He snickered and hung up.

Quentin arrived on my doorstep at the appointed hour wearing a black suit, red tie, and white shirt. When I whistled, he swirled in a Quentinesk pirouette and curtsied.

"Come in. I'm almost ready. Just gotta finish braiding my hair."

"I invited Alan to come too, but he'd already planned to clean out the garage. I knew he'd say no, but I asked anyway. He's being such a bear." Quentin plopped down on my couch.

"Watch out for cat hairs," I said before leaving.

When I returned to the living room, I found him brushing his backside. "You ought to clean this place once in a while," he fussed.

"I just cleaned. But the couch is hopeless. Let's go."

We drove to Bridgestone in my Honda. Although gentlemanly Quentin wanted to drive, I insisted on air conditioning. After all, I was the one in pantyhose. The day dripped with humidity, and the sky was cloudy and moody, perfect for mourning the premature death of a young woman.

Quentin flipped on the radio and fiddled with the dial until he reached an NPR station humming with a Yo-Yo Ma cello concerto. He leaned back his head. "Ah, that's heavenly. What I'd give for a radio like this."

"You could put one in the Dodge."

"You aren't serious, love. That car is just a piece of junk, but I've grown attached to the ol' devil. Putting in a sound system like this would be like putting a thirty-year-old heart in a seventy-year-old body. It'd just frustrate the old bag."

I laughed.

Cars jammed the funeral home parking lot. When a young person died in Athens, people turned out.

"What do you want me to do?" Quentin asked before opening the car door.

"Mingle. Pretend to be one of her teachers. Who knows, you might even have been one. Besides, someone here might shed some light on the tragedy of all this."

He saluted and got out of the car.

My stomach did a somersault as we walked up the sidewalk. When I was ten, my father died from a massive heart attack. At the funeral Mom held my hand, and I held my little sister's. Lou was eight. I'd never forget staring at the casket and wondering if my daddy was really inside. Tears sprang to my eyes.

"Here. You might need some of this." I withdrew a Kleenex from my purse and handed it to Quentin.

"Whatever for?"

"It's a funeral. Some people get a little emotional."

"Quite right." He stuffed the tissue in his pocket.

We entered the darkened parlor. I signed the family's book while studying the other signatures, looking for any familiar names. Then from the back of the chapel, I surveyed the crowd.

I recognized no one, particularly from the back. One woman, who sat in the last pew, wore sunglasses, which struck me as odd since thick clouds blocked out whatever sunlight might have peeped through the stained glass windows. The woman was dressed completely in black with a huge hat that shadowed her face.

A middle-aged man in a red and green plaid jacket sat directly in front of the woman in shades. He caught my eye because he wore that strange jacket. There was no sign of Detective Watring or Courtney, but I presumed both were among the crowd.

I led the way into the chapel. We settled on a pew midway down the aisle. I shivered, regretting having worn a sleeveless dress. The air conditioner was working overtime.

"Is that her?" the man in front of me whispered to his female companion.

The young woman turned and studied someone at the back. "Can't tell with those shades. But it could be her, if I had to guess. After all, it's the second one in less than a week. She had to show up."

The man squirmed and glanced back in the same direction as had his companion.

It took all my strength of discipline not to turn as well. Quentin patted my lap and shot me a warning glance that said, "Don't."

"Ladies and gentleman," the preacher began, "such a tragedy to lose someone so young." Then he droned on about the mystery of God's ways. Finally we sang "Amazing Grace." Tears streamed down my cheeks. That song never failed to make me cry. Quentin passed me his unused Kleenex. Afterward, while filing out, I glanced around. The woman in shades had vanished.

The mourners kept reverently silent until we reached the parking lot. I still saw no sign of Courtney. Surely she was somewhere among this crowd, perhaps keeping a low profile.

I sidled up to the young woman who had sat in front of me. She had long dark wavy hair and thick red lips. Her short skirt revealed rather muscular quadriceps. Quentin wandered away into the crowd, clearly ready to exit.

"Such a tragedy," I said.

The girl's head swung around. "Yeah."

"We worked out together—Fran and me, I mean," I hurriedly explained.

A quizzical look crossed the woman's face.

"At the Y," I added, hoping I'd hit an accurate note.

"Fran wasn't much for organized exercise. Jogging was her thing." She looked away as if searching for someone.

"You're right about that. She didn't come too often, only in spurts."

The young woman half smiled. "I used to bug her to come to a spin class I teach, but she was hopeless."

"My name's Jenna Scali."

"I'm Rita Garcia."

I glanced at the man standing next to her.

"This is Bill Jordan," Rita said.

"Pleased to meet you," I said. "Gosh, can you believe it? Who would murder Fran?"

"Some crack head," Rita said.

Bill yanked on his tie as if wearing it felt like a chain around his neck. His mousy-brown hair hung over his collar. "I've got an idea or two," he mumbled more to himself than anyone else.

Rita elbowed him.

"And Marty, too. I can't believe it," I said, hoping to get them talking.

"I didn't know the other girl," Rita said as if it was okay for her to have gotten killed.

I decided to change the subject. "Did you see that weird woman in shades at the back of the chapel? Wonder who she was hiding from?"

Rita threw Bill a warning glance. He looked away and readjusted his tie for the hundredth time.

"Fran got herself caught in the wrong place at the wrong time." Bill finally said. "It could happen to anyone. Right, Rita?"

The look Rita shot Bill would chill a jalapeno. She said, "Let's split."

"Good to meet y'all," I said to their disappearing forms. Whoever taught them manners missed big time.

I surveyed what was left of the crowd. The older man in the plaid jacket had left. A few young people stood in knots as if protecting each other. Quentin had his head bent talking to a tall fellow in a khaki suit.

"I've been there about five years," Quentin was saying when I walked up. He shot me a look that said, *Get Lost*. He was flirting, not showing the least bit of concern for Fran.

I reached for Quentin's elbow. His muscles tightened, but I gripped harder.

"We'd better go now, sweetie." I fluttered my lashes at him.

Quentin frowned.

I yanked on his arm. "Tell your friend goodbye." I tugged him away.

"Hey, Jen, are you daft?" A pout spread across his face.

"Somebody's gotta look out for Alan's interests. By the way, did you learn anything about Fran or simply that guy's phone number?"

"I didn't learn much," he muttered and yanked off his tie.

"Let's get out of here. I've got to go to Starr's party soon, but need to shower first."

In the car, Quentin asked in a slightly mollified tone, "So, what did you find out?"

"I found out the names of the people in front of us. Rita and Bill. And they were definitely hiding something. I'd bet one of my cat's nine lives that woman in the shades had more to cover up than her face. I'd love to talk to Rita some more. But she sure didn't act like the chatty type."

"Maybe the good detective should talk to her," Quentin suggested.

I shrugged. "If she won't talk to me, what makes you think she'd talk to the police?"

"They have persuasive powers you don't have. And anyway, who wouldn't talk to that copper." He grinned.

We turned the air on full blast as we headed home and I braced myself for Starr's do and an encounter with Steve.

Chapter 11

At 5:00 P.M. I DROVE into Starr and Steve's driveway. They lived in a duplex located on what most Athenians called the university side of town. Georgia bulldog emblems adorned all the mailboxes within sight, except for the Andrews who didn't have the least interest in anything UGA. Clutching the chocolate peanut butter delight dessert I brought for the party, I retrieved the morning newspaper and rang the bell.

"Thank the good Lord you're here," Starr said when she swung open the door.

"Here's your paper, but the news is probably old by now."

"I know. I haven't had time to get it, much less read it. Aunt Mabel and Uncle Horace stayed around, jabbering like magpies all morning. Finally, they left a few minutes before noon. Then I had to get the living room back to normal. You'll need to help me with the couch. I just finished vacuuming, but I've got to wash up the dishes in the kitchen."

"I thought this was your birthday party." I set the dessert on the kitchen counter. "You're not supposed to be working so hard."

"Who else is gonna do it? I don't have any fairy godmothers, unless you know something I don't."

There was no sign of Steve.

"Tell me what to do."

While we shoved the sofa back under the window and washed the dishes, I told Starr about the latest developments in the e-murder mystery. She clicked her tongue and uttered "Oh my Lord" several times.

"Even though I told you to keep out of this," Starr said, "it sounds as if you're slap dab in the middle. You had no choice but to tell the cops every dad blasted thing. Sooner or later they'd've been knocking on your door, wondering why you hadn't come to them first. One of our patients must be involved clean up to his armpits. First thing in the morning I'm gonna go through the files like my mama used to go through my diary. Surely there's somebody in there we can identify who's nutty enough to do this. Then I'll sweet talk Dr. B into helping us narrow the possibilities."

"Good luck. He's been none too helpful."

She wiped her hands on her jeans. "What were the cops like? Did they give you a lie-detector test or put you in an interrogation room?"

"You've been reading too many mysteries. It was pretty boring actually. Quentin showed up, he said to give me moral support, but I suspect to make sure I went. The police were actually nice—much nicer than when I called them. The detective practically danced on the desk when I told him I work for a shrink." I put the last glass in the cabinet. "You can help, though, by going through the files. That's something I've been wanting to do but haven't had much of a chance."

"Sure thing, sweetie."

The backdoor slammed. A moment later Steve sauntered in. The heat flushed his pockmarked face, making him look as if he were covered with red blotches. His narrow, dark eyes glared straight at me as soon as he stepped into the kitchen.

"Hello, pretty ladies," he said with a slur that suggested he'd unearthed a bar willing to sell him beer on Sunday. He reached a finger toward the chocolate dessert.

"Steve, you buzzard," Starr said, slapping his hand away. "We've nearly finished with everything. Leave it to you to disappear."

I imagined him hiding in the garage, guzzling beer and pawing over a shoebox full of Marty's stuff.

He leaned forward and kissed Starr on the cheek. She reddened. I wasn't sure whether her change in pallor came from anger or embarrassment. I'd feel both if Steve were my husband.

I decided to catch Steve off guard. "Did you hear about Martha Meeks getting herself killed?"

Starr looked at me as if I'd gone crazy.

Steve jerked his head up. "Who?" he stammered, but his eyes did a quick dart as if he were looking for a place to run.

"Martha Meeks. She was stabbed to death the other night. I thought you might know her."

"How would I know her?" His voice was unnaturally high-pitched.

"Steve doesn't know her. You know that. What a funny thing to ask." Starr gazed at me with a deep frown.

I tossed the dishtowel over the back of a chair. "I was simply curious. Her family's been in Athens for a long time. Just figured Steve might have run into her. Maybe she needed her cable fixed."

Steve straightened his slumped shoulders. He leaned toward me, his beer breath overwhelming. "Was she as pretty as you, darling?"

I turned away.

Steve let out a harsh laugh. "Your friend is an ice princess, Starr. But I love to watch ice melt."

"Get out of here, you old dog." Starr shoved him toward the door. "And get yourself cleaned up before our guests arrive. By the way, Jenna and I moved the couch back already."

Steve gave me a sideways glance and winked before he limped from the room. My stomach tightened.

Starr faced me. "What was that all about?"

"Nothing. Just a misunderstanding" I blinked and turned away from Starr, not wanting her to see the suspicions on my face. "Hey, don't we still have food to put out?"

"My gracious alive, the rolls!" Starr grabbed for the freezer. "I forgot to thaw them."

An hour later when the guests arrived, I steered clear of Steve. But his dark eyes pierced right through me even from across the room. Fortunately Frank's arrival drew me away from Steve's penetrating glances.

"Did you finish all your research?" Frank whispered and squeezed my hand.

He looked so concerned I caught my breath.

"I'm nearly done. Thanks." I hoped he wouldn't hear the flicker of guilt in my voice for having lied to him last night. Instead of working on the paper like I probably should have, I'd gobbled down delicious hamburgers with Quentin. Now that I thought about it, Quentin and I were both having trouble with our significant others. Wonder what that meant?

After we pigged out on country ham, potato salad, and homemade rolls, Starr banged a knife on a glass. "Hey, y'all, I'm about to cut into the luscious desserts. Hope you saved room 'cause we're gonna begin the tasting."

Two women I didn't know flanked Starr on each side. One held a dark-chocolate cake and the other a plate of assorted cookies. My mouth watered in anticipation.

Before I realized what happened, Steve sidled up next to me and grabbed my arm.

"Hey there, Green Eyes, how 'bout a taste of you?" he whispered in my face, spraying me with spittle.

His rancid breath nearly knocked me down. I twisted to free myself, but he clung tighter, pinching my arm. He touched my hair. I pulled my head away from him and searched for Frank while Steve slobbered a wet kiss on my neck.

"Stop it," I cried.

"Relax, princess. How'd you know about Marty—"

His expression crumpled when Frank smashed a fist into Steve's face. Blood splattered from his nose onto my newly-laundered white cotton blouse.

"Good God, Frank," Steve said and winced. "I wasn't doing anything wrong. If it weren't for me, you wouldn't even know Jenna. I was just being friendly is all."

"Like hell you were," Frank said. His face burned with anger.

People stood around, watching us as if we were the evening's entertainment. I escaped next to Starr, wishing I could find a convenient mouse hole instead.

"I'm sorry," Starr said. "He's drunk. I never know what he's gonna do when he's boozing."

"You'd better get some ice for his bloody nose," I said, and squeezed Starr's hand. I knew better than most how she felt. Michael drunk was so different than Michael sober. I loved one and hated the other. "I'm going to run cold water on my blouse before this stains permanently."

When I returned, people milled around the dessert table, filling their plates. Starr circulated among the guests, trying to ease everyone's embarrassment. I spotted Frank outside, smoking.

Steve gave me a petulant stare under a makeshift ice pack next to his nose. "How do you know Marty Meeks?" he asked in a nasal tone, calling her Marty as if he'd known her all his life.

"I didn't say I did. Like everybody else, I read about the murder in the newspaper."

He narrowed his eyes at me, clearly trying to read more into what I said.

"Stay away from her," Frank said, coming up behind us.

Steve slithered off.

"Come on, Frank, you've clearly made your point. We'd better leave."

"But we haven't even tasted any of the desserts yet."

I cocked my head at him and motioned toward the door.

Outside, Frank said, "I don't get it. Why'd we have to leave?"

"I'm wiped out. Between Steve and Starr and everything else, I'm going home and crashing."

Frank pounded his fist on top of the hood of his Volvo, putting a tiny dent in the shiny black finish.

I gawked at him.

"You're blowing me off again," he said in a whiny voice. "I can't believe it. Don't you know how I feel about you?"

"Listen, it's not like we haven't seen each other this week."

"But Friday night you went home early. Last night you cancelled out on me. It's only nine o'clock for God sakes. I feel like you don't want to be with me. I seem to have to beg to see you. What the devil is going on?"

I scratched my toe in the gravel. "I'm not ready for this kind of intense relationship. You're suffocating me. I need time to sort everything out. I can't even think about how I feel about us with you constantly on my case. Please understand. You've got to give me more time."

"If you loved me, you'd know it. You wouldn't need time."

The streetlight next to Starr's apartment shone on his head like an actor spotlighted in a small-time play.

He forced a smile. "Maybe I could go to your house and soothe whatever is bothering you. I've been known to give a great back rub."

Moving closer to him, I took his hand. "You're not listening to what I'm saying. I need some space. Maybe we need to chill for a while to give me a chance to think things through."

His grip on my hand tightened. I tried to twist away, but he held firm. "Don't do this to me," he begged.

"Only for a while. I don't want you to believe I can be something I can't, and right now I don't know what I can be to you."

"But that's not fair. You're blaming me for what Steve did. He deserved a punch in the nose."

"This has nothing to do with Steve. This has to do with you and me."

His shoulders sagged in resignation. He dropped my hand. "How long?"

"I don't know. A week maybe."

"So I can see you next weekend?"

"Call me and we'll see, okay?"

He nodded.

Quietly, I slipped into my car and drove away.

That night, I dreamed about Marty Meeks, picturing her as a tall girl with long wavy hair, like Mel, the girl who'd been with Timothy. Marty jogged along a tree-lined path. Suddenly she tripped. A man stood above her with a rope in his hands. She screamed, and the man grabbed her and tied her hands and feet. He pulled out a huge butcher knife. Seconds before he plunged the knife into her heart, I woke up.

My nightgown stuck to me. Stalin was walking on my chest, clearly disturbed by my restlessness.

I moved the cat, turned over, and glanced at my watch. 2:57 a.m. Switching on the light, I walked into the bathroom. The mirror reflected deep-purple rings under my eyes.

In my dream I couldn't see the man who was about to stab Marty, but his voice rang in my ears, and I could smell the beer on his breath.

* * * *

The next morning when Starr walked into the office at 8:50 a.m., the telephone was ringing, I was talking with a patient, and another person was leafing through a magazine in the waiting area. Starr grabbed the phone.

When she hung up the receiver, she mouthed, "It's nuts around here."

I shrugged, scheduled an appointment for the patient at the window, and returned to my desk.

"Looks like you survived last night."

She rolled her eyes and took over the front desk.

I moved into the back room to make copies of a stack of insurance forms.

"Lordy," Starr said when I returned, "the sky must've opened up this morning, and everybody and his brother decided to call us. What in the world happened? Full moon last night or something?"

"Dr. B came in late. Said he overslept. So we're backed up. I've got to do a couple of things on the computer before I exit for my seminar. But if things calm down, maybe you can pull those files we talked about yesterday."

"Will do." She saluted. "Was Dr. B furious when you told him you went to the police?"

I lowered my voice. "He didn't say much, but we didn't really have a chance to talk. I'll probably get read the riot act when he's free."

I switched on the computer, answered several routine e-mails, grateful to see nothing from Finland, and then e-mailed Frank.

Sorry about last night. I've been thinking about what you said—if I loved you, I'd know it and wouldn't need time. That's probably true, but I can't tell for sure. It's not that easy for me. After Michael, I no longer trust myself. You don't seem to understand that. I really think we should stop seeing each other for a few weeks (not just one). Maybe when I get back from the break, we'll see. By then all this craziness with the e-mail murders should be over, and I'll have a good start on my prospectus. You may think I'm not worth it and want to move on. If so, I'll respect that. But right now that's all I can do. Sorry. Love, J

I got an instant response.

Jen, I'll do whatever you want, but I'm not happy about it. You've helped me get over my mother's death. You understand me like no one else does. I depend on you so much. Do you get that? When you gave yourself to me, I thought that meant I was special to you. Don't push me away. I'll wait for you, but I won't stay away. I can't. Love, Frank

I cupped my head in my hands and sighed. Dealing with Frank was taking its toll.

After a few minutes of feeling sorry for myself, I glanced at the computer list the detective had reluctantly given me. I entered each name into our databank. As I went down the list, I came across Rita Garcia. So, she was hiding something, but what? I had no idea what this list was, but apparently it had something to do with the murders. I continued entering names. If Dr. B had seen any of these people in the last three years, the computer would tell me. To find out if he'd seen them before that time, I'd have to go through the files manually. Of course, he'd kill me if I told the police about any of them. Even so, I plowed my way through the list, deciding I'd deal with that when I saw what popped out.

As the computer gurgled and gulped, conducting its search, I paced. After seven minutes, I saved the data to a thumb drive, aborted the search, and grabbed my backpack.

"I should be back in about two hours," I told Starr. "Let's hope the police don't show up before then."

Starr's eyes widened. "Lordy me, I hadn't thought about that."

I left her frantically going through the patient databases for potential e-murderers.

The shady magnolia trees, antebellum buildings, and neatly manicured quadrangle of the university did little to ease my tension today. All I wanted to do was get back to my desk and search for the killer. A time bomb was ticking inside me, making it hard for me to concentrate on anything else.

When I returned from the seminar, I found Starr in the back eating a sandwich.

"Things calmed down after you left," she said. "I managed to pull a few files. They're on your desk." She swallowed some Diet Coke and handed me half a sandwich. "It's chicken salad with low-fat mayonnaise."

"No, thanks, I wolfed down some peanut butter crackers in the car."

At my desk, I restarted the computer search. While waiting for matches, I turned to the patients Starr had identified as possible e-murderers. They were all men, and none had seen Dr. Bingham recently. Each had corresponded with us via e-mail or tended to text the doctor, which at least suggested a geekishness that might characterize an e-murderer. On first glance, I remembered nothing about any of them.

"I added Mark Campbell to the group 'cause he worked for the Computer Center at the university," Starr said, returning to her desk. "But that's his only suspicious link. He didn't see Dr. B long, and he never was hospitalized. The other three spent some time in the psych hospital. If this killer is as sick as his messages, I'll bet my granny's last dime he's done his share of time as an inpatient somewhere. Also, all of them except the Computer Center dude are people who had trouble with women."

She flicked a mascara smudge off her cheek. Dark circles marred her usually bright expression. "By the way, I'm sure it's a man. None of our women patients look the part. They're all too concerned with their marriages or other normal kinds of stuff, like finances or children. Most have inferiority complexes, big time, but that's about it. Depressed people usually don't murder, at least if you believe what Dr. B tells us. So I ruled them out. I rejected several alcoholics because I don't believe somebody who's merely a drunk would stab anybody so brutally. But that's only my opinion, for what it's worth."

Sure hope she's right. Otherwise Steve is definitely tops on my list of suspects.

"Wow, Starr, I'm impressed. My behavioral psych professor would give you an A+. How did you find these so fast?"

"I entered a profile in the databank and then sorted through what it spit out."

"But you hate the computer."

She tapped the top of the desktop as if she'd made peace with it. "It's the least I could do after last night."

Before I could respond, the telephone rang. After finishing the call, I took a look at the files. "This guy, Samuel Willis, hasn't seen Dr. B in two years. He may not even live in town anymore."

"I thought about that. Dr. B will know if these fellows have murderin' potential. After he looks them over, I thought we'd try to track them down."

"We?" I said with raised eyebrows. She shrugged before catching another call.

The phone rang off the hook. Finally I asked Starr, "Shouldn't we tell the police about these people?"

"Lan' sakes alive, Jenna. We don't know anything about them."

"But that detective said the cops often follow dead ends before something connects. I think they'd be grateful for any lead. Furthermore, if one of them is the killer, I'm not sure we want to sashay up to his door with a howdy-do."

"Have you lost your ever-loving marbles?" Starr asked. She swiveled around in her chair and put her hands on her hips. "We're not gonna sashay up to anybody's door, but Dr. B would have a dying-duck fit if we gave the police names of patients. Don't you remember that speech he gave us when he hired us?" She lowered her voice, mimicking Dr. Bingham. "'Confidentiality is the most important value in this office. If I hear that you broke a patient's confidence, I'll consider that grounds for immediate dismissal . . .' blah, blah, blah."

"But, Starr, you forget two women are dead."

"I've forgotten no such thing. I'm trying to use the good sense my mama taught me. These people are probably as innocent of those murders as you and me and Dr. B. How'd you like it if your trusty shrink gave the police your name because of some stupid hunch about your character? Come on, Jenna. Think."

Starr was right. That good-looking policeman had rattled me. "Okay, calm down. I'll take these to Dr. B as soon as he gets a break."

"Good luck. I don't see him getting a break till Christmas."

I turned back to my computer, which obediently churned out several names matching the police's printout. Starr's reminder about giving names to the police rang in my ears. But these people weren't pegged as the killer; they were potential victims, a persistent little voice said in the back of my mind. I bit my lower lip. My choice was clear—lose my job or watch another girl die.

I printed out the results, stapled it to the list, and stashed it all in my backpack. I resolved to tell the detective about Rita Garcia, who had never been a patient, but that was it, no more. My lips were sealed so long as I worked in this office.

Bing. A message arrived in my inbox. My stomach dropped as I read:

I thought killing would help. But what would really help me is to know you understand. When my head begins to hurt, I have to do something. Sometimes I feel like I'm about to explode. Have you ever felt that way? That's when I do it. I can't help myself. All this can stop if you'd just listen.

With a trembling hand, I printed out this latest message and stuffed it into my backpack.

Chapter 12

LATER THAT AFTERNOON, I CORRESPONDED directly with Johon Pvirtius in Finland to see what I could learn about sending anonymous messages. Pretending to be a potential client, I asked him a question about his service. A response popped up immediately.

I can give you complete anonymity. When you send your mail messages to me, my system automatically allocates you an ID of the form anNNN and sends you a message containing the allocated ID. This ID is used in all your subsequent anon mails. The messages become anonymous once they reach my machine. Even I cannot trace their source.

The service destroyed all headers indicating the true originator. I asked him about malicious senders. Johon wrote back that the system depended on a built-in trust. He wasn't responsible for malicious senders. Defensiveness spilled from the curt nature of his response. I hoped the police could get more out of him.

My desk overflowed with dictation that demanded attention. And if my focus wasn't placed on the billing soon, Starr and I could forget about our paychecks this week. Fortunately, the afternoon seminar was canceled, giving me time to catch up.

Before tackling my desk, however, I headed for Dr. B's office, which looked tornado-ravaged, evidence of a very hectic day. The carefully arranged files and papers of the morning spilled everywhere. Dr. Bingham was fumbling through a stack of folders at his feet.

"Can I help you find something?" I asked.

He turned. "I was looking for the telephone number for Miss Willesden's mother. I thought I had it here."

"How you can find anything in this mess, I'll never know." With my help, we finally stumbled on the scrap of paper he was looking for. "Before you make that call, I need to talk to you about my trip to the police."

"What's there to talk about?" He didn't look at me, and his voice sounded sharp.

"I know you wanted me to wait till today, but I felt I'd waited long enough."

"I see. Did you solve the mystery?"

"No," I shot back with a snort. Two could play at this game. "But, the police appreciated the information. I gave them a copy of the article on sending anonymous messages online that Michael sent me, the message the guy who hosts the anonymous e-mails just sent me, and all the messages we'd gotten so far. Maybe they can track down this so-called e-murderer."

He rose from his desk and led me out. "When can I expect them here?"

"I don't know. They probably won't even come."

"Don't be coy with me, Jenna. They'll have a field day with my patients. I've talked with Ed Atkins again, and he assures me I'm legally bound to protect my patients' right to privacy." His usually soft-brown eyes bore into me like spears.

I felt like a child slapped by a beloved parent and handed him the folders. "Starr pulled some files for you to look at. Maybe if the police do show up, we'll have someplace to steer them rather than them looking helter-skelter at our records."

Dr. Bingham brushed past me without taking the folders. "They're not coming near my records without a court order, and I'll even fight that," he said, marching into the waiting area where he called his next patient.

When I returned to my desk, one of the files caught my eye. The patient's name was Luke Miller. Something about the name triggered a distant memory. I opened the folder and read.

Luke Miller came to see Dr. Bingham after he'd been through a bad divorce. He lived with an overly protective mother. Before he married, things seemed okay. But once married, he showed signs of psychosis. He'd been hospitalized three times and had seen Dr. Bingham in the office twice.

Images of the man came to mind. He was on the short side and had leathery skin like a blue-collar worker who toiled outside. The couple of times he'd seen Dr. Bingham, he'd been so quiet I didn't hear him come in. He'd startled me when his face peered into the reception window, never smiling, or, from what I recalled, talking. Something about Luke Miller made me shiver inside.

Dr. Bingham had written: "Becoming increasingly suspicious. Diagnosis: paranoid state."

Would a "paranoid state" kill?

Starr placed another message from Frank under my nose. His third call today. Cooling things with Frank rivaled getting across town on a football Saturday—next to impossible.

I picked up the telephone.

"Outdoor Advertising," the receptionist intoned in swallowed Southern sounds no one could understand unless they knew what she was saying.

"Hiya, Donna. Could I speak with Frank?"

"Omigod, Jenna. He's been trying to call you all day. What did you do to that man? He's been an absolute bear."

"Sorry about that. We've been busy around here, and I couldn't call. Is he free?"

"Damit all. He's with a client. I could interrupt him, but this is a biggie."

"No, don't do that. Tell him I called and ask him to phone me tonight after nine, not before. Thanks, Donna." I hung up and wondered what I'd say to Frank when he called.

As the day marched on and patients came and went, I expelled a long sigh of relief that the detectives hadn't paid their expected visit. As soon as the next-to-the-last patient exited Dr. B's office, I took some letters for him to sign.

He was dictating into his handheld machine and motioned for me to sit down. "...I'll plan to see her in another month period," he recited into the online system.

I glanced out the window at the wind rustling the leaves of a dogwood tree that had turned a deep shade of green. I also spied a huge mimosa visible from this spot. Dr. Bingham's patients enjoyed a nice view.

"What a day," he said, once he finished his dictation and turned off the machine.

I crossed my legs and relaxed. "You've got one more," I told him.

"Didn't you have a seminar this afternoon?"

"My professor canceled to give us time to work on our projects. They're due next week."

"I see."

I moved the stack of letters toward him. "Could you sign these? We need to get them out to the insurance companies today. I'll run them by the post office on my way home."

He scrawled his name on the letters with the usual doctor's penmanship that no one could read. "I'm sorry about my outburst," he said, not looking up. "With everything else going on, I suppose I bit your head off."

"It's okay. You were probably right, though. The police didn't pay too much attention to me. Otherwise they'd have responded by now. Whatever." I shrugged. "I did my civic duty." I gave him a half-hearted smile he didn't return and handed him the folders Starr had pulled. "Could you look at these? I mentioned them earlier."

He rifled through the pages while stuffing his pipe with sweet-smelling tobacco. "If you're looking for homicidal tendencies—I'm using laymen's terms here—as I told you Friday, without more to go on, this exercise is purely hypothetical. Even so, I doubt Harrison or Miller are candidates. Harrison's afraid of his own shadow, and Miller's not much better." He puffed some smoke in the air. "But, Jenna, I don't want any of these patients disturbed." Puff, puff, puff.

"Of course not. Starr is going to help me find out where they are now. That's all. If the police do come around, we won't say a word about anyone unless we uncover something suspicious. And then only after we've talked to you."

"I'm serious about this. I know how exciting it is to be acting like a detective, but I have an obligation to protect my patients' right to privacy. I do not intend to leak anything to the police unless I truly believe one of my patients is putting someone in danger."

I nodded and gathered the letters and the files. "I'll be careful. I promise."

At the reception window, I spotted a tall deliveryman with a huge bouquet of yellow roses.

"Are you Jenna Scali?" the man asked.

When I nodded, the man placed the flowers in my arms as he might a baby.

"My gosh! There must be three dozen there," Starr said, sniffing the aroma.

The young man winked at me. "You're a lucky lady," he said and departed.

The card read, *I miss you already. Please call. Love, Frank.*

"Are the flowers a peace offering?" Starr asked, while peering over my shoulder. "Steve always sends flowers when he's in the dog house."

I sniffed the deep, sweet fragrance. "Undoubtedly."

Starr giggled. "From the look on your face, I'd say they worked."

I sent Frank a text, and he called immediately.

"The flowers are beautiful."

"No more than you."

"Are you trying to win me with flattery?"

"If that'll work, I'll try anything." He laughed a warm, tender laugh.

"I still think we need to cool it for a while." My nose twitched from the flowers.

"Jenna, I promise not to pressure you again, but I've got to see you. Please. Don't leave me out in the cold, not after all we've been through. I know you're the one for me. I'm convinced we're right for each other."

"As I told you in my e-mail, we need some space."

"Jenna, I can't. I—"

"You can." I was twirling my hair with my index finger, causing tangles that would take hours to undo.

A long silence. "Okay. If that's what it takes, you win. I'll do whatever you ask of me."

I hung up, feeling like a rat. But with everything else going on in my life right now, I didn't need Frank's pressure. I arranged the flowers in a vase, added water, and placed them in the reception area.

Starr had been watching me. "He's got it bad, like a wild boar with the hots. The man's crazy in love with you."

"Yeah."

"Is he putting pressure on you for a commitment?"

I began restacking the magazines that patients had mauled all day long. "He wants to get married," I told her. "But I'm not ready."

Starr reached for her nail file to trim down one of her acrylic claws. "Do you love him?"

"I wish I knew. My life is so nuts. How could anyone think straight? I told him that, but he doesn't understand. According to him, love is obvious —you either know it or you don't. Plain and simple, black and white." I pushed two escaped strands of hair off my face. "And the way he acted at your party floored me. He shouldn't have hit Steve."

"I'm not so sure. Frank was rescuing the woman he loved. I wouldn't blame him for that if I were you. Men have fought duels over less. They used to call it gallantry. Steve was a real sorry ass, but that's nothing new." She worked away at that nail with increased vigor as if she imagined Steve's neck in its place.

I returned to my desk. "But they're friends. Steve introduced me to Frank, for God's sake. Why would Frank punch him like that? I simply don't understand men."

Starr cackled. "Don't be asking me."

* * * *

The next day began without any interruption from the police. For a time, I even put the e-murderer out of my mind. Being a Tuesday, I worked in the library all morning and returned to the office around 2:00 p.m. Voices drew me from the copy room to the front office.

Standing in the hall, peering into the reception window were Detective Richard Watring and a squatty, middle-aged man with bushy eyebrows that grew toward his nose. Even without the plaid jacket, I recognized him.

"Hello, Miss Scali," Detective Watring said. "This is my partner, Sergeant Lewis."

"Pete Lewis," the other man said in a deep voice. His eyes took in everything like a tiger on a hunt. "Where have I seen you before?"

I shifted under his stare. "Fran Knotter's funeral."

He blinked. "Of course."

Starr stood at her desk like a private awaiting orders from her commanding officer.

"Hiya, fellas," she said with the high Southern lift to her voice that seemed to rise with nervousness. At the moment, she sounded like a squeaky bird in heat. "We've been sort of expecting y'all."

"Is the doc in?" Lewis asked Starr.

I responded. "Yes, sir, but he's got a patient due any minute."

"We won't take long," the sergeant answered, and marched down the hallway.

Detective Watring trailed after him.

"I'll just buzz him," I said to the two disappearing backs. "Two detectives are here—"

"Yes," Dr. Bingham cut me off. "I see that."

Starr grabbed my arm. "My Lord in Heaven, Jenna! You didn't tell me one of them looked like Mel Gibson in the flesh. I couldn't flat out take my eyes off that man. He's simply gor-jee-us. And as far as I could tell, not married."

I re-tucked my shirttail into my pants. "Leave it to you, Starr, to peel away to the heart of the matter. Dr. B's going to kill me. I had hoped the police wouldn't come until we had time to check out these patients. Let's see what we can find out about Willis and Campbell while they're in talking and before Mrs. Warner gets here."

Starr grabbed Samuel Willis's folder and picked up the telephone. "Mrs. Warner is probably gonna be a no-show."

Dr. Bingham had ruled out Harrison and Luke Miller. I couldn't remember too much about Harrison, and nothing in his record jarred a memory. I glanced at Miller's file again. A shiver ran down my spine. Clearly something about Luke Miller gnawed at me.

What did Dr. Bingham know about this man that wasn't written in his chart?

Chapter 13

THE DETECTIVES MARCHED OUT OF Dr. Bingham's office just as I had reached a dead end as far as Mark Campbell was concerned. I slipped his folder under a pile of magazines.

"Did you have a chance to match any patients with that computer list?" Detective Watring asked me.

"Not yet," I said, looking everywhere but at him.

"I'd like that list back as soon as possible. Meantime, please call if you get any more anonymous messages on your computer." He wrote his cell number on the back of his card.

"Actually, I did get an e-mail yesterday." I pulled the copy from the top of my desk.

"Your doc isn't too respectful of Athens's finest," Sergeant Lewis said. "Maybe you can convince him we need his help to catch this gruesome murderer."

I glanced at my computer screen. An e-mail had come in. I clicked on the message. The two policemen didn't seem to notice.

Jenna, I've shared my private thoughts with you and only you. When you betray me, my head hurts. It's hurting really bad right now. You know what happens when my head hurts.

My throat tightened

"What is it, Jenna?" Detective Watring asked.

"Another message," I choked out.

The two men lunged around my desk almost instantly.

If my heart pounded any faster, I was sure I'd have a heart attack.

"What does it mean?" My voice shook.

"If we take it at face value, Miss Scali," Lewis answered, "we're going to have another homicide on our hands soon."

"But he seems to think I've betrayed him somehow. Why does he think that? How could he know I've talked to y'all?"

The two policemen exchanged a glance. "Have you any idea who might be writing these messages?" Detective Watring asked.

Michael's face flashed in my mind. He knew about the anonymous server, and he was in town when Marty was killed. But, Michael could never kill anyone. I'd bet my life on that one. Furthermore, why would he kill these women—he didn't even know them. Then there was Steve. He'd acted so bizarre at the party, and I was convinced he knew Marty Meeks.

I stole a glance at Starr, who stood at her desk, watching and gnawing on a fingernail. Both detectives stared at me. Finally, I shook my head. "No, I'm sorry. Not a clue."

Lewis shifted his gaze, but the young detective continued to eye me as if I'd killed the girls myself.

Finally I said, "Maybe y'all had time to look at that email I forwarded you from the guy in Finland. He got pretty defensive when I asked him about malicious senders. Are y'all having any better luck?"

"We've got someone in the department who knows people in Finland." Lewis' response was brusque, almost annoyed. "He's been in contact with a buddy of his from the FBI Academy. We should hear something soon. In the meantime, please make a copy of the message you just received."

I complied.

"We'll be in touch, Miss Scali," Detective Watring said as the two men exited.

Moments earlier, he had called me Jenna. I had disappointed him, but what could I do? I didn't know who this nut was. Michael might pull some stupid joke that involved anonymous messages—probably full of porn and such—but he wouldn't kill anyone. As for Steve, I had nothing but vague suspicions, and what could I say with Starr standing right there?

"Do you really think another girl will be killed?" Starr asked.

My eyes met hers. She was clearly frightened.

"If the police think so, what can I say? Did you find out anything on Samuel Willis?"

"He's moved to California. I suppose we can rule him out."

"And this other one," I said, "Mark Campbell, left the university and is working somewhere in south Florida. That leaves Harrison and Miller. But Dr. B vetoed them." I continued to watch Starr's face.

"What're we gonna do now?" she asked.

"I don't know. Dr. B doesn't want me to do anything. He ordered me not to say one word to the police about our patients. But I feel like I have to do something. Another woman's life might be in danger."

Starr walked to the window as if checking to see if anyone were listening. She rubbed her hands over her bare arms. "Jenna, you'd better be careful."

"Whoever is killing people has gotten me involved. For some reason this nut is using me as his contact. Finding out why is my first priority because I'm terrified this maniac might be a friend, someone close to me. That scares me more than anything else. Who can I trust? Everyone looks suspicious to me. Lately, I haven't been able to concentrate or study. Images of those poor women and how frightened they must have been keep flashing in my head. I'm starting to lose my mind."

Dr. B buzzed my desk. "I've been beeped," he said through the intercom. "Mrs. Warner is probably not coming. I'm gonna leave through the back. I'll see you tomorrow."

"Okay. Are you checking out for the evening?"

"Yes. Snipes is covering call tonight." Dr. Snipes was a local psychiatrist who shared call with Dr. Bingham.

I told Starr Dr. B was leaving. Then I wrote down Luke Miller's address on a slip of paper. Harrison lived thirty miles northeast of Athens, but I jotted down his address, too, just in case.

Just then Mrs. Warner flew through the front door like a gale of wind. "Oh my. Oh my. I'm sorry. Is Dr. Bingham still here?" As she huffed and puffed, her face beamed redder than a University of Georgia T-shirt. She was forty minutes late.

I lifted the telephone to ring the doctor's office in an attempt to catch him. No answer.

"Sorry, Mrs. Warner, but Dr. Bingham had to leave on an emergency call."

She let out a long, tired sigh. "There was so much traffic and I couldn't find my cell, you see—"

"It's okay. We'll just reschedule you for next week."

By the time I locked the office behind Starr, the sun had shifted in the sky, spraying the front office with spokes of late-afternoon beams.

On an impulse I took a detour before heading home.

Luke Miller lived on the north end of the county off Nowhere Road. I drove the distance in bumper to bumper rush hour traffic. Even though the Honda's air conditioner worked like a Trojan, sweat crept down my backside; it was like sitting in a puddle. No wonder people pulled guns on one another in stalled freeway traffic, especially in August.

Nowhere Road was unfamiliar to me. Upon first moving to Athens, I bought fabric scraps from a shop on the corner of Nowhere Road and Danielsville Road, but that shop had long since closed, and now a video store, strung with year-round Christmas lights, stood in its place. I maneuvered the sharp turns and steep hills. Not many people lived in this part of the world. A scarcity of houses dotted the landscape.

Turning onto Smoky Road, I was struck by the country feel of the two-lane, hilly highway. Michael and I lived in a similar setting on the eastside of town. We had a small duplex off the Athens bypass, near the super Walmart. It, too, was in what had once been the country—hog and dairy farming country, that is. Dogs sat on front porches free from fences or barriers. Our closest neighbor was a mile from us. Here, several small wood-frame houses, a few duplexes, and a handful of lone mobile homes clustered together like sheep, leaving long stretches of empty pasture.

A large, black BMW parked in front of a convenience store on the left caught my attention. It resembled Dr. Bingham's. car. On pure intuition I pulled into the store lot, eased up to the front, and got out. I peered through the glass window. The psychiatrist was talking to a bone-thin, middle-aged man. Dr. Bingham had his back to the window. The other man was shaking his head and rubbing his palms together when Dr. Bingham grabbed the man's arm.

I stood there as though watching a television program. What was Dr. Bingham doing here? He'd told me he'd been called away on an emergency. In our jargon that meant the hospital had called him, not some strange man in a convenience store across town. Curiosity nagged at me with such persistence I almost barged through the door. But, I stopped myself and tore away from the window to find a better place to watch.

Noticing a secluded dirt road a few hundred feet to the right of the store, and partially hidden by a weeping willow tree, I tucked my car under the drooping branches to wait for Dr. Bingham to emerge. As I sat, I impatiently switched the radio stations from country rock to gospel. The sky remained bright and the sun intense, but my air conditioner remained off because I didn't want to run the engine and risk calling attention to myself. I pulled my legs up to keep them from sticking to the seat and glanced at my watch—6:00 p.m. Belly-dancing practice would begin in thirty minutes, and Quentin wouldn't be any too happy if I arrived late.

Dr. B's part in the events over the last week tumbled around in my head. The e-mails came to our office. He knew Fran Knotter, who'd been a patient. He argued himself and me into a tizzy to prevent me from going to the police. And not long after the cops had shown up, he popped up in the neighborhood of Luke Miller, whom he claimed couldn't be the killer. I couldn't imagine Dr. B a murderer, but he was definitely up to something.

Not many vehicles passed this way. So far I'd counted three cars and one motorcycle. I yawned and was about to give up when the door to the convenience store flew open. Dr. Bingham raced out, got into his car, and pulled away like a man on a mission. Without hesitation, I followed his

BMW north, keeping my eyes glued to his rear bumper until losing sight of the car over a hill. Upping my speed, I almost passed the black BMW parked in front of a small, run-down house about three miles north of the convenience store.

I slammed on my brakes and eased into a spot across the street, keeping an eye on the front of the shack. Again, I waited while the clock ticked away. With each minute Quentin's angry curses sounded in my head.—*Where the devil are you, Jenna?*

The house looked abandoned. A rusted-out car without tires sat in the drive. The paint on the outside of the house peeled off, and several of the shingles on the roof dangled loose. The front screen porch had gaping holes. I wiped sweat from my brow with a worn tissue. When had Dr. Bingham made house calls? But that was the only explanation my weak mind could conjure up as I waited and sweated.

Dr. Bingham finally trotted down the front steps. He backed out and drove down the road in the direction he'd just come.

I fumbled around for the piece of paper with Luke Miller's address on it, finally retrieving it between the seats.

Slipping out of the car, I didn't bother to close my car door. The sun had moved behind a cloud darkening my path toward that run-down shack. On the rusted mailbox at the curb appeared faded but still legible numbers: 7-3-0.

My stomach sank. The numbers matched the address I'd written on the slip of paper before leaving the office, those of Luke Miller.

Chapter 14

I REACHED MY HOUSE AFTER ten o'clock that evening, exhausted and too confused about the day's events to think. Quentin left me alone during practice, clearly sensing my distress. Putting the key in the lock, I fully expected to be bombarded with at least one hungry cat. By now Churchill would be searching the kitchen table for scraps, and Stalin would be pacing the back step like a wanton panther.

I walked through the living room to the kitchen, but neither cat was anywhere, inside or out. I was certain Churchill stayed in this morning. A thump sounded outside as if someone leapt off a ledge, too heavy for a cat sound.

My stomach lurched.

Gulping down the panic inside me, I grabbed a carving knife and tiptoed toward the bedroom door. With my heart thundering and using the door as a shield, I peeked around the edge. The window next to my bed stood wide open, and the curtains flapped in the wind. Moonlight flooded the room. It looked like a scene from a cheap horror movie. Motionless, I stared at the gaping darkness when reality hit me square in the face. Someone had been inside my house.

This time, my imagination wasn't working overtime.

My mind screamed, *Someone broke into your house. The person might still be in your yard. Wake up, Jenna.* At the window, I knelt down so as not to be seen from the outside, peered out, saw nothing, rose, and slammed it shut, bolting the lock. Otherwise everything looked exactly as it had that morning, including the scattered papers on my bed.

My cell phone buzzed. It was my mother. I switched it off, planning to deal with her later.

I rifled through my purse for Detective Watring's card. I might be independent, but no dummy, and this was definitely a time to call in reinforcements. I dialed his cell.

Seconds later he answered with a strong hello, drowning out the background noises. Was he in a bar? Watching a Braves baseball game? On a date?

"I'm sorry to bother you so late. This is Jenna Scali." My insides jumped as if I had drunk ten cups of coffee.

"No problem, Jenna. What's going on?"

"I think someone's been in my house this evening. I was about to call 911, but thought I'd try you first."

"Where are you now?"

"I'm at home."

"Are you safe? Do you need to go to a neighbor's house?"

"No, I'm fine. Whoever it was is gone."

"Okay, then, I'll be right there. Give me your address again."

I told him and hung up.

While waiting for the policeman, I paced the apartment and periodically called Stalin who'd been out all day. The cat didn't show up.

To distract myself, I called my mother back.

"Lou called," Mom began with no preamble. "She's coming home a week earlier. From what she knows now, she'll be here about a month before she goes to Somalia. I told her you'd come see her."

"I'm not sure I can now." A piece of my brain actually functioned. *Amazing.*

"What? You said you would."

"But things have been crazy around here. Besides, you said she wouldn't be home until the end of the month." I clinched my fist to keep from bursting into tears. Something inside me wanted to run home to Mommy, but that was no longer possible. My life had moved way past that point a long time ago. Even after Michael left, I didn't run home. Lou and I both were independent sorts. Losing our father at a young age helped us realize that nothing in life lasted. Even though the little girl in me wanted to tell my mother about the e-murderer and all the threats, that couldn't happen. She'd insist on coming here or my going there, and I rejected both those options.

"Jenna Marie," she began, in a voice that told me a lecture was coming. "You said you could come home at the break. By my calculation, that's two weeks away—exactly when Lou is arriving. I can't believe you'd tell me you can't come all of a sudden. It's been three years since Lou's been home. The least you could do is come see her. She's your sister, after all. I would have given my right arm for a sister."

My mom, an only child, never ceased reminding us of our good fortune in having a sibling.

I listened to my mother's words with half an ear. Churchill wandered into the kitchen. He crouched low to the ground as if expecting to be attacked. Seeing the cat's erratic behavior brought back the reality—a stranger had been in my house, picking through my things. Clearly, Churchill smelled the intruder.

"Tell Lou to come here," I said, interrupting her lecture. "If she's got a month, she can make a trip. We can have a great visit, the two of us."

Silence, until she finally said, "Well, we'll see. Did you get the recipe?"

"Starr loved it," But I wondered if Starr had even tasted it. Frank and I had left the party so quickly, neither of us had a chance to enjoy the dessert tasting, and Starr had said nothing about the chocolate peanut butter masterpiece. For some reason other things demanded our attention at the office.

"Good. I'm sending you a Martha Grimes mystery you'll enjoy. Let's play it by ear when Lou comes. Okay, honey?"

The doorbell rang as soon as I disconnected.

My anxiety drained from me as soon as the detective appeared, and it took all my strength not to fall into his arms.

"You okay?" he asked.

"Not great, but thanks for coming." I moved from the door. "Please come in."

Churchill peeked around the corner to check out this new visitor.

"Howdy, fellow," he said to the cat, and reached down to scratch his head.

Churchill rubbed against the doorjamb.

"So, what happened?" he asked, while petting the cat.

"I got home about ten when a movement through the front window startled me, but I figured it was Churchill, my cat. My other cat, Stalin, went out this morning. Anyway, once inside, something felt wrong, strange. Usually the cats greet me as soon as my foot hits the front entrance, but Churchill was nowhere around. A noise sounded from the bedroom. That's when I discovered the window open. It hadn't been open when I left this morning."

"Let's take a look."

In my bedroom my jeans and tennis shoes from the day before rested near a chair, brushes and hairpins littered the top of the chest, and books and papers covered my end tables.

The detective didn't seem to notice the clutter. He approached the window, opened it, and peered out. He felt around the window frame. "It doesn't look forced."

"No, I suppose I hadn't locked it," I said, folding my jeans.

He rose from the window. "And you're sure you didn't leave it open? Your other cat may have jumped out making the noise."

"It's never open, unlocked maybe, but never open."

"Okay. Is anything missing?"

"Not that I can tell, right off, just looking around. The stereo and TV are still here."

To my utmost embarrassment, the detective peered in all my closets, and then he did a quick search outside and doubled checked all the doors and windows. When he finished, he returned to the living room.

"Everything looks clear right now," he said.

"Thanks so much. Could you stay a minute? I'll get us a couple of Cokes, unless you'd like something stronger." *Please say yes!* His presence felt like a snugly down comforter in the dead of winter.

"Sure, Coke sounds fine," he said. As soon as the detective sat, the cat jumped on his lap.

"I hope you like him as much as he seems to like you."

"I'm partial to most animals." He rubbed his hand down the cat's back. "Especially cats."

Churchill responded with a low guttural meow that indicated as much pleasure as I would have felt if the detective had done the same thing to me.

"I'm worried about Stalin. He always greets me at the backdoor as soon as I get home. He wasn't there tonight."

"Cats have a way of surviving," the detective said, and massaged under Churchill's neck.

I went to the kitchen, opened the backdoor, but saw no sign of Stalin. I returned to the living room with Cokes for both of us and settled down across from him. An amused look crossed his face.

"Probably I should have pegged you for a mystery fan," he said, referring to my shelves of paperbacks.

"In books I can always figure out the killer. It's nothing like this."

Detective Watring studied me while he drank the Coke. "No, this isn't fiction. And, Jenna, this killer isn't too nice. If you're holding anything back, think twice. You were smart to call me tonight. So far he's killed two young women, and he's threatened to kill another. I don't want you to be next."

"Believe me. That's my biggest worry, too, but he's writing me notes. Who would he write to if he killed me?" I hoped to be more convincing than I sounded to myself.

"Well, that's a point. But I've learned with these things, logic doesn't always work. Who do you think tiptoed around your house this evening?"

I looked away. Churchill moved to his favorite spot on the arm of the couch and was busy washing his stomach.

"Do you really think the murderer was here?" My stomach clenched at the thought.

"Since nothing is missing, we can rule out robbery. I suggest you get dead-bolt locks on all your doors, and be sure to latch all your windows."

I drank from my Coke and tried not to imagine the murderer prowling around my house. "Why would he come here? What in the world does he want from me?" Panic began to strangle me.

"Take it easy. We can't say for sure who was here. I just want you to take precautions."

"What did Dr. Bingham say about the killer?"

"We told him what we know, and he suggested some possible personality types."

"Like what types?"

"I can't go into all that now." He rubbed his hands over to the top of his khakis.

I set down my glass and crossed my arms. My nape prickled with, what, oh yes, *fear*. "You want me to take precautions but precautions against what? How can I find out who this nut is if you won't tell me anything?" My face flushed with anger and frustration.

"Much as I'd love to have you along for this investigation, we usually operate alone." His smile looked a bit like a smirk. He paused, drank some Coke, and then said, "If I tell you a thing or two about this perpetrator that information must never leave this room. Understand?" His tone was dead serious.

I nodded agreement.

"The reason I'm telling you anything is that Pete and I agree there's got to be a connection with you, somewhere, somehow. And, if your break-in tonight is related, that would suggest the killer knows you better than you think. Perhaps I'll say something that triggers a distant memory—some link to someone you know." He made that little speech as if to himself.

The pitter-patter of rain against the roof reminded me of Stalin's absence. It wasn't like him to disappear particularly on a rainy night.

"These murders are definitely the work of a sick, angry person. Both girls were brutally stabbed. Our autopsy reports show that one or two knife wounds would have killed the victims, but the perpetrator stabbed them at least ten times. He mutilated their faces and their genitals with an X-mark.

The pathologist, however, found no indication of sexual assault even though he masturbated on their corpses."

I blinked, my throat dry, my heart thundering. With a trembling hand I sipped more Coke, but didn't feel it go down my constricted throat. Who would do such a thing? I closed my eyes and tried to will away the dizziness that overcame me.

"I'm sorry. I've clearly shocked you. But you wanted the gory details. It's not a pretty picture."

"No," I managed to choke out, opening my eyes and swallowing hard. "I'd suspected anger but not such base violence. From the e-mails he seemed sort of lost—confused maybe."

The detective studied me. "Do you want more?"

I nodded, beginning to twirl some loose hairs at my neck.

"After killing the victims, the perpetrator confiscated both girls' underwear."

My hand tightened around the arm of the sofa, and the panic inside me rose to my voice. "Their underwear?" Gulping hard...*Don't shriek, Jenna. Stay cool.*

"I know it's strange. Dr. Bingham suggested the underwear represented some type of trophy, apparently a common fetish among sexually disturbed personalities."

Yes, that made sense. I'd read that many killers, particularly serial killers, took trophies. But underwear? That was a new one.

"I suppose the fact that this guy masturbated on the girls but didn't rape them means something." Pause. "Like he does have some kind of sexual screw loose."

"Can you think of anyone you know who seems, well . . ." He looked away and his face flushed.

"Sexually out there?" I added for him.

He nodded.

"Perhaps a patient or two. But you'll have to talk to Dr. Bingham about patients. Anyway, he rarely puts a patient's sexual fetishes in the notes."

"Your doctor wasn't exactly what we'd call helpful in that regard. He threw more questions at us than we did him." The detective drank more Coke. "Wouldn't a patient tell his doctor if he had an underwear fetish?"

"Not necessarily. Maybe he's a transvestite and is embarrassed that he sometimes wears women's undies."

Detective Watring emptied his glass.

"Do you want another Coke?"

"No, I've got to go. It's late."

"Thanks for coming." Gosh, I hated to see him leave. He'd told me the man who broke into my house might be an underwear-thieving, girl-mutilating, sexually disturbed, cold-blooded killer. I felt as if I'd just finished watching a horror movie, and now it was bedie-bye time. *Pleasant dreams, Jenna.*

"Maybe you'd like to call someone to stay with you tonight."

I shook my head. *Bothering Quentin at this hour, not a good idea.*

"I really don't think you'll have any more intruders tonight," he added. "But keep all your doors and windows locked, and be sure to get those bolts tomorrow. If you hear anything suspicious, call me."

Churchill lifted his head.

The policeman scratched him behind the ears. "You feed this fellow well," he said with a laugh. Then he dashed to his car in a useless attempt to stay dry.

The rain came down heavier now. I went to the back to call Stalin. Nothing. A lump of fear filled my throat. He always came home. Praying he'd found a dry place to spend the night, I shut the door.

After rechecking all the locks on my doors and windows, I went to my bedroom to undress, opened my bureau drawer, and gasped in horror.

"I'm sorry to bother you again so soon," I told Detective Watring. "But, it seems the intruder had indeed stolen something,"

"Yes?"

My voice shook as the words fell from my lips.

"All my underwear is gone."

Chapter 15

THE DETECTIVE RETURNED WITH A forensics team. I gathered up Churchill and the two of us spent the night on my neighbor's couch. The next morning after everyone had left, I returned to my house to search for Stalin. Again, no cat. The knot of fear in my stomach tightened. My cat had only been gone one day, I reassured myself. Churchill meowed to go out, but no way.

"I've lost one cat. I won't lose another." The frustrated feline was glad to be home but didn't appreciate the confinement.

At 7 a.m., I arrived at the office in the hopes of catching Dr. Bingham before the onslaught of patients.

I put my backpack in my desk and walked back to his office where my boss had his head buried in the *Physician's Desk Reference*.

"Good morning."

He jerked up. "Good gosh, Jenna. You startled me. What are you doing here so early?" He put the weighty book aside.

"I wanted a few minutes to talk."

"Great. I'm dying for a cup of coffee. Let's go get some."

A moment later, I slid comfortably onto the BMW's leather seats. My heart thudded with worry about what I'd say to my boss. The smell of the car and the odor of his pipe tobacco mingled reassuringly of his innocence. How could I doubt this man? A man I've worked with for over five years. And yet...

As he pulled into the early morning traffic, Dr. Bingham said, "How about the Waffle House?"

"Fine."

Several blocks later, he negotiated the car into the parking lot. Inside, the place clamored with activity even though my watch read not quite 7:15 a.m. Apparently lots of people came here on their way to work for a grease fix—sausage and grits loaded with butter. Great for the cholesterol level.

"Howdy, Doc," the waitress called to us.

"They know you?" This man continued to surprise me. The Waffle House didn't exactly fit with my image of his style. Nor, for that matter, did Luke Miller's side of town, a voice in my head reminded me.

"I sometimes come for a cup of coffee before going to the hospital," he admitted as if embarrassed. "How 'bout a booth, Maggie?"

"For you, Doc? You betcha."

She ushered us to the last available booth. The way she beamed at Dr. B I had no doubts she'd have run someone off if all the booths had been occupied.

The restaurant hummed with a gentle buzz. People conversed across tables and up and down the counter, like one big, happy party.

"Coffee?" Dr. Bingham asked me.

"Please, with cream. I'd also like some toast. I left this morning without breakfast." Who could eat after what I'd been through, and come to think of it, my stomach still felt queasy.

He motioned for Maggie and placed the order while the waitress poured coffee into our mugs.

The hot liquid tasted bitter.

"So tell me what happened yesterday?" I said after Maggie left.

"Yesterday? What do you mean?"

"I mean, Mrs. Warner came, and I tried to reach you at the hospital, but you weren't there." Okay, so I didn't try to reach him at the hospital, but I knew for a fact he wasn't there, and sometimes little white lies were in order, right?

He shook out two sugar packets before responding, "There was a minor emergency with a patient. Did you reschedule Mrs. Warner?" I loved the way psychiatrists never really answered your questions.

"She's coming back next Tuesday."

I studied his face while he stirred the sugar into his coffee. The frown between his eyes deepened. Could this man kill? He himself said anyone could kill given the right circumstances.

"Jenna, all this business with the murdered college girls is causing tension between us. Lately, I feel as if you're cross-examining me. I've nothing to hide. I thought I made myself clear about my position regarding my patients."

I pursed my lips under his gaze and shifted in my seat. For five years he'd been good to me. But why go to Luke Miller's house yesterday? Maybe Miller threatened suicide or something. Usually Dr. B told us when a patient became suicidal. We often had to notify the sheriff and the hospital in case he had to commit someone. I've never known him to go to a patient's house without telling anyone. It was too bizarre.

He pushed back the lock of hair that flopped over his eyes and sighed. "It's too bad I can't tell you everything. That's the nature of my work."

"Tell me what the police said."

Maggie put the plate of toast in front of us and winked at Dr. Bingham.

"How's the Misses?" she asked, and glared at me as if I were a threat to all the world's happy marriages.

"Fine, Maggie. This is Jenna Scali, my office manager."

"You're working for a great man. He did a miracle on my husband's niece. She flat out changed her ways after just a couple of visits. Never seen her so happy."

Two weeks ago, I would have heartily agreed. Now doubts clouded my mind. Who was this man? What had he been up to when I followed him? I wasn't sure about anything.

"Don't y'all hate all this rain?" Maggie added, turning back to Dr. B as if planning to pull up a chair.

"It's been good for my yard," he said.

"You got that right. And leastwise it isn't raining today." Maggie gave him a light pat on the shoulder before someone waved to her from the counter and she left.

Four men with sparse gray hair and wearing shirtsleeves gathered in the booth directly in front of me. They drank coffee and munched on bacon and sausage. They looked like retirees who didn't know what to do with their early morning hours now that work wasn't an option.

"Ain't what's happening to them college kids awful," one said in a loud voice.

"You mean those girls that got theirselves kilt?" another replied. "I'm carrying my granddaughter to Macon during the break. We want her far away from this messed-up town."

A third chimed in, "Good idea. I don't know what the world is coming to. I remember when a fella could walk anywhere in this town without a worry. Must be all them folks coming from Atlanta."

Instead of talking about the Braves' pitching game, these guys were jabbering about the murders. Amazing. I sipped from the steaming mug of coffee and waited for Dr. Bingham to answer my question.

"The police seem to think the killer is some kind of sex maniac," Dr. B said in quiet, measured words. "He brutally killed the victims. Because they found no sign of forced entry at the second girl's house, they believe he knew her and possibly the other one, too. Apparently the girls were friends." He nodded toward my toast.

"Have some," I said, pushing the dish closer to him. He ate a piece.

"Could you help them in any way?"

"I did what I could. I explained that the killer sounded like a person with a deep-seated hostility toward women, possibly an obsessive personality. The knife wounds were particularly brutal, but careful. They showed me pictures." He put down the toast. "The killer is probably paranoid. I don't think he's psychotic. Clearly he's a very angry person."

"Do you think it's someone who wants to be caught?"

"The messages coming to you suggest so." He drank from his mug. "I gave the police a sketchy profile. They seemed satisfied for the moment."

"So you agree the person sending me the messages is the killer?"

"From what the police said, it appears so."

I ate half a slice of toast but couldn't eat more. My stomach constricted. "What about Luke Miller? Didn't you diagnosis him as a paranoid state?"

He jerked up his head and blinked several times as if considering what to say. Then, he put another packet of sugar in his coffee and stirred.

Silence.

Plunging further, I said, "Don't you think you should mention him to the police?"

Dr. Bingham's face turned beet red, his eyes narrowed into thin, fierce slits glaring at me, and making me feel two inches tall. He shook out his spoon with unusual vigor, splashing drops of coffee onto the table. "I have no proof Luke Miller or any of my patients had anything to do with those murders. My patients have entrusted me with their confidences. I have no intention of violating that trust. Furthermore, I told you Miller's not a likely candidate. You've got to get over your obsession about this. I'm tired of arguing with you."

I leaned back in my seat. "It's more than an obsession. Someone broke into my house last night and stole all my underwear."

Dr. Bingham gasped. "My God."

"I'm going to meet with the detectives as soon as Starr comes in this morning."

"No. Go now. I can manage."

We left the restaurant a few minutes later.

At the police station, I told the cops everything I could. And yet, they weren't exactly making nice.

"If there's anything you're holding back, think twice." Sergeant Lewis spoke to me like I was a first grader. "You have no business meddling in a police investigation. Do you understand that, Miss Scali? It's up to us to decide what's important and what isn't, not you."

I nodded.

"There's a very sick killer on the loose, threatening the life of another innocent young girl." His gaze pierced right through me, causing me to tremble in my sandals.

Detective Watring stared at the tops of his shoes and didn't say one word.

I couldn't tell them about Dr. B's trip to Luke Miller's because Miller was a patient. Besides, that incident might not be related to the murders. But what about Steve's visit to Marty's house? I didn't know for sure if the intruder I'd seen had been Steve, but, I did see an intruder.

"There is one other thing," I began. "On Thursday night I saw someone leaving Marty Meeks house—"

"What were you doing at the dead girl's house?" Lewis broke in.

"She lives around the corner from me. I drove by on my way to Kroger and that's when I noticed someone there. I have no idea who it was. For all I know it was a family member or even a police officer. It was pretty late, though."

Detective Watring took notes on his iPad.

"There's more," I added on a roll now. "Have y'all talked to Courtney Jenkins?"

The young detective leafed through his notes. "She's a friend of Martha Meeks, right?"

I nodded.

"Actually, she knew both victims. She called me Saturday morning, and I went to see her. She's scared but otherwise okay. I'm worried she might be the next victim." I didn't explain why I visited her or how I found out her name. Some details are best left unsaid.

"Got it," Watring said, and flipped the iPad cover.

"And Rita Garcia? She was on that list you gave me. I met her at Fran's funeral. She wasn't one of Dr. B's patients, at least not in the last three years."

"We've talked to her," Lewis answered. "Anyone else from that list?"

"I'm still working on it." I lifted my backpack to go.

Detective Watring walked me to my Honda.

"We're going to put surveillance on your house, starting today," he said. "Also, we'd like you to take a quick look at Fran Knotter's belongings. We've thoroughly combed her house, but you might see something that jars a memory."

"Sure. When?"

"How about tomorrow evening around six. I'll text you."

I nodded agreement and quickly took off, glad to be away from that imposing building and from Sergeant Lewis' intense gaze.

At noon, I raced to a locksmith to arrange for new locks on my house. He promised to have them up by the end of the day. Target was next on my list where I quickly bought underwear, not as nice as Victoria Secret but more in my price range. Then I spent the rest of the day in the library, trying to concentrate on anything but e-murderers.

I returned to the office after six o'clock to finish up some work I'd started earlier. It took just two hours to complete three days of patient billings. I got so much done without telephone calls and patient interruptions. Why in the world did I ever come in during regular hours? As soon as the printout of the last invoice finished, the computer beeped an e-mail.

Tomorrow night. And, Jenna, quit looking for that damn cat.

He's keeping me company now.

Tears sprang to my eyes, making it hard for me to punch in Detective Watring's number.

"He's got Stalin," The words tumbled out as soon as he answered.

"Jenna, where are you?"

"I'm at the office. The message just came in. He's got my cat. Stalin's been missing since yesterday." My breath caught in my throat. The knot in my stomach tightened.

Silence.

"Did you hear me?" I said, wondering if the good detective was still on the line.

"Yes, I'm thinking. Why would he take your cat? It doesn't make sense. What's your cat got to do with anything?"

I propped my head in my hands and rubbed my temples.

"Read the message word for word to me," he asked.

I read it.

Silence.

Finally, he said, "Look, Jenna. He's not gonna hurt your cat. Why should he? Anyway, we don't know if he really has your cat or if he's throwing out an empty threat to get at you. Who did you tell about Stalin's absence?"

"Just Starr and my neighbor."

"Look," he continued. "This guy kills people, particularly young women, not cats. But he said tomorrow night. It looks as if we'd better step things up. I need to talk to Pete. Are you gonna be okay?"

Sniffing and sobbing, I could barely choke out, "Yeah, I'm leaving for belly-dancing practice in a few minutes."

"Good. Keep your cell phone close by. And, thanks for alerting me."

Uncertain about what the next few hours would bring, I checked to make sure my cell was fully charged. Then, I washed my face and left for practice.

On the way, my mind kept replaying the incidents in which sociopaths killed animals just for the fun of it.

Get a grip, Jenna!

Chapter 16

LATER THAT NIGHT, MUSIC FILLED the stage. My head swirled from the sounds, concentrating on the routine, counting the motions—one, two, three, step right, one, two, three, step left. *Stalin!* Turn and dip slightly. A tear trickled down my cheek.

Lucille danced next to me and Doreen in front. This was our dress rehearsal for the dance festival tomorrow. We'd been through the motions umpteen times already. Even with the threat of a killer lurking around me, I didn't miss a step. *He kills people, not cats. Please, God, bring Stalin back to me.*

"Let's quit," Quentin called out. "You ladies are great. If you promise you'll dance like that tomorrow, I'll let you go home and get your beauty sleep."

"Thank God, Quen. My muscles feel as if they've been through a wringer," Doreen complained, lifting her hair off her shoulders. The sweat glistened on her smooth, chocolate skin.

"Wait till Frank sees you in that getup, honey," Lucille said to me. "You look like an exotic dancer if I've ever seen one."

I had no idea if Frank would come tomorrow night, and, to be honest, whether or not Frank decided to grace me with his presence was the least of my worries.

"For real, black is a good color for you," Lucille continued. "You should wear more of it instead of that mousy brown you usually traipse around in."

"You're sounding more like my mother every day."

I pulled in my stomach. It would take a bucket load of courage to stand on a lighted stage, facing an audience in this getup. The top was no more than a bra with fringe hanging off. The bottom consisted of shiny beads on a strip of elastic fitted around my hips, fringe dangling off the panties and scarves hanging to the knees. I wore black mesh stockings cut off at the ankles.

"Maybe Starr needs to give me that pedicure she keeps nagging me about," I said, staring at my naked feet.

"You're worried about your toenails, standing there with a flat belly and neat hips. Must be nice. Me, I'm gonna have to starve myself for a lifetime before feeling comfortable in this itsy-bitsy excuse for a costume." Lucille tugged at the ring of fat around her thick waist.

"Ladies," Quentin said, "what's all the fussing? You all look quite dishy. Tomorrow night will be a huge success. Wait and see."

"Can we go now?" I asked.

Quentin acknowledged my question by motioning us off with a flip of his wrist.

"Are you still dealing with those threatening e-mails?" Lucille asked.

I drank some water to avoid looking at her. "Yeah. But I've been in touch with the police, and they put protection on me now." *But not my cat. They aren't protecting my cat.*

"That's a relief. These murders have everyone on edge. Let me know if you need anything," she said before disappearing toward the back.

"Have you seen that gorgeous copper lately?" Quentin asked, coming up behind me.

"Actually I saw him last night. I had a slight problem at my house."

"Slight problem? Oh my God, what happened?"

"Someone broke in." I took a deep breath to steady myself. "But the police are watching my house now, Quen, so don't freak out."

"Don't bloody freak out! How can you tell me that? What do you mean someone broke in? Did the bugger nic anything?"

I bit my lip, not sure I could say the words. "Quen, let's not talk about this now. Something worse has happened." I swallowed hard. Tears pricked my eyes. "He's got Stalin."

"Who's got Stalin?"

"The killer."

Quentin's eyes widened. Mine filled.

"Oh, Jen." He took me in his arms. "He's probably just gone missing. I'm sure he'll be okay. That cat's smarter than you and me. And don't forget they've got nine lives."

I sniffed and wiped my eyes, but more tears flowed. "He e-mailed me. He has Stalin. There's no doubt."

"All you know then is the anonymous e-mailer has a cat," Quentin said, rubbing my back. "Maybe it's Stalin and maybe not. Besides, we don't really know if he's the killer, now do we, love? So relax. Stalin will find his way home."

He dried my eyes with a tissue.

"I'll bet that gorgeous detective agrees."

"He did say mostly what you said."

"What detective?" Doreen asked, coming up to us and rolling up the sleeves of her blouse. Doreen in her jeans and a tight red shirt didn't look as if she'd spent the last couple of hours sweating.

"Wait till you see him, Dor," Quentin said. "Jenna went to the police Saturday morning *finally*," he added with a roll of his eyes. "That's when the man of my dreams appeared in the flesh."

"Your dreams?" I laughed. It felt good to laugh. "I thought he was the man of *my* dreams."

"And he's a cop?" Doreen asked. She poured herself a drink of water from the cooler. "Don't go messing around with any cops, Jenna, girl. They're bad news. Better stick with steady-as-they-go Frank. Hear me?"

"I'm not messing around with anybody." I wiped the sweat and remaining tears from my face with a towel, which turned a dull shade of brown after it connected with what little makeup was left.

Doreen turned away to answer her cell, which never seemed to stop buzzing, and waved good-bye to us while she talked to some unknown admirer.

"Want me to spend the night with you?" Quentin asked.

"No, I've got a police car on my doorstep." I moved toward the backdoor. "I'll be fine. Besides, you've got Alan to think about. But there is something."

"You name it, love."

"Do you have plans tomorrow evening, say around six?"

"Good Lord, that's two hours before the show." A stricken look crossed his face. "You're not going to do anything stupid, are you?"

"Detective Watring wants me to look at Fran's house. He thinks I might see something useful. I could use your help."

"Will the cute copper be there?"

I winked at him. "Probably."

Quentin moaned and shook his head. "Even so." He put his arm over my shoulder. "I suppose if I go with you, I can make sure you're not late."

Twenty minutes later when I pulled into my driveway, I spotted the dark-blue sedan across the street and waved to what looked like a lone figure behind the steering wheel.

After unlocking my new deadbolts, I found Churchill stretched out on the couch as if he'd been there undisturbed the entire day. From the looks of things, there'd been no intruders.

I walked directly to the backdoor and called Stalin. No cat. A deep sob echoed from the back of my throat. *Please don't hurt my cat.*

I pulled out my cell to check missed calls. Timothy left a voicemail. I also had an odd message from Steve.

"Call me at this number, Jenna. It's important."

What could be that important? I dialed Timothy first.

"Hello," his voicemail said, "you've called the right number, but the wrong time. You know the drill, beep, name and number."

I did as instructed and then called Steve. He answered on the second ring.

"Hiya, purdy lady," he said. "Sorry to bug you so late, but Starr tells me you've gone to the police about all this e-mail stuff."

"Yeah, why?"

"I wanted to talk to you, uh, private-like."

I hesitated and then remembered the police car sitting outside on the alert, ready to come to my rescue in an instant.

"Okay. But come here."

"Wow, that'd be great."

"Don't you dare get any funky ideas." The thought of being alone with Steve in my house gave me the creeps.

"Scout's honor, I'll be a good boy. Can I come now?"

"In twenty minutes."

I pulled books and papers from my backpack. Tomorrow my social psych professor expected a paper on bystander apathy, of all things. Imagine such a thing as an apathetic bystander. That was definitely hard for me to wrap my brain around, being about as apathetic as a nosy neighbor. My schoolwork had taken a backseat lately. How could I concentrate when a murderer was writing me gruesome letters online and my cat had disappeared? *Excuses, Jenna, get to work.*

By the time I'd prepared an outline for my paper, the doorbell rang.

Steve stood on my doorstep with his hands in his tight jean's pockets and a grin plastered on his face. He shifted his weight from side to side.

"See that car over there?" Pause. "It's a policeman. So watch yourself." I hoped the man inside could hear me screaming if Steve went homicidal.

"Cool it, Jenna," Steve said, shifting his gaze toward the car.

With a reluctant sigh, I moved aside.

"Hey, this sure is a nice place you've got. The white furniture is pretty cool."

He'd been drinking. Had I ever seen him sober? No wonder he and Michael were such good buddies.

"So what's the problem?"

Steve plopped down on my couch and caressed the pillows.

Churchill slunk into the room.

"That one's a big cat," Steve said. He stared at Churchill as though he were a white tiger about to pounce.

"He's trained to kill. I just have to say the word. So, come on, Steve. Get to the point."

He looked around like a man with something to hide. "I don't know how you knew it, but I did know Marty Meeks. We were sort of friends." The muscles in his neck twitched.

"You mean you lied about knowing her."

"What'd you expect? You asked me in front of Starr." Steve was too old for baby talk, but he sounded like a three-year-old whose mama caught him with his hand in the candy dish.

"So, you're saying Starr doesn't know Marty, and she didn't know you knew her." For a brief moment, I enjoyed toying with Steve's discomfort.

"We kinda had a thing going," he mumbled.

"My God, Steve." I moved away from him and shivered. "I suppose you expect me not to say anything to Starr."

"Please. You gotta know Marty meant nothing." He moaned now, sounding younger than a three-year-old. "Starr'll flat out divorce me. I know she will. I need that woman, and she needs me."

Yeah, right, like she needs a brain tumor. "If she divorces you, it's in her best interests as far as I'm concerned."

"Yessum, maybe you're right. But have a heart." By now his dark eyes were wet with tears, his brow covered with sweat.

"Why are you telling me this?"

Steve ran his hand across his head, rumpling his matted red hair. "I don't want the police snooping around. I don't think they will, but I was afraid you'd tell 'em something. How'd you know about me and Marty, anyway?"

"It was a lucky guess."

He gasped. "You mean you didn't know about us?"

"Nope."

"Oh, my Lord." He moaned and swayed. He'd be great at an African American funeral.

"Okay, Steve, I won't say anything to Starr right now, but you have to tell me everything you know about Marty and her friends."

My stomach tightened at the thought of betraying Starr. Finding out about Michael's unfaithfulness just about did me in, threw me into a tailspin for months mainly because everyone knew about his shenanigans but me. It took years to forgive some of my friends. And here I was making the same reprehensible promise to a jerk like Steve.

But, the murdered girls took top priority, even over my friendship with Starr. More was at stake than her marriage. Lives were at stake. The only way for me to get information from Steve was to promise him my silence.

Steve crossed his legs and licked his lips. "You got any beer around here?"

"No, and as far as I can see, you've had quite enough. Now are you going to talk or not?"

"There ain't much to tell. I'd been seeing Marty on Tuesday nights for about eight months."

"Tuesday nights? Why Tuesday?"

"That's the only night she had open—well, she was busy, you know with school and I don't know what all else. It was her way, I suppose. She was so beautiful, long wavy hair and a body to kill for. The mole on her face looked like Cindy Crawford's."

I withheld the urge to vomit.

"I would have done anything that woman asked," he continued. "So Tuesday nights it was. I told Starr I had a meeting at the Y. She believed me 'cause it was always the same night."

He caught me frowning at him, reddened, and looked away.

"Go on." Could I get through this true confession without punching him in his already bruised nose? My jaw clinched in response to the anger boiling inside.

"I met Fran who was a fox, too. I got to Marty's a little early once, and she was there. I'd seen her other friend, too, Penny somebody—Jamison, I reckon. Anyway, I figured they were a threesome, what with all of 'em in school. And I suppose Marty jogged with the two of 'em. I reckon they were the ones that, well, that found her."

"What was Fran like?"

"Loud and a brassy broad with bleached-blond hair, but she had a helluva body—legs as long as Florida and a deep, sexy voice. Penny was short but with huge jugs....oops....sorry." He stopped and rolled his eyes.

"Pretend you're talking to Frank." Exasperated hardly described my feeling at the moment.

"Well, Penny was the kind of girl you wanted to squeeze. She wore a blue jogging suit, and looked soft, kinda...not tight like Fran and Marty. Get my drift?"

"How did you meet Penny?"

"One night when I got there, Marty was on the phone with Penny. She needed to borrow something from Marty—some school stuff, I reckon. Penny came over to fetch whatever it was. Marty acted embarrassed for her to see me, but Penny didn't give a crap. If I didn't know better, I'd have sworn Penny was flirting with me. She laughed a lot, seemed like one hot babe. Maybe you could talk to her about Marty now that Fran is, well, you know."

I frowned and wondered if he might contact Penny, now that Marty was, well, you know. "I will."

He rubbed his freckled hand over my sofa.

"So, Steve, what made these 'foxy' ladies notice you?"

A muscle jumped in his neck. "What d'ya mean?"

"I guess if these women looked as good as you say..." I shook my head as if in total wonderment. "What made them show interest in a married man?"

Married jerk was what I wanted to say. What was there about Steve that might attract anyone, much less a girl like Marty? But, then again, who could account for people's tastes?

"Don't be stupid. They didn't know about me being married. I never wore my ring." He rolled it around a couple of times as if to prove it was still there. "Oh, there's one other thing," he added. "Marty told me about Samson."

"Who?"

"He was the dude who lived with her before we started seeing each other. If you ask me, she still had a thing for him even though she said she didn't. I hated it when she talked about him, but being married and all, there wasn't much I could say." He shifted in his seat, uncrossed his legs, and looked at the floor again.

"Is Samson still in town?

"You got me there. But, he's some type of painter. He used to draw Marty naked. Boy, I'd love to see one of those pictures." He said *pictures* with a disgusting slur and a sideways grin. "Samson smoked pot all the time, and to hear Marty tell it, complained 'cause his pictures didn't sell. He made Marty pose in weird positions with mirrors and Coke bottles—crazy stuff like that. She didn't go into much detail about what happened, but it sounded sorta kinky. She broke up with him."

"What's Samson's last name?"

He shrugged. "Who knows? God, I still can't believe she's dead." He glanced at Churchill who was asleep on the arm of the couch.

"What about the shoebox, Steve? Where is it?"

Beads of sweat dotted his upper lip. He ran a hand down his jean legs. "What're ya talking about?"

"Don't play games with me. You've told me about Marty. Now fess up. What was in that shoebox that was so important?" I forced myself to look directly into his dark, jittery eyes.

He squirmed in his seat.

"Well..." I crossed my arms and leaned back on the couch. "The police would probably be very interested in finding out what was in that box. Bet they would, wouldn't you?"

"No, Jenna, don't," he said, falling back on the sofa as if I'd shot him. "How come you know about the shoebox? I don't get it. Geez Louise, are you some sorta witch?"

I stared at him, determined to break him.

Finally, he said, "Marty was awesome. I couldn't believe my good luck. So I started writing her letters. It was stupid, but I couldn't help it, and the letters made her laugh. She kept them in the back of her closet under a board. She showed me once, all proud. Said no one had ever written her love letters before."

Steve the romantic. Who would have thought?

"I sneaked into Marty's house after she died and fetched them," he continued. "I didn't want them getting in the wrong hands."

"Like Starr's?" I interjected without remorse.

Steve rubbed his palms together. "I destroyed them, Jen. They're gone."

"What?"

"I tossed them into the Oconee River."

The Oconee, a narrow river that bordered our town, was so muddy no one had seen the bottom in years. Anything thrown in there was history.

"Did you find anything else in that box before you threw the contents to the fishes? For all you know she may have stashed other letters in there, maybe even some from the killer." What an idiot he was.

"So maybe there were other letters, but mostly from her folks in Michigan. Nothing to take notice of." His glance darted.

"Steve, you're not telling me everything."

"Jenna, the letters have nothing to do with nothing, and they're gone now. Forget it."

Realizing I'd gotten as much out of him as possible, I got up.

He lifted himself from the couch and moved toward me. His mouth was so close the smell of onions on his breath made me twitch. *Don't you dare!*.

I led him to the door and latched the new dead bolt behind him.

Before returning to my paper, thoughts about Steve and Marty intervened. Marty had been his "lover." Why kill her? Maybe she'd threatened to tell Starr. But even if that were true, would that be motive for murder? And what about Fran? And why e-mail me? God, what a mess. I gave up that angle but found Penny Jamison in the phone book and made a mental note to tell Detective Watring about her and about Steve's visit.

At 3 a.m. with my paper finished, I went to the backdoor with hopeless anticipation. Stalin wasn't there.

I hugged Churchill before glancing out the window at the police car. A flash of light glowed in the dark. Probably the policeman was smoking a cigarette to stay awake. What a miserable job.

Before drifting off to sleep, Steve's face flashed in my head. He knew both girls. And, by God, he knew me. That was the link, the connection I'd been searching for. My eyes flew open.

Love letters? Give me a break. No matter what Steve had vowed and declared, there had to be more in that box than love letters.

Chapter 17

THURSDAY MORNING GREETED ME WITH a trumpet blasting from my clock radio. I clamped it off with a groan and crawled out of bed. My body ached from head to toe—too much hip movement during last night's dress rehearsal and too little sleep.

The thought of dancing again tonight sent a shiver up my spine. When I stepped into the shower, my landline rang. My God, who would call at this hour?

Frank's voice sounded on the machine. "Jenna, I know you're there. Your cell's turned off. Pick up, please." Frank refused to give up.

The warm water caressed my aching body.

After dressing, I called Detective Watring, only to be told he was out and so I left a message telling him about Penny Jamison. I didn't tell him everything Steve said, wanting to talk to him instead so asked for him to call me. While on the phone, I checked for my missing cat. No luck. E-mailing Frank from work seemed like a better choice than calling him now. He never had much sympathy with me as far as my cats were concerned.

I barely unbolted my front door when my cell went off.

"Jenna? This is Courtney."

"Courtney, what's the problem?"

"I remembered something that might be important, but don't know if it'll make any difference."

"Everything might make a difference. What exactly did you remember?"

Water ran in the background. Was she cooking breakfast, washing clothes?

"First thing this morning, I remembered a photo of Marty with some man. You know how sometimes you wake up and remember stuff."

"What about this photo?" Getting information out of this girl wasn't easy, and it was time for me to get to work.

"Well, it was at Marty's house a few weeks ago on her nightstand. In it she was standing with a man, not someone I'd seen before. He was a really cute guy. Anyway, I asked her who the hot guy was. She snatched the picture from me. 'When will you learn to mind your own business?' she said. She'd never talked to me that way. It really hurt my feelings. Later she apologized and said she was having PMS. I didn't think much more about it."

"So why now all of a sudden do you think this picture might be important?"

"I'm not sure. It's just that I've never seen the guy before. Maybe he could be the one that killed her."

I frowned. "I really doubt it. Do you know where the photo is now?"

"Well, I think Samson has it. Samson's Marty's old boyfriend. He used it for one of his paintings since she wouldn't pose for him anymore. What about going to see him?"

"Why?"

"I have this feeling about that man in the picture. You see, he wasn't smiling. And it's really bothering me now. If Samson still has the photo, maybe we can find the man."

"You mean the police can find him, not us. Have you talked to the police yet?"

"Not about this because I just now remembered. Don't you think we should get that picture from Samson before he does something with it? It may be important."

I balled up a fist, held it tight, and let it loose—a technique that sometimes helped stop a headache.

"How do you propose doing that?" I said through clenched teeth.

"I thought you might go to his place with me. He's usually never home during the day. We could look around."

"No, Courtney, that's not a good idea. I'll call my friendly police detective. Let him handle it." I had enough to worry about with my missing cat and with a murderer lurking around my house without adding breaking and entering to the list.

"Well, if you don't want to go with me, I guess I'll have to go alone."

"What's that supposed to mean?"

"I have this feeling about that man. You told me to think hard about who might have killed Marty and Fran. I've done that."

"Why don't you tell the police about all this if it's so important?"

She let out a long, dramatic breath. "I talked to some cop yesterday and told him I couldn't understand why Marty and Fran were killed. He showed me some list, but I didn't know anybody on it except them. He acted like he didn't believe me. Then he told me to watch myself. Duh. As if I wasn't already scared to death. So give me one good reason to call that cop again. Besides, I just remembered that man in the picture, not that anybody cares."

Sighing, I asked, "When do you plan to go to Samson's house?"

"Today."

I should call the detective again right now and tell him about all this. Courtney seemed hell-bent on finding this picture. Maybe the guy in the photo was the killer, and maybe my seeing him would help me recognize him. And maybe it was nothing but a ridiculous and possibly dangerous undertaking. But one thing was for sure, Courtney shouldn't go to Samson's house alone.

"Where does this Samson live?"

I ignored Churchill who meowed to go out.

"He lives off Jefferson River Road. I went with Marty a couple of times to return some things he'd left behind."

I reached for a pad and pencil. "I don't suppose you have the address."

"No, but it's easy to find. His place is at the end of the fourth dirt road on the right. It's a small wood-frame shack. Looks like an old barn. He's never there and it's never locked."

"Couldn't we call him and ask about the picture?"

"I'm pretty sure he doesn't have a phone. He's weird that way."

"Okay. I'll meet you at his house at twelve-fifteen."

As soon as Courtney got off the phone, I raced to my car while texting Detective Watring. Frustrated that he didn't answer, I tossed my phone on the passenger's seat and took off for work.

Throughout the morning my e-mail and my phone remained quiet.

Nothing from the e-murderer and nothing from the good detective.

At noon, I said to Starr, "I've got an errand to run. And then I'm off to the library. Is it okay if I leave a little early?"

She eyed me. "No worries, but what're you up to?"

I grabbed my backpack.

"Just the usual, you know, coffee with friends, checking out the sales at TJ Maxx, and catching killers."

Her laughter rang all the way to my car.

I still hadn't reached the good detective and wondered about beeping him. Surely he got my text to call me.

I drove along Jefferson River Road, a street on the west end of town. I counted the dirt roads, driving nearly five miles before reaching the fourth one.

Although I've lived in Athens five years, I was still amazed at how much open country surrounded our city. It didn't matter where I began—north, south, east or west—if I drove from town, I'd be on a country road in less than fifteen minutes. That was where I found myself now. I turned into the drive and spotted the barnlike structure Courtney had described. A skinny striped cat slept on the doorstep. The house appeared empty with no sign of a car. My watch read twelve-twelve. I waited. This entire rendezvous seemed pointless.

At twelve-thirty with Courtney still missing in action, I dug into my backpack for my cell phone to call her. Not there. Probably at the office on my desk. Great. Now what? *Get the hell out of here,* my good self said. My bad self got out of the car and walked up the muddy path.

The rainy summer had left grooves of deep puddles on this road, forcing me to leap from one to another to avoid ruining my shoes.

On the mailbox appeared a single hand painted word—*Samson.*

I peeked in the window and then knocked on the front door. It came ajar. Inside, the place couldn't have been more deserted. I pushed the front door farther open. Country people must not worry about intruders.

Samson lived in a single-room structure with a twelve-to-fourteen-foot ceiling. The place smelled of turpentine and paint. A small cot with crumpled sheets fit snugly against the far wall. A rusty space heater stood in the corner. Blue jeans, T-shirts, and underclothes cluttered a few folding chairs and spilled onto the floor. The most up-to-date piece of equipment Samson owned was a toaster oven on a card table adjacent to the bed. No evidence of the modern world. No computer, no TV, not even a radio. Definitely no phone.

"Hello. Anyone home?" *Dumb question but...*

Canvases of all sizes filled the room. The style of art appeared pretty primitive to me, laden with harsh colors—putrid greens and overly bright oranges. But the paintings held my attention. I gazed at one easel in the middle of the room. He'd painted a woman, who looked vaguely like Marty, with her back to the viewer. She wore a thin, transparent dress. Her hair consisted of fruits—oranges, apples, grapes. Bananas hung from her ears.

Jars of liquids, tubes of paints, and old brushes sat on small tables all over the room. I spotted a dirty commode and sink in the back corner. So where did this guy take his baths. The place reeked of turpentine mixed with pot. Little green plants lined the windowsill. His personal supply?

By now my watch read 12:45 p.m. Where the devil was Courtney?

I edged over to a card table covered with papers and looked for the picture Courtney had described. I'd just lifted a handwritten letter when the door flew open.

The biggest, hairiest man I'd ever seen faced me, hands on his hips, nude from the waist up, with one towel draped around his neck and another around his torso.

"So, what have we here?" he asked in a gruff voice.

"Are you Samson?" The words oozed out of my tight throat in a voice I barely recognized as my own.

"That I am, and who are you?"

He approached me. I backed up a step or two, maneuvering myself closer to the front door, which he blocked with his massive body. He had tiny, bright blue eyes peering from beneath thick black eyebrows stretching across his Neanderthal forehead.

"I'm a friend of Marty's."

Courtney knew what this man looked like, and she'd sent me here. I felt like a lamb being fed to the lion.

He inched closer to me. Gosh, he must be six foot three or four, and what muscles!

"What may I ask are you doing in my digs, going through my stuff, Marty's friend?" A touch of amusement laced his words.

The tension in my body eased a drop. "Surely you heard about Marty."

Samson moved a step closer to me and reached toward my face. I jumped backwards, stumbling over a canvas.

"Hey, chill. I'm not gonna hurt you. It's just that—well, turn to the left and let me see your profile."

I stood perfectly still.

"Ah, come on. I want to see your profile in that light, exactly where you are." He reached for me again.

This time I didn't jump. When his cool fingers touched my chin, my breath stopped, but I willed myself to remain still. He turned my head.

"Whoa. You're like a real-life goddess. I've never seen anything quite so . . . Romanesque. Stay still."

He fixed my head to face the side window. My first impulse was to run, but my muscles wouldn't comply. Papers rustled. I turned to peek at him.

"Don't move," he barked. "One more minute." He was sketching madly.

He put a folding chair under me. "Sit."

I complied.

After about ten endless minutes, I said, "My name is Jenna Scali. I'm sorry to have barged in on you like this, but the door was open, and I—"

"Shut up."

Time passed. My nose twitched and begged to be scratched. My neck ached. My back screamed. Nonetheless, I stayed fixed in place.

Finally, he said, "Okay."

I twisted my head to remove the stiffness. "Marty was killed about a week ago. I thought you'd have heard."

"Do I look like a man who listens to CNN?"

"Aren't you sorry about Marty?"

"Not really. Haven't seen her in almost a year. What's she to me? Dead, alive, it's all the same." He had seen her a few weeks ago according to Courtney.

He shuffled over to a tiny refrigerator where he removed a beer and popped the top.

"I came here hoping to find something that might explain her death."

"Did you?"

"There's a photograph of Marty that you used for one of your paintings. She was standing with a young man. Do you have it by any chance?"

He shrugged, and took a swig from the beer. Clearly I wasn't going to get the photograph.

"I would really appreciate it if you'd look for that photo. It could help the police."

He gazed at the floor. Had he heard me? If I was going to escape, now was the time.

"Thanks for your time, and sorry to have bothered you." I edged toward the door.

He didn't get up. I raced out to my Honda, dodging the mud holes. I'm sure I didn't breathe until reaching the office to retrieve my phone.

I called Courtney, but she didn't answer. A bad feeling settled over me.

* * * *

Before leaving the library at 3p.m., I finally got Detective Watring.

"So where'd you go this afternoon?" he asked.

"I tried to call you all morning. I would have told you about it, but you never called me back."

"We had a man on you. He said he didn't believe you were on a shopping spree."

God, I'd been followed and didn't even know it.

"I went to visit someone Courtney thought might have some information. He's got a photo of Marty y'all ought to check out. He wouldn't give it to me."

"Courtney Jenkins, right?"

"Yeah"

"We'll follow up. Thanks for the tip. By the way, we'll be stuck to you like Velcro tonight."

"What if he kills someone else?"

"We're paying attention to the other leads. Give us a little credit, Miss Scali." His voice sounded edgy.

"Did you get my message about Steve?"

"We know he paid you a visit last night if that's what you mean. We ran his plates. What'd he want?"

"He wanted to tell me about his relationship with Marty Meeks. He's scared of what Starr might do."

"Anything else?" I wondered if he'd followed up with Penny Jamison, but now was not the time to ask. My friendly detective didn't sound too friendly.

"Are you coming to the dance tonight?"

"Can't, but someone'll be there. I'm also sending an officer to the Knotter house to let you in at about six. Take your time in there. If you see anything that might connect you to her, text me right away."

"You mean you won't be coming?"

"I've got a full plate today. Remember, though, call me any time. And if I'm not here, you can always get me on my cell or beep me. By the way, any sign of your cat?"

"No."

"I'm sorry," he said.

I believed he meant it.

Hanging up, a wave of fear fell over me. I put my head in my hands and cried for Stalin.

At five o'clock I raced home to whistle for Stalin, but Churchill came instead and wrapped himself between my legs. I left Churchill inside and walked out the backdoor. Despair gripped me.

I sat on my back step and gazed at the woods. How many times had Stalin come running home from these woods after his catly escapades among the trees and shrubs?

Returning to the house, I played my voicemail. Three annoying deep-breathing messages gurgled from the machine. The last one ended with a bone-chilling guttural laugh. I hit the delete button to remove it forever.

A scratch sounded at the back screen. My heart jumped. Stalin stood on the step with his tail held high as if he had won a blue ribbon.

His fur was matted, and he smelled rancid as if he'd urinated on himself, but I grabbed him in my arms and held him close. My lips quivered and then the tears flowed down my cheeks. He squirmed out of my arms. I opened a can of salmon buffet, his favorite, rousing Churchill, who didn't seem as happy with Stalin's return as I was. He hissed and growled in a most ungrateful way. The prodigal cat ignored his brother and went at the food like a starving bear at the end of hibernation. Stroking and talking to him as he ate, I waited until he signaled he was finished by putting his paw to his face to wash up. Then I examined his body for wounds.

"I wish you could tell me what happened to you."

He purred while I palpated his stomach. As far as my amateur veterinary skills could tell he was fine except for being hungry, which for Stalin wasn't unusual.

I sent the detective a text about my cat's return, which got an immediate response. "That cat is one lucky creature."

I wrapped Stalin in a blanket and carried him to the bedroom where he began washing away all traces of his misadventure.

Chapter 18

I PARKED IN FRONT OF Fran Knotter's house at 5:50 p.m. The assigned policeman hadn't arrived, nor had anyone else, including Quentin.

Fran's place looked run-down, not neat like Marty's. Weeds choked the front yard and covered the sidewalk. The screen door had holes in the bottom as if a dog had fought to get outside, and the white paint had yellowed. A rusty trashcan leaned next to the side of the house. A hungry-looking brown mutt eyed me from the driveway. Could the dog belong to Fran? If so, who would feed him now? A snappy red BMW convertible was parked at the back of the house. Nice car, Fran. Just then Quentin pulled in behind me.

"Hi. Sorry I'm late. I had to pop over to Michael's for sequins for the headbands."

"I'm not wearing a headband."

"You must, love. They'll bring out the sparkle in your eyes."

As we walked up the broken sidewalk to the front door, I told him about Stalin's return.

"Do you really think the killer had him?"

Finding the door locked and the place blocked with crime-scene tape, I peered in through the window. The outside of the house begged for repair, and the inside didn't look much better. "I'm not sure what to think. The e-mail said so, and Stalin sure looked as if he'd been through a war, but he wasn't hurt."

"That nails it. This bugger must be someone you know."

I shivered at the thought.

"I wonder how Stalin escaped."

"I hope he scratched the blazes out of the guy."

Athens's Finest pulled up in Fran's driveway.

"Shush. We'll talk later."

A uniformed officer in his mid-forties lumbered up to us.

Quentin elbowed me. "Where's my handsome copper? You got me here on false pretenses," he whispered.

I shrugged with my hands open.

"I'm Officer Kelley," the policeman said, fumbling through his pockets for keys and fiddling with the lock. "Detective Watring told me to keep track of anything you uncover." He unlatched the door. "But I've gotta tell you, we went over this place from top to bottom." He spoke in clipped words with eyes downcast. Clearly he disapproved of the detective's request to babysit us.

"I don't believe Detective Watring expects us to find anything that you missed," I told him. "We're looking for whatever might mean something to me. I didn't know either victim, but for some reason the killer is sending me messages. Or at least we believe they're from the killer."

"We have no idea what we're looking for," Quentin added helpfully.

The officer moved aside. "Take your time. If you need me, I'll be out here." He reached inside his shirt pocket, withdrew a package of Salems, and settled on Fran's front porch step.

We entered the semi-dark room.

"Oh, my Lord," Quentin said when his sneakers touched the chalk form drawn by the homicide team onto the dingy brown carpet. "She must've been done in right here."

"I guess they don't remove their debris when they're finished," I said with a tight voice, an octave too high. "You'd think someone would have come in and cleaned this place."

Flashes of what I imagined happened to Fran right here at my feet filled my head. Dark bloodstains on the carpet made my stomach turn. I opened the curtains, and the room filled with low-lying sunlight.

Quentin giant-stepped over the chalk figure. "Do you have any idea what we're looking for?"

"Anything. I'd like to get a sense of who Fran was, and Detective Watring wants us to find a clue of some sort that links her to me."

He handed me a photograph. "Maybe this will help."

I studied the woman's face. She had a lengthy sharp nose and huge hazel eyes with a sparkle as if she knew a secret. Her long blond hair was clearly bleached as Steve had described. The half smile on her face looked almost evil. Even though Fran had seen Dr. Bingham and the woman in this picture had an unforgettable look about her, nothing about her jogged my memory. I put the photo back on the fireplace mantle with a sigh.

"I had an interesting visit with Courtney Jenkins Saturday morning," I told Quentin.

He prowled through Fran's books. "You went back there? You didn't say."

"She called me after she'd read in the paper that Fran'd been killed."

"Quite right."

"She told me about some sort of ring."

Quentin moved from the bookcase to survey the CD collection. "This chick liked Jimmy Buffet and R.E.M."

"Everybody in Athens likes R.E.M."

"Not me," Quentin said.

I moved aside a collection of old magazines and newspapers and dropped down on the couch with a stack of scribbled notes that looked like reminders to call people or some sort of code about appointments. *M at 6 on 16, W at 7 on 18.* I deciphered nothing from her scribbled shorthand.

"It appears Marty and Fran were mixed up in this ring, whatever it was. Courtney didn't know much about it."

As Quentin and I sifted through the dead girl's possessions, my stomach somersaulted. The thought of someone being alive one minute, listening to Jimmy Buffet and reading articles in *Cosmo* about how to keep your man, and then dead the next seemed surreal.

Quentin turned toward me. "A drug ring?" he whispered as if someone might hear him.

"Dunno. I'm merely speculating. But we might find something here that could tell us. Mrs. Sosbee told me she saw a shiny black car the day Marty was killed."

"You didn't tell me that either," Quentin said.

"Didn't I? Sorry. So much has been happening. I wonder if the car and the ring might be connected to some big drug operation."

I poked around the edges of the couch, not really expecting to find anything except dirt and old gum wrappers. I wasn't disappointed.

"Have you told the good copper about all this?"

"Not yet, but I did tell him about Courtney, and they've talked to her." I thumbed through the *Shape* and *Vogue* magazines on the table next to the couch, searching for hidden messages.

"The police might already be on to the drug angle. You need to tell them what she said."

"Courtney can tell them if she wants to. It's no more than hearsay from me."

Quentin groaned. "You're impossible."

I decided against telling him about my visit to Samson's. He'd have a fit.

"Jen, if someone is stalking around your house, maybe you ought to come stay with me and Alan."

"That's not necessary. And besides, how would it look to your neighbors? A threesome?"

"My neighbors can sod off."

"I told you a policeman is protecting me now. I'll be fine. Besides, I stayed with the Hudson's next door on Tuesday night. They said for me to call them again if need be. Trust me. I don't want to face this killer any more than you do. I simply want him caught, and fast, before he snuffs out another young life, mine in particular."

"Right-o."

I followed Quentin up the narrow stairs to the bedroom.

From the looks of the clothes in Fran's closet, she paid close attention to high fashion. How could someone, who lived in such a run-down place, afford a BMW, classy magazines and the clothes they depict? Besides a Chanel suit, I pulled out a fabulous Vera Wang dress, a leather St. John's jacket, snazzy pink Pumas, and a pair of Manolos to-die-for. I cupped one of the Manolos in my hand. Size 9, too bad, a bit large for me. It looked only slightly worn. Starr would flip out over this hoard.

Clearly Fran didn't frequent TJ Maxx and Target. Maybe she shopped on e-Bay or maybe her rich parents sent her gifts from Paris, or maybe drugs were her game.

A photograph of three young women, barefoot and wearing sweatshirts and cut-offs sat on the bedroom dresser. By now I recognized Fran and Marty. From Steve's description, the other woman must have been Penny. She was short, with a wide smile and huge—yes, va-va-voom breasts. She'd put Dolly Parton to shame. Why hadn't I asked Courtney about Penny? Naturally, I'd forgotten. I was probably flunking Detective 101.

Quentin sneezed. The cluttered house hadn't been dusted or vacuumed, I'd say, in months. The bed looked rumpled as if she'd just finished a rather wonderful romp with a lover. Fran, of course, wasn't expecting company, especially company who'd paw through her closets and drawers.

Quentin's second sneeze came along with a call, "Jenna, come here."

He faced an open drawer with his mouth agape.

"Wow," I said, staring at a collection of multicolored condoms. They resembled an assortment of Lifesavers—yellows, reds, greens, and various shades of purple. Yummy.

"This was one busy lady. First drugs, now sex," Quentin said between snickers.

"Cut it out. We're not certain about the drugs, and remember you're referring to a dead person."

A distant memory tugged at the back of my mind, something about Fran.

"Don't we have a date tonight?" I asked.

"Did you know Trojan made 'Magnum' for big men?" Quentin said, fumbling with the condoms.

I closed the drawer.

"We'd better go."

On the porch we found Officer Kelley still smoking. "We didn't find anything, sorry," I told him.

He snuffed out his cigarette as if that information didn't surprise him.

At home, I finally got Courtney to answer her phone.

When I asked her where she was today, she said, "I didn't go to Samson's because I chickened out. Besides, you didn't seem to want to go."

"I'd have appreciated a phone call."

"I did call but didn't leave a voicemail 'cause I figured you'd be at work, but when I called the *Flagpole*, they didn't know who you were." Her voice sounded tight.

I swallowed. *Ouch.*

"It's our new receptionists. They change every week. She never gave me the message, sorry."

"Oh, yeah."

"I didn't find that photograph, by the way, and I asked him about it," I said, hoping to take the heat off me.

"He's got it. He just didn't want to give it to you. He probably still has a thing for Marty."

Doubtful, considering his cavalier response to her death.

I ended the call glad Courtney was okay but increasingly curious about why she'd sent me to Samson's house alone. What was so important about that photo?

* * * *

People jammed the Athens Community Dance Festival later that night. Dancers from all over the ten-county area came to perform. There was everything from ballet, modern dance, tap dance to belly dancing. I suspected the audience consisted mainly of family and friends of the multitude of dancers.

While gyrating through our routine, I strained to see who had come, but the bright lights facing the stage blinded me. Starr made her presence known when she hollered, "Way to go, Jenna!" I'd also seen Timothy before the performance. He gave me a kiss on the cheek and a single red rose for luck. There was no sign of Frank, and he hadn't responded to the text I'd sent him asking him to come. Squinting, I'd tried to spot the cops who I thought would be there, but if any came, they were inconspicuous —perhaps in plainclothes.

When we finished our belly-dance finale, Quentin beamed with delight. I hugged Doreen and Lucille, quickly changed out of my costume, and exited through the backdoor, too keyed up to mingle, and determined to get to the office to check what was nagging me about Fran.

When I drove into the dark parking lot, a wave of fear passed over me, causing me to slump low in my seat. Maybe this wasn't such a good idea. Glancing around, I searched for my police escort but spotted no one. Fran's half smile, which I'd seen today in that photo at her house, jumped into my mind. I'd waited too long to help her. That couldn't happen again. I mustered all my courage, took a deep breath, and fumbled for my keys to enter the office. Surely the policeman would arrive behind me shortly.

Once inside, Quentin's words about the killer floated into my mind: *It must be someone you know.*

I wanted to believe the killer was one of Dr. B's patients who happened to hone in on me because I worked in the psychiatrist's office. But too many things suggested otherwise. He knew about my cats. He knew my first name. The way he addressed me in his e-mails hinted at familiarity. Who then? Steve? Dr. Bingham? Michael? What about Timothy and Frank? Each was computer savvy. God, I shook my head, frustrated with myself, but trusting no one.

As soon as I switched on the lights and retrieved Fran's file, a noise came from the outside, sounding like a car door closing. *Oh my God!* My stomach—none-too-steady since Fran's house—lurched. I inched toward the side window. Everything outside looked black. A car sat in the lot, but the darkness prevented me from making out who, if anyone, was inside. That had to be my police escort finally arriving.

I let out a small sigh of relief and returned to the back room to begin reading Fran's file. I'd hardly started when the lights in the office flicked off. I gasped.

Footsteps approached.

Damn. Didn't I lock the door? *Good grief!*

I crouched low. The room was black as ink. The footsteps neared. No one called out. My heart pounded on warp speed. Where the devil was that policeman? He was supposed to be watching me. I crawled toward the door and groped for the light switch. When I turned it on, nothing happened.

Someone had flipped the fuse.

My legs tingled with stabs of numbness, but I managed to stumble into the hall and creep toward the back entrance. The floor creaked under my feet.

Arms wrapped around me like a snake. I kicked and struggled when a large sweaty hand covered my mouth, muting the scream in my head.

"You bitch," a voice whispered. "You wouldn't stop, would you?"

The smell of onions overpowered me before everything went black.

Chapter 19

"JENNA, FOR GOD SAKES, WAKE up."

The voice sounded far away, as if on the opposite side of a mountain. A pain shot through my head. I opened my eyes. Detective Watring leaned over me, his face near mine.

"Thank God," he said. "Can you tell me what happened?"

I moaned in an effort to lift up. Pain pierced my head like a sword. "Whoa." I lowered myself back down.

The detective turned to the anxious-looking cop who stood behind him. "Get a cushion from the lobby." Returning to me, he said, "Just relax. We're going to get you to the hospital. The ambulance should be here any minute."

"Ambulance?" I concentrated on the Sheetrock ceiling and tried to figure out how I ended up in the middle of the floor with an eye-splitting headache and two policemen staring down at me. "What's going on?"

"That's what I'm trying to find out. Officer Kelley was supposed to watch you, but he lost you after the show." The detective passed the hapless policeman an accusing look. "Apparently you disappeared, and he didn't see you leave."

"They wouldn't let me backstage," Kelley said in his own defense.

A glare from the detective quieted him.

Watring added, "Someone must've attacked you, Jenna. Thank God, you weren't killed."

I winced when he placed the pillow under my head. "I can't remember," I said. Everything inside my head was floating around like a bunch of lost puzzle pieces.

"Don't try now."

The EMS people burst through the front door with a loud clank.

"Back here," Detective Watring called. He moved away.

A man and a woman dressed in black slacks and white shirts with hospital emblems on their sleeves came toward me.

"Don't try to get up," one said, while the other took my pulse.

A piercing light flashed in my face. I blinked and shut my eyes.

"Don't think I could if I wanted to," A queasy feeling washed over me.

"She's got an ugly head wound," the detective told them.

"I'll get the stretcher," the man said.

"We're going to put you in a neck brace. Relax here for just a sec and then we'll ease you onto the stretcher. Try and keep your eyes open," the woman EMS said as she fitted my arm with a blood pressure band. "Pressure's down," she told her partner when he returned. "Tell me where you hurt."

Her soothing voice reminded me of my mother's when she told me bedtime stories. My eyes drooped.

"My head," I mumbled.

"Open your eyes, honey."

She turned my head sideways. "There's some blood. Pretty nasty. It looks like the bleeding has stopped, but let's bandage it anyway. What's your name?"

"Jenna Scali."

"Who is the US President?"

Mechanically I responded to her questions, wincing while she wrapped the bandage around my forehead. The man fitted me with a large plastic neck brace and lifted me to the stretcher. They carried me down the hallway toward the door. A water stain marred the ceiling. Had it leaked in here at one time? I'd need to tell Dr. B about that. I kept my eyes glued to that stain as the medics maneuvered the stretcher.

"I'm gonna ride to the hospital with you," Detective Watring said.

"You'd better call Dr. Bingham," I told the detective, who took my hand in his and walked beside the stretcher. "I can't leave the office unattended and open."

"Don't worry. He's already on his way here. Do you want me to call anyone else?"

The movement of the lights on the ceiling made me dizzy and sick. "Quentin."

Contrary to all medical advice, I closed my eyes.

The ride in the ambulance was a total blur. Detective Watring kept a hold of my hand, and he talked to me, too, but I had no idea what he said.

I awoke in a bed separated by curtained partitions, lying on white sheets that must've been washed in an entire bottle of Clorox. The dank, sick smell told me I was in the hospital. Quentin sat in a chair next to my bed, thumbing through a *People* magazine with Prince William on the cover.

"Quen?" I whispered.

He moved closer to me. His gray eyes surveyed my face as if he'd never seen me before. "What do you know?" His face broke into a wide grin. "The girl is coming to life. How are you, love?"

"I could be better. What brought you here?"

"Your friend, Detective Watring, rang me up. Woke me from one of the best dreams I've had in God knows when. But hearing his voice made my little heart flutter. He said you asked for me."

"I did?"

What happened remained fuzzy except being carried by stretcher to the ambulance and the feel of the detective's hand in mine.

"You're still in the casualty department. The doctor said you suffered a concussion from a bash to your head. Jen, what the devil happened to you?"

"Someone attacked me in Dr. B's office. I went there after the show because something was bothering me that I wanted to check." I lifted myself up on my elbows. My head pounded as if it were the main theater for Patton's march on the Germans. "There was a noise, but I thought the policeman had followed me so I wasn't too concerned. Then the lights went out and someone grabbed me from behind."

"Oh, bloody shit," he exclaimed. "The killer probably attacked you. I can't believe it. This was bound to happen. I bloody well knew it would. You're lucky to be alive. How could you go there alone like that in the dead of night? What were you thinking? You've got to be more careful, love." He took my hand. "Detective Watring told me another girl was murdered last night."

My stomach sank. Gasping, I tried to catch my breath, feeling as if someone had put a huge rubber band around my chest. Fighting the urge to vomit, I said, "Please, God, no. Who?"

"I dunno. He didn't tell me. You know how tight-lipped the police can be. Of course, I didn't ask, did I? I wasn't thinking about that, being more concerned about you. You looked like a corpse when I first saw you, pale and wrapped in white bandages with that big neck brace on. But they promised me you were merely asleep. You scared the devil out of me, Jen." He tightened his grip on my fingers.

"When are they gonna let me out of here?"

"Wait till you see the doctor. He's quite dishy. You'll want to set up camp."

"Give me a break. Not another heartthrob. Can't you think of anything else?"

"Hair as black as night. Deep green eyes with lashes like spiders. Blasted all, he's wearing a gold band and seemed all business even though I flashed him my very best dimples."

"Dear heart, don't want to burst your bubble, but you don't have dimples."

"Not those dimples, love." He turned his back to me and thrust his fanny out. "These."

My laughter turned into a wince as a pain stabbed through my skull. "Gosh, you're incorrigible. Now, when can I go home? I need to find out who was killed and if another message came from the e-murderer." Furthermore, the cats! I had no idea how long I'd been unconscious.

"You need to do no such thing. You're confined to my care for the moment. Besides, Dr. Casey said he wanted to examine you after you woke up. But I expect they'll keep you here awhile."

"Dr. Casey? Like in Ben Casey?"

"That's the one. I don't actually know his name."

"What time is it?"

"Seven-thirty."

I nearly jumped out of bed. "In the morning? Ouch! My head." I eased back down on the bed with my arm over my eyes.

"Good Lord, Jenna, calm down. You're supposed to take it easy."

A dark-haired man in blue scrubs with a stethoscope tucked in his pocket appeared at my bedside. A smiling nurse trailed behind him.

"Looks like you decided to wake up," he said. He lifted my wrist to check my pulse. Why do doctors always take the patient's pulse?

"How long have I been out?"

"The EMS team brought you in around midnight. You were pretty much out of it then. We examined you, but you didn't look too inclined to run a marathon. How are you feeling now?"

"My head hurts."

His nameplate read Dr. Millstone.

"Still dizzy?"

"Nope. I don't think so. But, I haven't moved much."

The nurse took my blood pressure and recorded the results. Dr. Millstone flashed a bright light into my eyes, giving me a good view of him. Quentin had exaggerated the man's good looks. Red splotches dotted his face where he had shaved too closely. He palpated my head and examined the wound. It took all my strength of willpower not to wince and scream.

"You'll be sore for several days. Looks like someone wanted to put you out of commission for a long time, but they didn't do any permanent damage."

"It's a good job they didn't," Quentin said, while batting his eyes at the oblivious doctor.

The nurse shoved a thermometer under my tongue. Meanwhile, the doctor dictated some medical lingo to her, none of which made sense to me. But at the moment not much made sense.

"We're not going to admit you. You suffered a mild trauma to the head. I want you to stay here and rest for another hour. If you're still not dizzy, you can go home. But I suggest you take it easy for several days. I'm giving you a prescription for Loratab. Ten milligrams no more than three times daily as needed for the pain. Take it for at least two days, particularly before bedtime. And, don't drive while taking the medicine."

"But, Doctor," I protested, nearly dropping the thermometer.

"Only a few days while on the meds," he repeated.

"No problem, Doc. I'll see to it," Quentin said.

"Good, I'll check back in an hour." He disappeared behind the curtain.

The nurse removed the thermometer, and once again recorded the results. "What might you like to drink?" she asked.

"Some apple juice would be great."

To Quentin, I asked, "Would you call Dr. B? They'll wonder what's happened to me. Also, Quen, the cats—"

"They called Dr. B last night. And, I rang up Lucille an hour ago. Woke the poor ol' bird from her beauty sleep. I knew you'd come out of it worrying more about the felines than yourself. Now you lie back down." He eased me toward the pillows.

I flopped down.

My eyes flew open. "Quen, how did Lucille get into the house? I've got new locks."

"She came by here, and we fetched the keys from your purse. Now will you lie down and get some sleep or do I need to bash you on the other side of the head?"

I smiled, closed my eyes and muttered, "Thanks. You're terrific."

My muddled mind tired to remember details about the man who'd hit me. Was he tall? Did he reach down or up to grab me? Did he clasp my waist? Memories floated up from my delirious state. Something nagged at me about my attacker but whatever it was floated around in the back of my mind like a blurry object on the bottom of a swimming pool, within my grasp but too far to reach. He'd spoken to me as well, but what had he said? His voice had a familiar ring, but his words evaded me. Darn!

* * * *

Quentin dropped me at my house at a little after 11:00 a.m. and fussed over me like an old hen—tucking me in bed, getting me pitchers of Coke to drink, checking the locks on all the windows and doors—until I finally ran him off. "But, Jen," he protested. "There's no cop outside. I can't just leave you here, unguarded."

"You can and you will. Maybe the poor man had to get himself some breakfast. Detective Watring will tell me what's going on when I call him. Don't worry. Now go so I can rest." He was making my head ache even more.

Finally he left but not before I promised to call him every hour.

I lay in bed and stared at the ceiling. My cozy home felt as if the place belonged to someone else. So much had happened since yesterday. Could it have been only last night when we had the show? Churchill peeked around the corner, ears flat, tail down.

"Hi," I said, and patted his head.

Then, against Dr. Quen's orders, I got out of bed and went into the kitchen. Uneaten Tasty Tuna buffet lined the cats' dishes. A note from Lucille sat on the counter.

The black cat insisted on going out. Hope that's okay. Neither ate much. Nor, I might add, did it look as if they needed to. Both could survive off the fat of the land for weeks. Hope you're feeling better. Call me when you get a chance. Love and kisses. L

I went to the backdoor and called Stalin inside. After his ordeal, he didn't need to be wandering the neighborhood no matter how much he protested.

"Good boy." I ran my hand down his black coat, feeling the rumble of his purr. His personal grooming left him looking as good as new. Satisfied that all was well with my felines, I returned to my bedroom.

Quentin had put my cell phone next to the bed. My voicemail signaled lots of calls, including one missed call from Frank but no message. A voicemail from Starr congratulated me on the show, and one from Timothy: "Hey, girl, you've got great moves. Give me a call."

Detective Watring had asked me to phone him once, "you settle in." I punched in his number.

"Are you feeling any better?" he asked.

"Lots. Sorry about last night." My stomach tingled when the memory of how he clutched my hand resurfaced.

"Hey, what are you sorry for? It wasn't your fault. It was ours. Officer Kelley to be specific. If you've got some time, I'd like to talk to you about what you remember. Sometimes even the tiniest detail can help us. But I don't want to tire you."

"I'm fine, but Quentin said another girl was killed last night. Who was it?"

"We can talk about that when you're feeling better. Don't think about it now."

"But—"

"I'll give you a call before I come. It'll probably be thirty minutes or so," he said, before cutting me off.

Next, I telephoned the office.

Starr paused after each word for dramatic effect. "Quentin—said—you'd—been—knocked—out."

"I got bashed in the head. Someone must've decided I'd poked my big, fat nose too far into their business." I hoped Starr would laugh.

She didn't.

"For the love of God, Jen. This is too scary."

"It might help if you'd look to see if I got any e-mails from this nut."

"Hold on."

I heard Starr talking to Dr. Bingham. Then he got on the line.

"Jenna, are you okay?"

"I'll live."

"Thank God! We were terrified for you. The police were all over the place last night and this morning. Tell me what happened."

"I came by after the dance. Must've been about ten-thirty. Someone sneaked in after me, deciding to knock some sense into my head. My only consolation is if the person had wanted to kill me, I'd be dead right now. I suppose they were trying to scare me off."

"Scare you off from what?"

"I figure I'm getting too close. Last night I was following up on a hunch. But I didn't finish."

"What hunch?"

I bit my lip. At this stage everyone was a suspect, particularly my sweet-talking boss.

"I'd rather not say. As you're so quick to point out, without concrete evidence, hunches hardly count."

"How did this attacker get in? Didn't you lock the door after yourself?"

"I thought so, but apparently not."

He sighed.

Starr squealed something in the background.

"Hold on a minute," Dr. Bingham said.

Mumbled voices came through the line. I strained to make out the words—*message, killer, help.*

"What's going on?" I demanded into the line.

Finally, Starr came back on. "You got a message all right. Looks like it came in about ten minutes ago. Want me to read it?"

My head throbbed. I would have been surprised if there hadn't been a message. "Please."

"'*YOU DROVE ME TO IT, BITCH.*' All caps, no less,"

"'*That damn cat escaped,*' Starr continued. "Did Stalin come home?"

I quickly told her about the cat's return, wondering if his lucky escape might have triggered my attack and the new murder. "Go on, please, Starr."

"'*That damn cat escaped, but you won't. NEVER.*' (All caps again) '*I warned you, but you wouldn't listen. Now you've crossed the line. I've done all I can for you. You won't get away with this. That whore didn't escape either, and she sure tried. When I stabbed her, she didn't die right away. I watched her bleed. No one will ever get away from me again.*'"

"Is that all of it?" My voice shook.

"Yes."

"Forward it directly to Detective Watring."

"Okay, but you'd better flat out take this crazy man at his word. He's coming after you."

"I know, but why didn't he kill me last night?"

"Who're you asking?" Starr's voice was high. "I may be crazy, but I sure can't figure out this loony tune. By the way, did you check on Luke Miller?"

"Not yet. I was planning to do that today, but I can't drive."

"Good."

"But, Starr, I can't tell the police about my suspicions of him. I've got nothing to tell them, really nothing. And yet,"—pause—"he might be the killer. Somehow I've got to get over to his house and see if he's left any signs."

"Like a bloody knife?"

"You're too gruesome. My head can't take your humor."

"I was being serious, not funny. If I were you,"—she lowered her voice to a whisper—"I'd say to hell with Dr. B and his rules about confidentiality, and I'd tell your police friend about Luke Miller. Let them check him out. You're in no condition, sweet pea."

"Two days ago you went ballistic when I wanted to report what we knew about Luke Miller to the police."

"Yeah, well, that was two days ago, before you got your little self attacked. Listen to me, now's the time to scream your crazy-fool head off. Dr. B or no Dr. B. If you ask me, he's just covering his you-know-what. What's more important, your life or a patient's right to privacy? Give me a break, for heaven sakes."

I giggled. "Let's not ask Dr. B that question. You're great. I love you."

"Does that mean you'll pay attention to what I said?" Starr's voice was as shrill as a siren.

"Quentin told me another girl was killed last night. Did the paper have anything in it?"

"Sweetie, you didn't answer my question. Are you gonna tell that Mel Gibson cop about Luke Miller?"

"Yeah."

Starr let out a long sigh. "Wait a jiff. I'll check out the paper."

She rummaged through the pages.

"Nothing in here. Must've happened too late."

"One more thing. I have an odd feeling about Fran Knotter. Could you get her file? It's in the back room. Just put it on my desk. I'm hoping it'll loosen my clogged memory."

"You got it. By the way, you were great last night. Steve hasn't stopped salivating after seeing you slink around the stage."

"Good grief." It had been embarrassing enough being up there in that teensy-weensy outfit without the image of Steve salivating. I wanted to throw up.

"See, my dear Miss Scali, in the right clothes with the right makeup, you send up firecrackers bigger than a Fourth of July bash. When are you gonna let me give you a makeover?"

Imagining Starr with all her jars of glob to slather on my face, I cringed. "May as well do it today. I've nothing better to do cooped up here."

"Do you think you'll be able to come to work later?"

"God, I hope so. That is if you'll come get me."

"Gladly. Oops, the phone. Don't go away. I'll be right back."

Starr put me on hold. After a few minutes, she returned.

"That was Mr. Porter. It seems Mrs. Porter fell down the basement stairs and broke her ankle. He's going to miss his appointment on Monday."

Poor Mrs. Porter. Except for talking too much, she was a nice enough lady.

"Yeah. By the way, Steve teased Michael like mad last night for letting you go," Starr continued.

"Michael was here?"

"You betcha. We assumed you knew. Steve figured you invited him."

"I most certainly did not."

"You don't get it, Jenna. Michael keeps tabs on you. I doubt he's over you."

"Well, that's tough because I'm over him."

"That's my girl."

I hung up with Starr, and before the meds took control of my conscious self, dialed Michael. After several rings, he answered.

"Hey, what a nice surprise. Usually you don't call until the late hours of the night when I'm in my jammies and curled up with a book."

And a glass of scotch.

"Can you talk now?" I clenched my fist to control the throb churning inside my head. Michael couldn't be the killer, but these mysterious visits to Athens needed explaining.

"Yep. Just returned from a staff meeting five minutes ago and don't have an appointment for twenty. What's up? Have you decided to marry Frank yet?"

"How did you know about Frank?"

"You told me."

"I didn't say who. How do you know Frank?"

"My bad. Why are you so jumpy? Who else could it be? Surely not Timothy. When you said you got a proposal and the man was eligible, I'm no dummy. Connecting the dots from what Starr and Steve told me about Frank, I had no trouble pegging him the winner. They like to rub it in. Starr hates what I did to you."

I swallowed hard. I didn't like what he did to me either, but that was beside the point.

"You're right. Frank does want me to marry him. But I've put that idea to rest, at least for the time being. We're cooling it right now."

"Oh, I get it. The way to a woman's garbage heap is to get down on your knees and propose. That's not what my mom taught me when she read fairy tales about princes and such."

"Your mother never read you anything, much less fairy tales."

He moaned. "Too true. Too true."

"Michael, when's the next time you're coming this way? I've got some of your books that you need to come get."

Silence

"Michael, are you still there?"

"Yeah, what books?"

Commotion sounded in the background.

"One minute, Jenna." He carried on a muffled conversation about deals and a meeting in five minutes. "You still there, Jenna?"

"I'm here."

"Now what were we talking about?"

"Your books. I've got a box of them in my hall closet, and I'd love to get rid of them. I wondered when you might be able to pick them up."

"Why don't you give the stupid books to Goodwill? By the way, did you get that article I e-mailed about the anonymous server?"

"Yeah. Thanks. It helped. Have you signed on with him?"

"What's wrong with you? Why would I need to send anonymous e-mails?"

"You could send me hate messages, and I'd never know they were from you." *Actually, I just might sign up and send you a few choice messages myself.*

"Sweetie, you know I don't hate you. In fact, I think we still sort of love each other in an odd, offbeat kinda way. We need each other but can't live together."

"I can't live with you and your bottle," I cut in.

"Oops, this conversation has lasted a bit too long."

"I'm sorry, but rumor has it you came to the dance last night, and it hurts my feelings that you didn't even call. Not that you have to, of course. But it would've been nice."

"Oh, I get it. This really isn't about the box of books, is it? My plans to come to Athens were sudden, didn't even know till after six last night. There was a client wanting to see me. A lot of my business contacts are still in Athens. You know that." He was making excuses. "I suppose Starr told you. I should've known. No secrets in good ol' Athens town."

"Like you said, they keep everyone informed." I leaned back on the bed with my arm across my forehead.

"Touché. Incidentally, you looked sensational last night. Had to bite my tongue to keep from screaming lewd remarks."

"Thanks for that. Catcalls have always gone straight to my heart. Oh, and Michael, my closet is overflowing with boxes of books here I'd love to get rid of. Let me know the next time you're in Athens."

"Sure thing, and maybe we'll go out for coffee. Gotta go, doll."

I lifted myself from the bed and shook my head, trying to dislodge the cobwebs. I'd been married to Michael for three years. I knew him better than my own sister. I'd bet my life he wasn't mixed up in these awful murders. But what about the facts? Michael knew about computers and even about anonymous e-mail. He'd been in Athens when at least two women had died. He got out of control when he drank. He'd never hit me, but he'd yelled plenty.

I blamed Michael's drinking on his anger toward his father for leaving him as a child. He was very close to his mother, but not in a healthy way. Little Mr. Perfect, as far as she was concerned. Part of Michael's problem was his inability to get close to anyone, especially women. I wish I'd known all this before I married him. But what difference would it have made? I'd have probably married him anyway. Young, stupid, and in love, that was what we were.

Michael certainly fit the bill for the murderer. Dr. B said the killer had a healthy dose of anger toward women. My eyes fluttered closed. No matter how hard I tried, picturing him brutally killing people just didn't jive with the man I'd married.

The pain in my head had lessened but the meds made me want to sleep. The last image in my head before drifting into unconsciousness was Michael's face.

Chapter 20

I AWOKE IN A DAZE, thinking I'd heard a noise. Had someone broken through my window? A closed window and sleeping cat convinced me otherwise. Returning to la-la land, I dreamed of variations on the scene of me running from some darkly clad attacker. The ringing of my cell pulled me awake.

"Hello," I choked out.

"Did I wake you?" Detective Watring asked.

"Yeah, the meds knocked me out."

"Gosh, I'm sorry. Things got crazy around here. You probably need to rest anyway, but I could be there in about fifteen minutes if you feel up to talking."

"Sure, but there's no guarantee I'll be able to hold my head up. I'm nodding off quicker than a couch potato watching the Braves."

"Don't be poking the Braves."

"Oops, sorry. I forgot I wasn't talking to Quentin."

"I'll take that as a compliment. But if you get too droopy," he said before hanging up, "I'll slip away into the night like a gentleman."

In anticipation of my visitor, I changed into fresh jeans and a T-shirt, combed my hair, and put on a touch of lip gloss. Even so, a zombie stared at me from my mirror, wide-eyed and with deep dark circles under the eyes.

I headed for the kitchen to make a pot of coffee. Stalin snaked between my legs, begging to go out. Instead, I tossed him a piece of cheese as a peace offering, still not wanting to release him.

The teakettle whistled and the doorbell rang at the same instant.

Detective Watring entered, alone, thank goodness. My head couldn't take a drilling from Sergeant Lewis.

"Welcome." As soon as the door opened, Churchill darted past me and out in the yard. "No Churchill!"

The policeman nabbed the not-too-pleased cat and brought him back inside.

"Sorry. I'm afraid the cats are driving me crazy. They're upset I won't let them out. But after Stalin's kidnapping, well, you see, they've gotta be prisoners for a few days. My guess is, too, they're restless because they sense something is wrong. Would you like some coffee? It's instant, I'm afraid, but I'm about to have a cup. Caffeine might keep me awake."

"That'd be great." He scratched Churchill's back, set him on the arm of the couch, and followed me to the kitchen like a friendly neighbor. "You're looking much better than you did last night."

"You're too kind. By the way, thanks for taking care of me and getting me safely to the hospital." *And holding my hand*, I refrained from saying.

"No problem. When I saw you lying on the floor—" He stopped and looked away. "Well, let's just say you scared the life out of me. But that's all over and done with."

When he sat down at the kitchen table, Stalin sniffed his leg and settled next to his foot. "Hello there," he said to the cat, rubbing the top of his head.

A man who talks to my cats. Geez, how perfect is that?

"Do you take cream or sugar?" I asked.

"One teaspoon of sugar. I've tried to drink it black, but my stomach can't take it."

"Mine either. I have to have lots of cream and sugar—more like a latte." Settling down in a chair next to him caused my already dizzy head to spin.

Our knees practically touched. I swallowed some coffee, trying to ignore the power of his presence. My palpating heart and sweaty palms made me feel out of control as if I might spill something, or fall on my face, or both.

Following a short pause, he said, "Tell me everything you remember about last night."

As I stirred my coffee, the color turned from black to khaki, and the color of my own nerves shot from red to blue. "Maybe I'd better fill in a few other things first since I haven't been completely straightforward."

He laughed, a rich booming sound that brought a smile to my lips. "Is that right?"

"You see, I didn't know what to tell you. There were so many odd things happening, and not knowing what was relevant and what wasn't…But after last night, it's clear you need to know everything."

I began with the visit from Steve. "He told me he went to Marty's house to get letters he'd written to her. It was Steve I'd seen the night of my late excursion to Kroger."

"Tell me about Steve."

"He's a real jerk. He and Starr married right out of high school. I've always suspected he was unfaithful, and now there's no doubt, and I expect Starr knows it too. But I promised Steve not to tell her. He told me he'd been having an affair with Marty for about eight months, and he seemed genuinely concerned about her death. Really upset."

"Do you think he killed Marty?"

"I don't think he's got the guts to kill a daddy longlegs. Seriously, he nearly wet his pants when he thought Starr might find out about his affair with Marty."

"Where are the letters now?"

I explained what Steve had said as well as my suspicion he was holding something back. "Maybe you can squeeze more out of him."

Detective Watring had removed a small pad from his pocket and was jotting down notes with a slim gold pen. Short dark hairs dotted the top of his hand.

I sipped my coffee and considered telling him about Luke Miller. Instead, I said, "There's something else. Courtney mentioned some sort of ring."

Detective Watring stopped writing and drank from his cup without looking at me.

"You know about this?"

"Just go on."

I shifted in my seat. "I don't know much more. Really nothing, just that she mentioned it. She's the one who needs to tell you what she knows. Looks like she maybe didn't?"

"Do you have that list I gave you when you came by the station Saturday?"

"Yeah, I'll get it.."

My backpack rested on my desk in the living room but the list wasn't there. It had been carefully tucked in the zippered section. Right after running the computer search at the office, I stashed it in there. Where the devil was it? Strange.

"I can't seem to find it," I said, returning to the kitchen.

"That's okay for the time being. Did you ever run that search you promised?"

A hot flush travelled up my neck. "Well, yeah, but, since they were patients, I didn't know what to do. Too bad, though, the names were stapled to the list, and it's disappeared."

"Try and put your hands on that information. It may be very important."

"What's that got to do with the ring?"

Detective Watring stirred the coffee, which had to be pretty cold by now. "Jenna, I can't tell you about that yet. Pete plans to fill you in a bit later. Are you going to work today?"

"Starr said she'd come pick me up."

"Why not let Pete and me take you? That way he can explain everything."

"Okay, but they're expecting me to be there by two o'clock so Starr can go home. She doesn't usually work on Fridays."

He nodded. "We'll be here before one-thirty. That should give us plenty of time."

"Is this ring some sort of drug operation?"

The detective shook his head. "Wait till Pete gets here, okay? When are we going to get to the events of last night?"

A pain shot across my head, forcing me to catch my breath.

"After the show, something about Fran kept niggling at me. It was a hunch or a feeling that came over me while at her house. She'd been a patient of Dr. B's so I went to the office, figuring whatever it was would come to me when I looked at her record. I didn't tell you about all this because divulging patients' names is a huge no-no."

"Even after they've been killed?"

"Never, if you believe Dr. B. What hit me was that Fran had syphilis. Dr. B had recorded information about her sexual history, including a note about her having several partners, so maybe one of the partners might have killed her. I never found out because someone bashed me in the head, giving me no chance to look at the record." I paused, and then added, "I could get fired for telling you about Fran."

"We'll be discrete, but you're right to tell me. You know that, don't you?"

I nodded, wanting to agree with him but doubtful Dr. B would.

"Do you remember anything about the person who hit you?"

"If only I could. His voice was familiar but sorta like hearing a distant relative you haven't talked to for a while and can't quite place. He whispered in a real low tone."

"That suggests he thought you'd recognize his voice."

My stomach did a flip. "You really think this killer is someone I actually know?"

"I'm only suggesting. What else?"

"I don't remember much else. He grabbed me from behind, around the waist, and then he hit me, with what, I haven't a clue. But it's strange. All that comes to me is the smell of onions."

"Onions?"

I fiddled with a broken fingernail.

"On his breath, maybe," I said.

"Do you remember what he said to you?"

"I can still hear the words. He said, 'You bitch. You wouldn't stop, would you?' That was it. Then everything went black."

Detective Watring closed his pad and placed the cover on his pen in slow, deliberate moves. I could practically hear his mind ticking away.

"Does any of this help at all?" I asked, twirling a loose hair with my finger.

"Everything helps."

Twirling a little more, I stopped, took a deep, fortifying breath before finally saying, "There's more." Then the words tumbled from me—the entire story about Luke Miller and Dr. Bingham's mysterious visit to his house. "Dr. B will fire me for sure, first for telling you about Fran, but she's dead. He might forgive me that one, but he'd never forgive me for telling you the name of a living, current patient."

"You need to face reality here. Worse things could happen to you than getting fired. We'll check out Luke Miller." He was writing again.

"How will you check him out?"

"We'll talk to the good doctor first. We won't bother Mr. Miller yet. Do you know if Mr. Miller might have access to a computer?"

"All I know is he sent us a couple of notes that looked like computer notes. There was nothing in his file that suggested anything else. Dr. Bingham doesn't say much about patients in the files except things related to their mental or physical status."

"What made you suspicious of Miller?"

"The way he acted when he came for his appointments. He seemed to sneak up on me. He had a low, quiet voice and vacant eyes. When he looked at me with that odd stare, it gave me the creeps. Most of Dr. B's patients aren't like that. They suffer from depression or they're going through a tough time after a divorce or a death of a family member. Luke Miller was different."

He closed his notebook again. "Jenna, leads like this and like Steve Andrews might help us break this case.

"By the way," he added, "that Mr. Pvirtius in Finland is a hard nut to crack. When he refused to budge, Pete threatened to get a subpoena. He snorted into the phone, saying an American subpoena meant nothing to him. Pete talked to the county attorney. Unfortunately, cyberspace is still poorly regulated. There are no legal precedents or guidelines. Pvirtius is free to do whatever he wants, and we have no recourse."

I rested my head on my hand. The throb had started again. "I'm not surprised. The guy struck me as obsessed with protecting his clients."

"The attorney did say we could impose international laws prohibiting the sale of pornography across continents or some such nonsense. But that would take too long and may not even work. Finally Pete called Pvirtius again and pleaded with him. He described the murders in detail. Even though the deaths affected the man, he still refused to tell us anything. Pete's friend with the Finnish police is hammering at him too. He thinks he'll break.

"The point is we weren't getting anywhere with this case until you came forward. Now that we've got a few suspects, we can get a court order to allow our computer nerds to check out their computers. Even though the messages were anonymous, they still leave a footprint. Or, we hope they do. I don't profess to know all the ins and outs, but we have people who do. It'll be a start."

"I got another e-mail after y'all left this morning. Starr dictated it to me and forwarded it to you. But I made a copy."

The detective read the sheet where I'd written the last message. "It looks as if he took your cat to get at you somehow, and when that failed, he freaked out and killed again." The detective carefully folded the sheet of paper. "Jenna, unlike the other messages, this one is a definite threat."

Swallowing hard to steady my voice, I asked, "Why didn't he kill me last night?"

"I can't answer that. But he did make a clear threat on your life. It looks as if this guy's trying to help us by pointing us toward you. The question is—how do we snare him before he strikes again?" He unfolded the paper and re-studied the words. "Do you have any idea what he means by 'You drove me to it'?"

"I've thought and thought. What have I done? I can't even communicate with him. My messages keep bouncing back. Who in the world is doing this?"

He laid his hand on mine. A current of heat rushed through me.

"Sometimes killers appear just like you and me. They don't stand out in a crowd with a big sign on them. Clearly though, this is a person who is very unstable."

"I suppose you've talked to Samson?" I asked, recalling his face with those piercing blue eyes.

"Who?" He released my hand and reached for his pen.

"Samson, the man Marty lived with."

"The man you visited yesterday? The one with the photo?"

"That's right."

Detective Watring flipped through his notebook and made some notes. "Right. I intended to pay that guy a visit this morning but got sidetracked."

"And what about Penny Jamison? Did you ever get a chance to talk to her?"

The detective stopped writing, his pen poised over his pad, his eyes on his pen.

"What is it? Have you talked to her?"

"Jenna," he said in a deeper voice, his eyes now on me. "Penny Jamison was murdered last night."

Chapter 21

WE HAD MOVED TO THE living room where I was pacing, unable to stop the jitteriness inside me. "But, I told you about Penny. How could you let this happen?"

"We did follow up, but it was too late. Listen, I can't tell you everything that's going on. Of course you're upset. That's understandable after all you've been through, but there's just so much we can do—"

"I don't understand. Did you give her police protection like me, hopefully not Officer Kelley? Gosh, it couldn't be her. Are you sure it was Penny?"

"Yes, we're sure, and I'm sorry. Now, sit down, Jenna. Have some more coffee. You shouldn't get all worked up like this."

I plunked down on the sofa. The throbbing in my head intensified.

The detective looked at his watch. "I really do have to go. We'll be back here in less than an hour. Will you be all right? Maybe I should call Quentin."

I shook my head. "I'll be fine." I eked out a smile, trying not to think about the bubbly, friendly, flirty Penny that Steve had described.

He rose, and squeezed my shoulder. "Sorry. I shouldn't have told you about Penny. Try and get some rest before we come back, okay?"

I nodded.

I didn't get up when he left.

* * * *

Still groggy, I barely got my teeth brushed before the two detectives walked into my living room. Although I'd had time to calm down about Penny's death, I still froze inside when imagining what had happened to her. The image of the girl with the shiny, happy face in the photo at Fran's house kept sneaking into my consciousness.

Pete Lewis wore the grim expression of a man carrying the weight two thousand men on his shoulders. Detective Watring smiled at me, but he too looked preoccupied. He didn't even notice Churchill who stood at attention next to the coffee table, hoping for a scratch on the head. When the two cops sat and I offered coffee, my landline rang.

I answered in the kitchen. Heavy breathing. Just as I was about to slam down the receiver, a voice on the other end of the line said, "You're next," and clicked off.

My hand trembled as I put the phone back and leaned on the kitchen counter, gulping for air. Whirlwind thoughts rolled around in my mind while I panted, trying to get my breathing under control. The pain in the back of my head re-emerged with a throbbing reminder of my recent bout with this maniac, but the murmur of voices from the living room pulled me back to reality.

At the sight of me, Detective Watring jumped up. "What is it, Jenna? What's happened?"

I sat across from them.

"I've been getting some annoying hang-up calls. I didn't think anything about them, but this one. Well——"

"You don't have caller ID on your landline?" Lewis asked.

I shook my head. "I hardly use that phone. My mom calls on it mostly. I have it for emergencies, and didn't want to spend the money for caller ID. Never needed it till now."

"What did the caller say?"

"Someone breathes in my ear and hangs up. But yesterday the person laughed. It wasn't exactly a laugh, more like a deep, creepy chuckle. I deleted all of them." I swallowed the lump in my throat and clasped my hands in front of me. "This time he said, 'You're next' and hung up.

What frightened me more than anything else was the voice. It sounded like the man who attacked me."

Sergeant Lewis removed a pad. "Describe the caller's voice."

I massaged my throbbing temple, and took a deep breath.

"A high pitch, but soft in tone and definitely a man's voice. Something about it seems familiar, but for the life of me I can't place what it is. Why is this happening to me?" Tears prickled my eyes. I squeezed my hands harder to keep from crying, but couldn't control myself.

Detective Watring moved next to me and covered my hands with his. I buried my head on his shoulder and sobbed. Penny's happy face kept floating in my mind.

The sergeant retrieved a Kleenex box from my bathroom. I blew my nose in a most un-ladylike fashion.

"Feel better now?" he asked.

I managed a smile. "Yeah. Sorry."

"Don't apologize. A lot has happened to you in the last few days. You've every reason to cry."

I stared at Lewis, not having realized he could be so sensitive.

"We'll put a tap on your phone and keep a man on you. Our surveillance failed miserably last night, but we've got plenty of reasons to be more cautious now." He shifted in his seat and glanced at the detective.

The moment of silence that followed weighed heavy with expectation.

"I have coffee ready for y'all, if you want some," I finally said.

The men nodded.

I fixed a tray with all the coffee trimmings and set it before them. They filled their cups in silence, the clatter of the spoons against the mugs sent ominous chills up my arm.

Pete Lewis began. "It appears you and Detective Watring had a good talk earlier. We're going to proceed quickly on the leads you gave us." He paused and stirred his coffee.

"You seem to be the bait for this killer," he continued. "He's struck three times, and each time he's directed his anger at you—that is, if we can believe the messages you're getting online. And we have no reason not to connect the messenger with the killer. I've talked with the district attorney's psychologist who is an expert on the criminal mind. She believes the killer is angry with you. You've done something to trigger him. She also believes he will eventually target you. My guess is that telephone call and the last e-mail you got are warnings. Not to mention last night's attack. That was probably a warning, too. Otherwise. . ."

"I'd be dead," I interjected.

Silence. Lewis drank from his mug.

"I need you to agree to cooperate with us in every way," he continued. "Will you do that?" He peered at me as if he were sizing me up for a new job.

I nodded.

"I know you're a strong young lady, and you've got brains. You've proved that. But I have to trust you. And I'm not real sure of that yet. You must do what we say and not go off half-cocked on your own. No more amateur investigations. No more withholding information. Agreed?"

Looking down at the crumpled tissue in my hand, I nodded again and then said, "There is one other person you might need to check."

Both men waited.

"I don't believe he could do anything like this, and I really don't think he's angry at me like you described. But…"

Pause. Silence. *Can I do this?*

"I found out my ex-husband, Michael Davis, was in town when two of the women were killed. He lives in Nashville now. I can't believe Michael could be capable of anything like this. I really can't. And he wasn't angry with me after the divorce—not the way you said. It was more the other way around. Me being angry with him. What possible motive would he have, anyway?"

Detective Watring exchanged a look with Lewis.

"We're already checking Mr. Davis out," Lewis said, "but you were right to tell us about him. You must tell us about everything you suspect, no matter who or what it is or how insignificant to you." He paused and then continued, "We know of one connection to each of the three murder victims. They were all part of a ring of prostitutes."

"Oh, my God."

Stalin looked at me, startled at the sound of my strained voice. I stared at Lewis, twirling my hair with my finger.

"I know it's hard to believe from everything you've learned about the young women, but it's true. In fact, this ring consists of a group of coeds who work with a select clientele, usually well-to-do men. That list Detective Watring gave you when you first came to the station named the girls known to have been involved with the ring. The clients are a closed fraternity. For example, if I wanted to participate, I couldn't without endorsement from someone else. That's one reason it's been so hard to break the ring." Lewis paused and drank some coffee.

"We know someone called Big Mama is the 'pimp' or the 'madam'—whatever you want to call her," Detective Watring added. "She arranges the meetings. The girls usually don't know anything about the men they're to meet except their first names and a number code. Some men select their partners, but basically the arrangement is up to Big Mama, who is apparently anonymous to everyone. As far as we can tell, none of the girls know her identity, but we suspect some of the clients do. This operation has thrived for at least ten years, maybe longer."

"But how? And why?" How could Marty Meeks, a young woman who had taken an old lady chocolate chip cookies, be a hooker? Penny Jamison looked like the girl next door if anyone did. My God!

"We know more about the why than the how," Watring said. "The beauty of the scheme is that the girls are fresh, young college students. They're clean…they're smart…they're attractive. No one suspects they're hookers. The clients are often young men with solid reputations in the community. Some are doctors, lawyers, judges, even ministers. Who knows? Actually no one knows except Big Mama. The prices run steep. Big Mama handles all the payments. We assume she scrapes her take off the top. We've recently learned this ring has extended to Alabama and is active in Atlanta." He glanced at Lewis.

"Before these killings, however," Lewis continued, "the Atlanta police were about to call in the FBI. We're glad they didn't. That's the last thing we need. Between us and the GBI, we're tripping all over each other as is. But that's beside the point." While Lewis talked, he fiddled with the pen in his hand, like a cigarette smoker who'd stopped.

My coffee grew cold while I listened to them with rapt attention. Could Steve be one of Big Mama's clients? If he was, where did he get the money to pay for Marty's services? Steve made a decent salary in his job, but enough to pay a hooker once a week? Could he have dipped into Starr's money? Maybe the bonus she got last year. The thought made me shiver.

"Jenna," Lewis said, "we believe one of Big Mama's clients is killing these coeds, and we believe this person knows you. He may have even dated you."

Timothy's reaction at the mention of Fran Knotter's name popped into my head. Could Timothy be a client? "Impossible," I whispered in answer to my own thoughts.

"You told me yourself that Steve Andrews dated Marty Meeks. It's not so impossible," Watring insisted.

I couldn't make sense out of all this. "Why would this killer murder three prostitutes if he's supposedly mad at me?"

"We don't know. Motive is the hardest part of any investigation to pin down," Sergeant Lewis continued as if he were teaching Criminal Investigation 101. "I've got ideas, but they're purely speculative. You've given us some possible suspects in Luke Miller, Dr. Bingham, this Samson person, Steve Andrews, and now Michael Davis."

"Dr. Bingham? That's ridiculous." My reaction came from the heart. Even though I'd suspected Dr. Bingham, I couldn't believe him capable of such crimes.

"No, it's not," Lewis said. "In fact, it's most likely. He's got opportunity, and we believe he's one of Big Mama's clients. He's also connected to you, and his actions and his behaviors have been suspicious."

And Michael? He'd been involved with prostitutes. Thoughts buzzed around in my head like flies.

"Jenna," Lewis said, sounding as though he were on another planet, "now that you know about all this. We have a plan to flush the killer out. We need your help. Are you willing?

My heart thundered and my throat grew dry. "What do you have in mind?"

* * * *

Thirty minutes later I climbed into the backseat of Sergeant Lewis' car, a medium-sized blue Ford model of some sort, looking as if it'd seen better days. Scratches marred the interior dash, and coffee stained the seats. The clock next to the steering wheel read twelve o'clock and looked as if it hadn't worked in years. When Detective Watring adjusted his seat for his long legs, my knees jammed into my chin. Papers and notebooks filled the opposite side of the backseat.

Even though the car was as hot as a sauna, my body shivered like a caffeine induced junkie. I had agreed to the policemen's plan, but that didn't keep me from feeling as if I were venturing into a dark cave full of bats.

"We need the names of all the men you've dated in the last year. We'll run them through our computer to see if any of the fingerprints are on file," Lewis said.

"Fine," I mumbled.

Hi, Frank, my mind played out, *the police are going to take your fingerprints and look over your phone calls to check to see if you're a murderer. Nothing personal, just routine. They're checking everybody.* And what about the men I'd gone out with once or twice? I didn't even know how to reach them. Inside, panic rose. Maybe after all this, they'd make the killer madder, and he'd murder me before they matched his precious prints.

"Jenna," Detective Watring said, breaking into my thoughts, "when we talk to Dr. Bingham, we want you in there with us."

"Why?" My voice sounded like a shriek. What more could they ask me to do?

He turned around to look at me, his blue eyes as soft as a summer sky. Why couldn't the two of us escape from all this and go to a nice little island in the South Pacific and live happily ever after?

"We want him to know you saw him so he won't deny his presence at Luke Miller's. You won't have to say much. Pete and I will do most of the talking. It will also help for you to watch him. You know him better than we do. You'll know if he's lying."

A tear rolled down my cheek before I could stop it. Detective Watring was asking me to betray Dr. Bingham.

As we drove past the university, students walked to and from class with backpacks flung over their shoulders. Some laughed and pushed at each other; others walked with heads bowed. Next week, finals began. I needed to be in the library at this very moment, compiling my literature review, taking notes, reading research, not riding in the backseat of a police car.

A rather loud, unladylike sniff escaped from me.

Pull yourself together, my mother's voice said. *More is at stake than your prospectus and a few final essays.*

Detective Watring turned to me and patted my hand.

The parking lot at Dr. Bingham's office contained two cars, Starr's and someone else's, probably a patient's. Dr. Bingham's BMW was parked alongside the building.

I unfolded myself from the backseat, ignored the cramps in my legs and the pounding in my head, and walked up the front porch steps.

"Are you okay?" asked Detective Watring.

"Fine." I was miserable.

"Did we throw too much at you at once?"

"Yeah, but I'm a strong-natured Italian woman, remember?" *Not a weak-kneed Irish girl.*

Starr opened the sliding glass covering the window to reception. "Thanks for bringing our girl."

"No problem," Lewis answered. "We wondered if Dr. Bingham had some time. We need to ask him a few questions."

Starr fingered through the book. "He's got an appointment after this one and another three after that. It's a nonstop day."

A wave of ridiculous guilt washed over me. When Dr. B was on call as he was this weekend, I worked and Starr stayed home. Today, she sported deep, dark creases under her eyes and her lipstick had faded. She hadn't even found the time to apply more—very un-Starr-like.

Detective Watring and Sergeant Lewis exchanged a glance.

"I'll wait in here," Lewis said, moving into the outer sitting room.

Detective Watring and I joined Starr behind the window.

"I need to ask you a couple of questions," he said, addressing Starr.

She switched the computer screen to sleep mode and covered the papers she was working on—precautions we always took when people invaded our workspace.

"I'll catch the phones. Y'all go to the copy room."

Starr saluted, tossed her head, and began an easy banter with the detective as they departed.

Once immersed in the office activities, I nearly forgot about the interview soon facing me and my employer.

The phone rang.

"Sorry to call your office, but your cell wasn't on." It was Frank. I hadn't seen or talked to him since when? Tuesday? Who could remember? The roses he'd sent sat next to my desk, their pretty little yellow heads bent, wilting.

"Actually I am glad you called because I'm thinking about going home this weekend and wanted you to know." My sixth sense told me not to mention the incident last night. He'd freak and want to protect me. I needed to keep my distance from Frank until all this was over, particularly since Sergeant Lewis had asked me to be available to the police for the next few days.

"I thought you were working on your prospectus and all that school crap."

"I am. But something's come up at home, and Mom asked me to make a quick trip. I can work there." I had become quite adept at lying to Frank.

Never one to give up easily, Frank pressed, "How 'bout I come over and cook dinner after you get back on Sunday night?"

"Frank, hadn't we decided to hold off, at least until after the break."

"You decided, remember?"

My eyes shut...tight. "I'm not sure when I'll get back or how I'll feel. I'll give you a call late Sunday afternoon and we'll talk."

Hanging up, I let out a long sigh. By Sunday maybe all this would be over. Ha, that would be more than too wonderful.

Dr. Bingham's patient walked out. His next hadn't arrived. The window of opportunity cracked open. What little energy was left drained from my body like air from a balloon. *Here goes.*

Detective Watring was still talking with Starr, but he got up when I appeared with Lewis at my side. Starr's face was pale even under her morning's thick application of blush.

"Sorry, Starr, but can you cover a little longer?"

She nodded. Walking next to the two policemen toward Dr. Bingham's office, I felt like a convict on the way to execution.

Dr. Bingham's face registered surprise when he saw me and the police walk into his office and close the door.

"I believe I've got another patient any minute."

"We'll not take long. Besides, your patient isn't here yet," Lewis said, and we both settled on the sofa.

Detective Watring chose the wingback chair facing Dr. Bingham.

"How are you feeling, Jenna?" my boss asked.

"I'm much better, thank you."

"We need to clear up a few matters," Lewis began without preamble.

Dr. Bingham swiveled his chair to face the sergeant. "Such as?"

I toyed with a thread on the couch. Dr. Bingham's face looked pinched, lips tight. A vein throbbed near his temple.

"You understand you can postpone answering our questions if you'd rather have your attorney present." The sergeant spoke as if he were reciting the latest weather report.

"This is nuts. Am I a suspect? Why would I want to kill those girls? I didn't even know them." Dr. Bingham's eyes darted from Lewis' face to mine.

I swallowed a lump the size of a mountain. He'd known one girl, and right now he looked pretty darn nervous.

"We are pursuing every avenue," Lewis answered.

"That doesn't answer my question. Am I a suspect?"

"Dr. Bingham, must I remind you that three young women are dead, brutally murdered? Everyone is a suspect."

The psychiatrist crossed his arms. "Okay, ask your questions. I've nothing to hide." The ice in his voice sent a shiver up my back.

"Where were you last night at about eleven o'clock?"

"Home."

"Can anyone attest to that?"

"My wife was with me." Knowing Mrs. B's schedule, I doubted his alibi.

"I see."

"Where were you Tuesday evening about five-thirty?" Detective Watring chimed in.

Dr. Bingham scowled. "What's that got to do with anything? Wasn't the last victim killed last night?"

"I thought you were answering the questions," the detective said.

Dr. Bingham expelled a loud, frustrated sigh. "I left the office early that afternoon in response to an emergency."

"What kind of emergency?"

The doctor turned to me. "Did you tell them about a patient?"

"About what patient?" I choked, wishing my voice hadn't cracked.

"Jenna, you know perfectly well what I'm asking."

"Leave her out of this for now," Watring said. "Tell us where you were."

"I can't see that my whereabouts on Tuesday afternoon has anything to do with your investigation."

Detective Watring glanced at Lewis who turned to me. "Okay, Jenna, tell Dr. Bingham what you told us."

Clearing my throat, I leveled my gaze at Dr. Bingham. The lock of hair that fell in his face was rakishly angled across his brow. He held his unlit pipe in his hand, twirling it around in his palm.

"On Tuesday afternoon," I began in a quiet voice, almost a whisper. "I went to Luke Miller's house."

At the mention of the patient's name, a muscle in Dr. Bingham's neck quivered. He blinked as if in resignation.

"I saw your car there."

"What did you do when you saw my car?"

"Nothing. Just waited for you to come out of his house. After you did, I followed you to a convenience store where you stopped. Then I left."

Silence weighed down the room. Dr. Bingham stared at me, registering his disbelief. I held onto the arm of the couch as if for dear life. A tear rolled down my cheek and fell on my skirt. I'd sure miss working for this man.

"Luke Miller is my wife's brother," Dr. Bingham finally said in slow measured words.

My startled eyes found Dr. Bingham's face. The words he said hung in the air like smoke from his pipe. Everyone waited for whatever he would say next.

"You realize," he finally began, "I don't have to tell you anything about what happened that afternoon. Even though I want to cooperate with your investigation, Luke Miller is not involved in any way, absolutely not." He stopped, obviously thinking about what to say next.

I gazed at him, wishing to ease the pain so evident in his face.

He pushed the hair off his brow. "I can see, though, you'll never believe me until you hear it all."

Detective Watring had his notebook poised to write. Pete Lewis fixed his gaze on Dr. Bingham. The psychiatrist lifted his pipe, filled it with tobacco, and began the lighting process.

"Beth beeped me at about four o'clock on Tuesday afternoon. She was hysterical." Puff, puff, puff. Smoke filled the room. "Apparently Luke threatened to kill himself. This isn't the first time Luke's made a suicidal attempt, and the last time he almost succeeded." He blew out two matches he held between his fingers. "The poor man slashed his wrists when he and his wife split two years earlier. He was hospitalized at that time. I saw him for a short while and then referred him to one of my colleagues in Atlanta. It's difficult to treat your brother-in-law." Puff, puff, puff. Dr. Bingham looked more relaxed with the pipe between his lips.

"Family issues go back to Luke and Beth's mother, who was probably bipolar. Luke's stepson, Dave Fitch, operates a Golden Pantry near Luke's house. I called Dave as soon as Beth telephoned, and he agreed to meet me at Luke's.

"To make a long story short, Luke vanished before we arrived. Dave refused to go back to his stepfather's house, saying he was basically fed up with him. I tried to convince him to support Beth, who feels very alone in all this. But he wouldn't budge."

I bit my lip in an effort not to burst out with an apology. Poor Dr. B raced out there to help his wife's pitiful brother, and I'd suspected him of such awful things. How could I have thought he'd hurt anyone—this man who always bent over backwards to help me and would do anything in the world for his patients?

"Later that night," Dr. B continued, "Luke called me. After we talked for over an hour, I convinced him to come into the hospital. He's now at Athens Regional on the psychiatric unit. His attending physician is my colleague, Dr. Scott Snipes. You're welcome to talk to Scott if you think that's necessary."

"We'll need to do that merely to confirm your story. It's routine, of course," Detective Watring said. This time his voice sounded matter-of-fact, almost kind.

"I understand, Dr. Bingham, you also saw Fran Knotter as a patient," Sergeant Lewis said.

Dr. Bingham shot me a glance that caused a flush of heat to travel up my neck. Again I had divulged a confidence. I'd be an old woman with one foot in the grave before he ever forgave me.

"She was."

"Tell us about her problems."

"I'm not at liberty to do that. In fact, telling you as much as I have is a violation of doctor/patient confidentiality. Because Luke is technically not a patient, I don't feel as honor bound to him as with my other patients, even though I did see him several times, but Fran was my patient. Without a court order, I can't tell you anything about her."

"Can you confirm what we already know?" the sergeant asked.

Dr. Bingham shrugged noncommittally. Clearly he wasn't going to cooperate on this one. He banged out his pipe into the big wide ashtray on his desk.

"We understand she was involved with a ring of prostitutes. Did she talk to you about this association?"

I shifted in my seat.

Dr. Bingham blinked but didn't answer. As far as I could tell, this information didn't surprise him.

"We think the killer was a client of Fran's. Did she ever mention any of her partners to you?"

"Believe me, Sergeant Lewis, it's my desire to help you with this investigation. But, I've told you all I can." He stood.

I got up with the two detectives.

"We may subpoena her records," Lewis said.

"That's certainly your option." Dr. Bingham turned to me. "Jenna, ask my next patient to come in."

At least he didn't fire me on the spot.

Chapter 22

"HE'S A COOL ONE," SERGEANT Lewis told Detective Watring as we walked down the hall. "Get on the telephone to Judge Carson for that court order," the sergeant added. "I want the Knotter file ASAP."

My stomach ached. Now I knew what Judas must have felt like.

Before the two policemen left, Detective Watring turned to me. "I'll come back about five-thirty to take you home."

I nodded consent, but wanted the two of them out of there. If I could find a hole to crawl in, believe me, I'd be in it.

To Starr, who was watching us from her desk, I said, "You can go on if you want. I can take over from here."

"I'm fine," she said, and then ushered Dr. Bingham's next appointment to his office.

I returned to my post and answered the telephone.

Later I asked Starr if she was okay.

"Yeah, you?"

"I'm not sure. This is all too much. What did Detective Watring say to you? You looked whiter than your linen jacket."

"He told me about the murders." She looked away. "In gory detail. Then he asked if I knew anyone who might do such a thing. Patients or anyone. Of course, I told him that talking about patients would get me fired for sure. He questioned me about Steve. He wanted to know how long we've been married and all sorts of stuff about his childhood. Why in the blue blazes did he want to know about Steve? It was nuts. I was glad when y'all rescued me." She shot me a half-hearted grin.

"Don't you wanna go on home and give yourself a nice pedicure?"

"Actually, I'd rather stay here," she said, passing me a Diet Coke. "It's almost four anyway. How's your head?"

"It still hurts, especially near the bruise, but otherwise it's fine." Then I told Starr everything about Luke Miller. "It's important for you to know what's going on."

I figured Starr would soon be running the office alone. If Dr. B kept me after my treachery today—not only for divulging confidential information, but also for doubting and betraying him, it'd shock the fire out of me.

"How 'bout that Dr. B, slipping out there like that and not uttering a peep to either one of us. What was he thinking? Why didn't he tell you about Luke Miller being kin and all as soon as you showed him the file?"

"He did rule him out, probably thinking that was the end of it. He didn't realize I'd pursue him like I did." The Diet Coke travelled down my parched throat. So cool and refreshing.

"Yeah, like a bloodhound after a rabbit. He should know you well enough to know you'd never quit, especially after you got all tangled up with those murdered girls." She had unwrapped a brownie and munched away.

"I suspect he knows that now."

We laughed, but there was a jumpiness about Starr that wasn't like her. Maybe Detective Watring had done more than ask questions about Steve.

Ten minutes later, I texted Timothy and was amazed when he immediately called.

"Maybe this is a good time to contact you," I teased him.

"I had a break from school and headed home before anyone could catch me," he said. "Are any more cops coming to hassle me today?"

"Cops?"

"This morning two uniforms greeted me on my doorstep before I had a chance to finish my java. They flashed badges and scared the hell out of me. I figured they'd come to collect my back taxes—or worse still, my parking ticket fines."

I moaned and rubbed my temple.

"As it turned out," he said, "they took me down to the station—even lowered my head when I got in the backseat, like a genuine criminal—asked me a bunch of questions, like my whereabouts on such and such a night. Geez, sure could of used a date book. Then they took my fingerprints. I've still got ink stuck in my thumb. Is this about those murders, Jen?"

"Sure is. I'm really sorry. I should've warned you. Being my friend has its liabilities."

"Liabilities? You're not kidding. At least they didn't give me a urine test. I'm not sure they'd've been pleased with the results."

"Probably not. By the way, there is one thing that's been bothering me. Remember when we talked about Fran Knotter getting killed?"

"Sure."

"You seemed to recognize her name. Was there anything you didn't tell me that night?"

"Man oh man, you're as bad as the cops. No, I've never heard of the chick, her or any of them."

"Okay, no worries. You know me, just trying to make sure."

"When you're finished playing Miss Marple, call me, and let's go out somewhere downtown. That is if I'm not wasting away in some jail."

"Great idea."

I ended the call with an image of the police escorting Timothy to the station. The e-murderer might not kill me but he was sure rubbing out all my friends, one by one.

As I pulled folders for the next week, Starr straightened the waiting room—an endless job, especially on a day like today when patients rotated through nonstop. Several must've brought their children because magazines and books were strewn from one end of the floor to the other.

Finally Dr. Bingham's last appointment left.

I had about twenty minutes before the detective would come for me. I knocked on the doorframe to Dr. B's office.

Head bent, writing a note, he motioned me in. "Are you really feeling okay?"

"My head is, but I'm not sure about the rest of me. Talk about really screwing up. My friends hate me. Even my cats are mad at me. I'm so sorry for everything."

"Not your fault. If I'd had my head bashed in, I might have done exactly the same thing. You frightened us all to death. Have a seat. Let's talk." He reached for his pipe.

I lifted my shoulders, prepared for the axe to fall.

"I know I've been acting like a bear," he said, bumping the pipe against the trashcan with a loud thunk. "I'm afraid my mind has been elsewhere. Sometimes I'm not a very good psychiatrist, especially with people like you who are usually so capable. But that's no excuse. Can you forgive me?"

"Me forgive you?" *What's going on here? Have I entered the Twilight Zone?* "I'm the one who did exactly what you told me not to do. Shoot me at sunrise and put me out of my misery."

He chuckled.

"But you waited until you nearly got yourself killed. I shouldn't have let it go that far. Of course, you had no way of knowing about Luke. I'm such a stickler about confidentiality it often gets me in trouble. Luke is harmless enough, though, to everyone except himself."

"I'm sorry about telling them about Fran. That clearly was going to upset you, but—"

"Jenna, it's my job to protect my patients' privacy. But Fran's dead. Legally I can't release her files without a court order. That's how the system works. You really had no choice and that can't be held against you."

I played with the sash on my dress. "You mean I still have a job?"

"Listen," he said, looking at me sideways, "I made some mistakes and so did you. Can we start over?" He extended his hand.

I gripped it with a smile.

We walked to the front office. How could anyone ever doubt this man?

"You two kiss and make up?" Starr asked with a big grin.

I nodded and winked at her.

Dr. Bingham headed out the door. "I've got to swing by the hospital. See y'all on Monday. Maybe next week we'll have fewer surprises. I hope y'all have a quiet weekend. Since I'm on call, there's no hope for me."

Starr offered to stay with me until my ride came, but I chased her out the door because she looked wiped out. Ten minutes later the detective arrived, right on time.

Gathering my backpack, I settled into the front seat of a small red VW Beetle. Snazzy and quite a change from Sergeant Lewis' rundown Ford.

"Could we swing by my house first so I can feed the cats, shower, and change? It's probably gonna be a long night, right?"

"No problem."

Once home, Churchill and Stalin followed me to their bowls, anxious for their dinner. After filling their bellies, they joined the good detective while I went to change.

In the shower, the water bounced off my skin—so cool and purifying, I almost melted. The spray on my head wound felt wonderful. Gingerly cleaning around it, massaging soap close but not directly on the injury, I managed not to grimace too much.

I toweled off quickly and braided my hair, trying to think of anything —even my sister's impending visit, instead of what lay before me tonight. Although the dark circles under my eyes reminded me of recent events, having reconciled with Dr. B gave me some relief.

Refreshed and dressed in a pair of jeans and a fresh white shirt, I returned to the living room. The detective sat on the sofa, leafing through a paper on social aggression with Churchill draped across his lap. The cat let out an annoyed growl when his human pillow moved.

"We just put that tap on your landline," Watring said. "If you get one of those harassing calls, we'll try and trace it. We need to keep him on the line as long as possible. From what you described, he doesn't stay on long enough. But we can try. You really ought to get caller ID, living alone and all."

"I've never needed it before. I guess I didn't want to fork out the cash." I made a mental note to call the phone company first thing Monday morning.

"And you should keep your cell phone charged and on all the time," he added. "You never know when you might need to call for help."

"Thanks," I said, feeling a bit foolish but glad to have someone worrying about me.

* * * *

When we returned to Watring's VW, the air hung heavy with summer heat and humidity, threatening a storm. He maneuvered the car down an unfamiliar narrow street behind the university. The sun peeked out from dark clouds like a giant fiery ball as it began its descent into darkness. After another turn, we were back on College Station Road, a main thoroughfare leading to the east end of the campus where the detective turned into a fastfood establishment.

"I thought we might need some take-out. It could be a long night."

The drive-through line wrapped around the corner.

We opted to go inside where we ordered two hamburgers, fries, and Cokes. Eating burgers was not my usual fare, but tonight my stomach insisted on being filled with something more substantial than lettuce or yogurt.

"Are you sure you want to go through with this?" he said as we waited for our order. "I wouldn't mind turning around and running you back home."

Thoughts of curling up with a nice book and a cat on my lap and forgetting about all these murders tempted me. Of course, knowing me, I'd hear sounds outside my door every second and freak out each time my telephone rang.

"I'm really feeling much better," I finally said. "I haven't taken any pain medication all afternoon."

He looked me in the face. "That doesn't exactly answer my question. Do you wanna go through with this?"

A couple sat at the table in front of us, their heads nearly touching. A lone man ate a burger in a booth by himself. People milled all about. Life as usual. No murders to worry about. Detective Watring continued to watch me.

I shrugged. "The game's afoot, as Sherlock would say."

A uniform-clad kid announced our order.

"Okay then. Let's go," he said.

After another few minutes of weaving in and out of back streets, we stopped in front of a duplex on the northeast side of Athens. A child's bicycle leaned against one side of the double apartment. The other side of the brick structure looked dark, as if the inhabitants had left town for the weekend or had gone to bed early. A plastic encased newspaper rested on the front step. A dog close by barked when our car halted.

Exiting the VW, we stepped across the flagstones toward the darkened duplex. I snatched the bags of food from the detective while he unlocked the door.

Once inside, he flipped on the porch light and the hall light. The place smelled damp, as if it'd been closed for some time. Mail and catalogues cluttered the table at the entrance. The medium-sized living room contained furniture Quentin would call early attic. Two stuffed chairs faced a couch, flanked by a scratched coffee table and a couple of floor lamps. Ruffled Laura-Ashley print curtains hung from the windows. Neatly stacked textbooks sat on the coffee table. A television on a cheap stand, that looked tired from the weight, faced the couch. The mud-colored carpet appeared lighter in spots from wear.

"Penny wasn't killed here, was she?" My voice quivered. Images of the chalk drawing at Fran's house flashed in my mind.

"No, we found her in her car. The guys removed the crime-scene debris this morning. We sped up the process so we could get in by tonight. Except for the print dust, the place is pretty much as she left it." He went around and flipped on more lights.

Penny's answering machine message light blinked.

"Should we see who's called her?" What would it be like to listen to chipper messages from people who didn't know Penny was dead? *Yo, Penny, let's go get a pizza tonight. Call me.*

"I'll do that later," the detective answered. "Right now how 'bout we eat this food before it turns into a cold, soggy mess—"

Before he finished talking, the front door opened and a tall woman in her late twenties or early thirties glided into the room as if she lived there.

"Rosemary, I didn't think you'd be here till eight-thirty." A twinge of annoyance cut through his voice.

"Pete told me to come on." Turning to me, she extended her hand. "I'm Sergeant Erwin, but please call me Rosemary. You must be Jenna."

"That's right. Glad to meet you."

Rosemary's short hair bounced as she turned from me to her partner-in-crime. She was dressed in jeans and a short-sleeved blouse. She carried a burlap backpack over her shoulder.

"Apparently Pete doesn't trust me to be alone with you, Jenna," Detective Watring said with a sharp laugh.

Rosemary winked at me. "I can see why." She removed her pack.

"Have you eaten?" Watring asked Rosemary.

"Actually, I'm fine. Y'all go on."

My appetite had disappeared during the last few minutes, but as soon as I unwrapped the foil cover from the hamburger, it returned with a vengeance—the kind of hunger that used to overcome me at the beach after a day of swimming.

"I know we've been through this before, but I'd feel better if we could go over the plan once more," I said between bites, wiping a bit of mustard that oozed out from the corner of my mouth.

"Sure," Rosemary responded. "At about nine o'clock I'm going to make the call."

"We got the number from a young girl who used to work for the ring," Watring added. "She told us most of what we know even though she's not been involved for over a year."

"I'm to identify myself and say I'm ready for company, nothing more," Rosemary continued. "We understand no one will speak. After about twenty minutes, a woman calls back and tells me the name and time to meet my company."

"What if the procedure has changed?" I asked, washing down a French fry with Coke.

"That's a risk we have to take," Watring said as he dipped his fries in Ketchup.

"And you're sure no one knows about Penny?"

"Just the neighbor who found the body, and we notified her family, of course. But the press agreed to keep her name under wraps through the weekend," Rosemary said. "We told them we were having trouble reaching her parents. Unless someone from the media leaks it, no one should know, except the killer, of course. I think everything will be all right. I know all about the case, having specialized in crimes against women. This one, naturally, is of particular interest to me." She shifted her small, bright hazel eyes from me to Detective Watring.

"When they call back," I asked, stopping to chew the last bit of burger, "then what?"

"The visitor will come here at the appointed hour," Rosemary went on, putting finger quotes around the word *visitor*. "When the doorbell rings, I'll answer it. You and Rich will be out of sight."

"Unfortunately, the man who comes here may know Penny," Detective Watring added. "We understand the ring tends to encourage repeat business. In other words, this man may be one of Penny's regular customers. If so, I'll quickly jump out and take him downtown. If he doesn't know Penny, Rosemary will find out as much as she can about his relationship with Big Mama."

"What about me?"

"You'll be standing about here." Watring stood to the left of the dining room behind the doorjamb. "All you have to do is take a good look at the man and see if he's someone you know. I'll be right next to you." He returned to his seat at the table.

"Do you think the killer will come?"

"That's highly unlikely," Detective Watring said.

"But how can you uncover the murderer this way? I don't understand. It sounds like you're trying to break up the ring. I thought we were doing all this to find the killer." Doubt crept up inside me. Would this really work? As far as I could see, only if I recognized him. My heart thudded with anxiety. If I don't, the killer remained out there murdering other girls like Penny.

"We have to get to Big Mama's client list," Rosemary said. "And only one person has that list. Somewhere among those names is our killer."

"Besides," Watring said, "if you recognize the person, that brings us closer to the killer. And it saves us precious time that might spare another life."

I sipped my Coke and nibbled on the fries. My stomach was content except for the knot of fear that wouldn't go away. If the killer did show up tonight and I recognized him, then what? But why would the killer come? Maybe to check out what was going on?

Apparently noticing my discomfort, Rosemary said, "Don't worry, Jenna, Rich and I have been through many operations like this. We'll take care of everything. All you have to do is lie low. If you're able to identify the client, we'll be one step closer to understanding how you're connected to these murders and maybe to identifying the killer. If not, we'll try again."

We passed the next hour with small talk until it was time for Rosemary to make the call.

The two cops seemed unperturbed at how time crawled by slower than a crab on a beach. As for me, I kept tapping my cell to check the hour even though there was nothing any of us could do but wait.

Chapter 23

Twenty minutes later when the phone rang, I spilled my Coke across the table. Detective Watring began mopping the mess with the paper napkins from our dinner.

Rosemary put her finger to her lips to quiet us, and lifted the receiver. "Yes?"

A frown creased her brow. She placed the receiver back in the cradle.

"So?" Watring asked, still mopping.

"Mark 141 at eleven. That's all she said. It was a woman's voice."

I walked into Penny's kitchen for a dishrag. She'd decorated her windows with frilly yellow and green curtains. Pots of herbs sat on the sills. No dishes were in sight except for a single glass that stood next to the drain. The backdoor appeared unlocked.

I found the dishrag under the sink, dampened it, and returned to the dining room.

Detective Watring was wadding up the burger wrappers in small, tight balls.

"Did you notice that glass in the kitchen?" I asked, while wiping the dining room table.

"What glass?" Watring asked.

"I'm sure it isn't anything, but there's a glass next to the sink. And the backdoor looked unfastened. Surely y'all noticed that, and it's probably nothing, but I just wondered."

"The crime team covered this house, but they left in a hurry. One of the officers might have left the backdoor open."

"Maybe," Rosemary said, her eyebrows lifted.

"Yeah, maybe," I said. "But Penny strikes me as a neatnik so she would have likely put the glass in the dishwasher or rinsed it out and left it in the drain. Again, it's probably nothing."

"Humm." Watring leafed through his iPad. He pulled up a photo of the kitchen, showing the single glass near the sink. "I'll ask forensics to take a look at it tomorrow."

While the two detectives sat in the dining room, I moved to the living room sofa to read, hoping to distract myself. I'd brought a paper about how children model violent behavior. All the studies lent support to the belief that young people who observed violence in real life or on film or television could suffer from harmful social consequences. In one study, kids practically battered a doll to death with no remorse. It was pretty scary stuff. With what kids saw on television nowadays or played on videogames, it was no wonder coeds got themselves murdered. I prayed the person who came tonight would be someone familiar. It could be Steve or Michael or Timothy or Frank, maybe even one of Dr. B's patients that Starr and I overlooked.

The slam of a car door jarred me like the blast from a gun, sparking me to leap toward the dining room. My phone read ten forty-five.

Detective Watring turned off the dining room light. He motioned me to one side of the doorjamb. The silhouette of his gun pointed upward and ready.

A stick broke under someone's shoe. A soft knock sounded.

My heart thudded as though it might burst out of my chest.

Rosemary opened the front door. Low, muffled sounds came our way. It was impossible to make out the shadowy images through the door crack.

"Stop!" Rosemary yelled.

Detective Watring leapt from our hiding place. Rosemary raced out the front door. A car skidded away.

"What the hell?" Watring asked Rosemary.

"I don't know. As soon as I opened the door, he took off."

"Do you think he recognized you weren't Penny?" I asked.

We walked back into the duplex. "That's one explanation, not having gotten a good look at him. He seemed young and in good shape and took off like a cougar."

Before we could speculate further, another knock sounded at the door. Detective Watring shushed us and motioned for me to get behind the doorjamb. Rosemary resumed her post at the front.

"Are you Penny?" a deep gravelly male voice asked.

My mind raced with questions. Who was the first man and why had he run?

Once Rosemary and the man moved inside, he said, "Hey, let's turn on some brighter lights so I can have a look at the merchandise."

"You're Mark," she said, not turning on any more lights other than the one already lit next to the couch.

"Yeah, that's me. This is my first time. You'll need to show me the ropes," he said with a chuckle.

Mark stood in the middle of the floor. He had large, bulging nervous eyes with thick brows that grew into a single line across his forehead. He covered his receding hairline with a few dark, course strands. I'd never seen this man before. Frustration and helplessness settled over me while the scene in the living room played out before my eyes.

"How 'bout a drink?" Rosemary offered.

"That'd be great. Got any beer?"

"Sure thing. I'll be right back."

Rosemary must've stocked Penny's refrigerator earlier in the day. She glided right past Detective Watring and me as if we were invisible.

The man in the living room removed his jacket, carefully folded it on the arm of the couch, and sat down.

Rosemary leaned through the kitchen door. "Regular or light?"

The man touched his stout belly. "Better have a light one."

Returning with a glass of white wine and a beer, Rosemary eased down next to Mark and sipped her wine. If it had been me, I'd have guzzled the entire glass in one gulp for fortification.

"So this is your first time?" Her voice sounded soothing.

"Not my first time with a . . . uh . . . well . . . you know." Nervous laugh. "But I just signed on with Big Mama's operation."

Rosemary stroked the man's knee. "How'd you find out about the ring?"

Yuck. How can she stand this?

"Like everybody else. I've got a buddy. He works with me at the bank. It took eons to get approved. You'd think I was applying for a million-dollar loan." He laughed again, a deep gravelly sound, like his voice.

"Maybe your buddy is one of my clients?"

"Maybe." He drank some beer.

Mark wore a gold band around his finger. I stiffened, recalling Michael's indiscretions. Shivers of anger ran through me. He'd been with a prostitute exactly like this. Had he taken off his wedding ring or worn it boldly like this man? Swallowing hard and focusing on the scene, I pushed my thoughts aside.

"You've got a nice setup here. What's your major?"

"I'm a grad student in journalism."

"What made you decide to go into this, uh, business?" He touched her knee.

She placed her hand on top of his. *Good move—keeps her in control.*

"I needed more cash. My parents barely had enough money to send me to school. During my freshmen year, some of my friends were going to Lauderdale, and I wanted to join them, but my cash supply was low. So one of my girlfriends let me in on Big Mama. That's when I started."

"So, you're experienced." His fingers caressed her knee.

"You could say that."

I shut my eyes. The way the man's hand moved on Rosemary's leg made me want to throw up. Detective Watring stood as stiff as a statue, not moving so much as a hair. Was he feeling a similar revulsion?

The man reached up to caress Rosemary's cheek. "You've got mighty pretty skin. And you smell so fresh, clean. Not like the other's I've been with. They usually reek of cheap perfume."

"Have you met Big Mama?" Rosemary asked, taking another drink of wine.

"Not exactly."

His hand disappeared on the other side of Rosemary's neck. She circled her head as though to arouse him, but actually dislodged his hand from her neck to her shoulder.

"Two of my friends think they know who she is," Rosemary said, the wine glass to her lips.

"I doubt that. Top secret, you know. That's what's so great about this setup; it's so protected." He gulped more beer. "I talked to Big Mama on the telephone, and she interviewed me, face to face, except her face was hidden. She's a cool one. I'd say she's really hot, too, if I had to bet on it. Such a sexy voice." He leaned closer to Rosemary, his lips near her ear.

Rosemary giggled.

Oh my God! Disgusting.

He bent over to untie his shoes. "Who do your friends think she is?"

"You tell me. Surely you've got some idea. I've heard the clients know. We girls have a bet going to see who can discover who she is first. I'm determined to win."

"Maybe I'll tell you afterwards." He slurred over the word *afterwards,* stuffing it full of innuendo.

Then he lunged at her.

The lights in the room flashed on.

Detective Watring stood in the doorway, his gun pointed. "Get off her, you weasel."

Mark crumbled next to Rosemary, who jumped out from under him and produced her police identification. I remained fixed behind the doorjamb.

Mark's eyes darted from one police officer to the other. "What's going on?" he asked in a small, shriveled-up voice, no longer gravelly.

"Come on, mister. You've got a long night ahead of you and lots of questions to answer." Detective Watring tucked his gun back in his underarm holster and yanked Mark from the couch. He marched the hunched-up man out of the room.

Once the front door closed behind them, the tension in my body dissolved, and I collapsed into a chair.

"Did you recognize him?" Rosemary asked.

"Sorry no."

"I'm not surprised. He was too green." She scowled and bit her lower lip, letting out a long sigh.

"What about the other guy. Who do you think he was?"

Rosemary shrugged. "It's hard to say. Maybe one of Penny's previous friends who bolted when he saw me."

We gathered our things, and Rosemary took me home.

"How 'bout I spend the night on your couch," she said when we arrived at my door.

"You don't have to. I'm fine, and besides, there's a police car watching my house."

"Yeah, but he's just surveilling. It's no bother really."

I shook my head. "Really, I'm fine."

"I'll just give the place a quick look, then." She poked around my place, forcing the cats under the couch. "Everything looks secure and if you're sure, I'll head out."

"Honestly, I am. You're the one who's amazing. How could you stay so calm? I nearly lost my burger when that creep touched you."

"We're trained to detach ourselves, but it's not easy. Don't let my cool exterior fool you. I was dying inside. But when the stakes are as high as this, you can make yourself do anything." She looked my age, but she sounded years older.

"Can you believe a person like Penny would touch a man like that? Just the thought of it freaks me out."

Rosemary's upper lip twitched. "I learned a long time ago not to try to figure out why people do what they do. It's hard enough to understand my own motives. I can't help but think, though, if those young girls hadn't been messing with fire, they'd still be alive."

"So you think the killer is after the women in the ring?"

"Pete isn't convinced. But it looks pretty likely to me. We're all anxious to unsnarl the ring. We've been working on it for two years.

Maybe the guy we nabbed tonight will help." Her voice didn't sound hopeful.

"I wish he'd been someone familiar."

She patted my shoulder. "I'm confident we'll have this wrapped up soon. For the first time in months I feel as though we're close." She paused. "You sure you don't want some company tonight?"

I shook my head. "I'll be fine, but please tell Detective Watring to call me and let me know what's going on."

When she left, I tumbled into my bed, fully dressed.

Images of a young man who ran like a cougar and killed like a lion kept me tossing and turning until sheer exhaustion overtook me.

Chapter 24

THE NEXT MORNING, MY TELEPHONE rang at 7:15 a.m., jarring me out of a sound sleep.

"Where the bloody hell have you been?" said a familiar English voice. "I've been daft out of my mind with worry."

"Hi, Quen. Sorry, I had something to do last night."

"I rang until one a.m., both your mobile and landline. Then Alan threatened to castrate me if I rang you up one more time. By then I'd rung up everybody, except your mum, but let me tell you she was next on my list if you hadn't appeared by this morning. Frank told me you said you might go out of town. Surely you'd have said something to me, wouldn't you have, love? By the way, he didn't seem to know about you getting bashed in the head—"

"I didn't tell—"

"I even rang the hospitals," he continued as if I'd said nothing. "For all I knew you passed out somewhere and were dead on the street. Starr told me you left with Detective Heartthrob, but that was hours and hours before. And you're supposed to be resting. Then I thought maybe you unplugged your phone and turned off your mobile. If it hadn't been for Alan, I'd have called the authorities and sent out the troops, mind you. Thank God you answered now, love."

"For heaven sakes, calm down. I'm okay. Really, Quen, I'm fine. But, now that I'm awake, you want to do me huge favor?"

"Anything."

"Go by Bojangles, pick up an extra large coffee and a couple of biscuits. Bring them here. I'm ravenous, and there's nothing to eat in this house except cat food. Let's have breakfast and talk."

"Can Alan come? He's feeling left out, and he's bitchy as an old bat."

"Sure. But give me thirty minutes to shower."

I hung up and quickly responded to the cats who'd been crying and walking all over me. The felines gobbled down salmon-flavored Tasty Buffet as if they hadn't eaten in a week, and shot me glances that rivaled the most adept Jewish mother.

Once the cats were fat and happy, I jumped in the shower. The warm stream running through my hair was as relaxing as a massage from expert fingers. I scrubbed, hoping to remove every trace of last night and what that yucky man represented. And to think, I'd been married to someone equally disgusting.

When I'd dressed and wrapped a towel around my head, the doorbell rang.

Quentin stood on my front step with Alan, one grinning, the other frowning.

"Did we interrupt your toilette?" Quentin asked.

"Just finished. Come in."

Alan had not seen my house and immediately began critiquing the decor. Although he said he approved of the white carpet and couch, he added, "This place must be a monster to keep clean. I'd have gone with a light tan in a Berber."

Who's asking for your opinion?

"Where'd you get this marvelous little print?" He fingered one of my wall hangings.

I unwrapped the towel and released my mop of damp hair. "I bought it in New York in the Village. Thought it had charm, and the colors worked in here," I said, and sipped the coffee, savoring the delicious effect of the caffeine.

Quentin passed me a biscuit and opened the hash browns.

"You've got great taste," Alan said.

Just then Stalin waltzed in. When the cat saw Alan, he stopped in mid-step, slunk next to the sofa toward me, and glared.

"Usually he's very friendly. This behavior is very odd. Maybe all the commotion has freaked him a bit. Sorry."

Alan's saucer-like green eyes glowered at the cat. "I'm not much of a cat person." He crossed his arms as if for protection and added, "I've been wanting to spend more time with you, Jenna. Quentin never stops talking about you." He tossed Quentin an accusing glance.

"Alan is a jealous chap," Quentin said with a laugh that sounded a bit jittery to me. "Don't let his banter bother you, love. How about a sausage biscuit, ol' man?" He handed Alan the peace offering without waiting for a reply.

Come on, guys. I'm the one chasing after killers and needing a little T.L.C. Have some respect, please.

"So did last night include a hot date?" Alan asked. He bit into the biscuit.

"You might call it that," I said, munching on a few hash browns. "I'm sorry Quentin overreacted."

"He's always wired when it comes to you, sweetheart. If I didn't know better, I'd swear he loves you secretly down deep in his gay little heart."

I didn't like the way he called me *sweetheart.*

Quentin burst out laughing, but his gray eyes looked steely.

"Have you seen the Adventures of Tintin, Spielberg's latest?" Alan asked me between sips of coffee and glares at Quentin.

Startled by the question, which seemed to come out of nowhere, I shook my head.

"Alan went to see it instead of coming to our show," Quentin said.

"Sorry, sweetie," Alan said. "But I had better things to do than to watch a bunch of women show off their navels and swivel their buns. No offense, my dear. And that Jamie Bell was worth dying for even in animation. Trust me."

Quentin threw down the biscuit. "I've had about enough of this rubbish. Something is gnawing at you, so spit it out."

I eased further down the couch, relinquishing my place in the middle of this domestic argument. The scowl on Alan's face could strike a hapless passerby dead. What possessed me not to tell Quentin to come alone? Next time I'd know better.

Alan turned to me. "Sorry, we've been at each other like an old married couple, and last night we didn't get much sleep." To Quentin, he said, "Let's talk about this later."

We finished eating in relative truce-like silence.

"I'm gonna pop over to the track for a jog," Alan said, rising and stretching his long legs.

"You're going to jog after gobbling down three sausage biscuits?" Quentin asked with his good ol' motherly tone of voice.

"All the more reason. I'll be back in about an hour."

Once Alan left, Quentin expelled a long sigh. "Whoosh."

"I believe I've messed things up with you and Alan." I patted Quentin's knee. "Sorry."

"Not your fault. It's been coming. I can always tell. I'd hoped this time things would be different. He's been nagging me like a shrew, night and day. Tell me, love, what's wrong with this picture—me escaping my own house to get away from his harangue?" He took a breath and turned toward me with a look full of concern. "You don't need all this rubbish. Are you really feeling better?"

"Fine."

"No more headaches?"

"Nope, and I quit the medicine yesterday afternoon. I'm gonna start driving even though your Ben Casey doctor probably would prefer my waiting a little longer. But, with no headaches and just a little soreness where he hit me, it seems foolish to sit around here full of pain meds."

"I suppose you can't tell me where you were last night?"

I shook my head. "Not yet. Maybe later."

"And I suppose it had something to do with Detective Heartthrob?"

The smile that leapt to my face at the mention of the detective answered Quentin's question.

"You lucky little devil," he said with a pout. "Are you doing any snooping tonight? The thought of spending the evening at home with Alan is giving me the willies."

"Quen, you're going to have to face things with him. Tonight is as good a time as any."

"Does that mean you're not snooping tonight?"

I grinned and cocked my head at him. "I've really got to study. I've barely opened a book since my head got creamed. And I sorta promised Frank a date tomorrow night."

"Yeah, yeah, rubbish, rubbish," he said in a singsong voice.

I gathered the breakfast debris from the coffee table. "By the way, Quen, you remember that list Detective Watring gave me the first morning we were in his office?"

Quentin rose from the couch, dug into the back pocket of his too-tight jeans, and retrieved tattered slips of paper. "You mean this?"

"How the blazes? It was in my backpack. I know it."

He scrunched up his face like Lou did when caught doing something naughty. "You did, didn't you? When I rummaged through your things for your keys after you got your head bashed, there it was and having recognized two of my students on the list, I took it. Didn't think you'd mind, and with all the excitement, I suppose it slipped my mind." He glanced at the shredded pages. "What is it a list of anyway?"

"Did you show or tell anyone about this list?"

Silence.

"You told Alan, didn't you?"

"Jen, he quizzed me about where I was and what I was doing. When I told him, he huffed and puffed, making me out for a liar. He demanded to know who the new man in my life was. To prove there was nobody, I showed him the list with the copper's logo at the top."

"Did you convince him?"

"Dunno. He snatched the papers from me. That's why they're in such a mess. We wrestled like a couple of dogs over a bone. He screamed at me and threatened to tear up 'my precious evidence'—his words, not mine. The bugger tore up the last page. Sorry. I copied over as much as possible but had to leave off the names that got ripped off. I almost chucked it afterwards, but it occurred to me the cops might ask for it back. Alan really has a temper."

"Why do you think Alan got so upset?"

"Beats me, love. My guess is he's angry at me for being gone so much. Of course, he doesn't realize I leave because he's driving me mad. How am I going to tell him that?"

A troubling thought hit me. "Alan knows all about computers, doesn't he?"

"I've told you he's a real techno nerd. I'm an idiot compared to him. I can't tell you much about what he does, but he's always talking computer stuff. I asked him about helping you block those anonymous messages. He didn't know much about that, though."

I paced in front of the couch. Both cats had curled up in the stream of sunshine that fell across the carpet. They lifted their heads at the sight of my restlessness.

"Quen, I've got to call Detective Watring. This might not be anything, but Alan could be involved in all this."

"You mean the murders?"

"Who knows exactly? But Alan's behavior doesn't make sense. The detective will know what to do."

Quentin followed me into the kitchen where I retrieved my cell and punched in the detective's number.

I eventually got through to the policeman and quickly told him about Alan.

He expelled a long sigh. "Okay, tell me his name and address. We'll check him out with the others." He sounded rather unimpressed with my detecting skills.

"But don't you think it's odd he tried to tear up the list of the ring?" I spoke as if the detective hadn't heard me the first time.

"Not really, Jenna. Ever heard of a lover's quarrel? When people get mad, they act in funny ways. How would he know what the list was? Now, give me his name."

"Quen, what's Alan's last name?"

"Masters."

I told the detective, and added, "I could get his fingerprints if you want them. He had breakfast here." Why was Detective Watring acting so peevish? Clearly Alan might be a suspect.

"Later, maybe."

I bit my tongue, annoyed and frustrated. "How are you doing with, you know?"

"As we suspected, he doesn't know a lot. Rosemary wants to try again this evening. We're hoping our mysterious visitor might return."

"Tonight?" My stomach did a somersault as the word squeaked out.

"You don't have to come. If we capture anyone, you can identify him here. We were hoping to save a bit of time, but if that'd suit you better?"

I twirled my hair not sure about going through it all again. Images of the three dead girls popped in my head along with Rosemary's words about being close to solving all this. I had such a small part to play.

"No, I'll come. Text me later."

When I ended the call, Quentin glared at me. "So, you're going to study, now, love, are you?"

I shrugged with my palms open.

"You're up to mischief. I feel it deep down in my bones."

Just then the front door opened, and Alan sashayed in all flushed and sweaty. I stared at him as if I'd never seen him before.

"I'd better not sit on your good furniture," Alan said. "Ready?" he asked Quentin.

"Thanks for the breakfast, y'all," I said.

Before departing, Quentin whispered in my ear, "Be careful."

My stomach tightened as my best friend walked down the sidewalk and got in the car next to Alan.

"You, too," I whispered.

Chapter 25

As soon as the boys left, I played the messages from the evening before. My mother complained that Lou wouldn't be home when expected and for me to call. Doreen telephoned to invite me to dinner on Thursday with her and her new boyfriend, Marcus.

"Bring Frank if he's behaving himself," she said with a laugh.

There was one hang-up, deep breathing, not long enough for any trace. Quentin left several pleas to "ring him up."

Finally Starr's anxious voice said, "Steve's been acting funny. Call when you can."

I telephoned Starr first. Her machine clicked on with a cheery "Hello," and promises to return my call. "Starr, your message said to call. Sorry. I've been covered-up with school stuff, and tonight I'll be out again, but call when you can." With a frustrated grunt, I hung up.

After a quick call to Doreen accepting her dinner invitation, I dialed Michael's number. He answered on the third ring with a breathless hello.

"Hold a sec," he said, "I was riding my stationary bike. It'll take me a minute to catch my breath."

Once he came back on the line, I said, "I've got to ask you something. Now, don't take offense at this. I'm not trying to delve into your personal life, but—"

"Good heavens, Jenna. You sound like my mother when she asked me if I'd 'done it' with Janie Norris."

I smiled. My ex-mother-in-law asking him that question struck a funny nerve. "Surely she didn't come out and ask you."

"You better believe she did. She's a woman of steel."

"What'd you say?"

"I fail miserably when lying to my mother. She sees through me in a second. So, I fessed up. 'Yeah, Mom, I screwed the luscious little sixteen-year-old in the back of a truck during a hayride with the good ol' Southern Baptists singing, 'Praise the Lord.' And Mikey liked it.'"

"Michael, you're hopeless!"

"What can I say? Now, what's up?" He'd caught his breath but was still doing something, probably untying his sneakers. No comment about a police visit, a good sign.

"I'm calling about those anonymous e-mails and the murder of three women."

"Three?"

"Yeah, another was killed on Thursday. Apparently the murdered women were involved in some kind of a sex ring made up of student prostitutes. Do you know anything about this ring?"

Silence. Whatever Michael had been doing, he'd stopped.

"All the victims were, uh, working as prostitutes?" he finally asked, his voice no longer holding a teasing edge to it.

"Do you know anything about this ring? It's important."

He sucked in air, not like the gulping pants from a moment before.

I waited.

"How much of this do you want, Jenna?"

"Everything."

"Some of what I'm about to tell you might hurt. Are you ready for that?"

"You can't hurt me anymore than you already have. Trust me. I'm ready for whatever you've got to say. Answers, Michael. C'mon."

The hum in the background, probably some baseball game on Michael's TV, stopped. I braced myself for what my ex-husband might say. A sharp pain shot across the side of my head, either leftover from Thursday's battering or the beginning of a tension headache.

"A number of years ago," he began, "I don't remember exactly, a friend told me about the ring. Basically it's an organization of prostitutes. But not your usual, run-of-the-mill whores. These girls are classy. They're all students or former students, young, clean, fresh, and hot. The ring began at the brink of the AIDS scare in the early eighties when three prominent men decided they wanted clean sex without ties. What better resource than UGA coeds? They formed a bond. A couple of years later others joined but only after intensive screening. They wanted to protect the young women, and also their own reputations were at stake. About fifty men participate now and some twenty-five young prostitutes, men and women, I might add.

"There's someone called Big Mama."

"The so-called founders needed someone to run the organization. They contacted a woman, someone trustworthy, beyond reproach, and with time on her hands. Whoever that person was stayed on up until around five years ago. At that point another person took over." Then he stopped, and in a lower voice, almost a whisper, he added, "I became part of the ring not long before you dumped me. But I'd wanted in for years. It's sort of a status thing. I'm sorry."

Although not surprised by this confession, I massaged my temples. The pain in my head quickened. "Did you know Marty Meeks or Fran Knotter?"

"I knew Fran. Usually we visited one girl, and we stayed with her, unless the client insisted on a different arrangement or, of course, when the girl graduated, but all that was worked out ahead of time. I couldn't see Fran more than once a week. Any rule violations and you were out, no questions asked. My last visit with Fran was December before leaving for Tennessee. I didn't know she'd been killed until my trip to Athens last week. Frank told me."

"Frank?"

"Jenna, Frank's been part of the ring forever. People say his father was one of the original three men who started it. Learning you were dating him shocked the devil out of me. I guess what goes around comes around."

Easy for you to say. My grip on the phone tightened until my fingers ached. Frank—a man I had considered marrying. My God! How could he? Were all men jerks? Or was it my inept selection skills?

"Are you still there?"

"Yeah," I managed to choke out.

"I don't know how active Frank is any more. We all tend to come in and out, so to speak. You need to ask him. I'm sorry about telling you."

"Frank knew Fran?" My mind tried to fit all the pieces together.

"I'm not sure how well he knew her, but he knew she was part of the ring, and that she'd been killed. We are all wondering why our girls were being attacked. Everybody's jumpy."

"Who else is involved?"

"I don't know. Really. None of us know the names of more than a handful of people. We have our suspicions, but nothing for certain. Sometimes at parties people let a word slip here and there. But really, I've no way of knowing for sure."

What a bunch of crap. I didn't believe a word of it.

"Is Steve involved?"

"Really, I've no idea. Ask Frank. He knows Steve better than me. Somehow I can't imagine them letting Steve in, though. Most of the guys are—what's the word—more discreet than Steve. We're people who can be trusted. Steve runs off at the mouth too much."

"Michael, the police believe whoever is killing these coeds is connected to the ring. They're trying to find out who Big Mama is because she's the only person who knows all the ring members. Do you have any idea who she is?"

Silence.

"Please, Michael, this is important. If you know anything, it might save someone's life. For God sakes, think about what happened to Fran."

"Jenna, I swore an oath on becoming part of this organization. It'd be like betraying my own family. Sorry. Don't ask this of me."

"For the love of God," I yelled into the phone, "you betrayed me when we were married without a second thought. This is a group of prostitutes." I was losing it but I couldn't help myself.

Silence.

I steadied my breath. "Michael, the killer is after me. He broke into my house. He captured Stalin. He bashed me in the head. He's threatened me in his e-mails. If you don't tell me, I may be next, and then how will you feel about betrayal?"

"But, Jen, you just said the murdered girls were part of the ring. You're not. Why would the killer target you?"

"You tell me if you know so much, but one thing he's made clear, he's after me. By the time we figure out why, you may be coming to my funeral." *Calm down.*

Silence.

"He's been calling me. The last time he said, 'You're next.' I'm desperate, Michael. You're my only hope. If you ever cared for me at all, please tell me who Big Mama is."

"God, Jenna." Another pause. "Can I call you back? I need to think about this."

I shook my head in disgust. How many scotches would it take for Michael to chicken out?

Once the call with Michael ended, I rang Frank's cell. His voicemail picked up. I disconnected without leaving a message, too mad to trust what might come out of my mouth.

Images of Frank caressing me as if he really loved me flashed in my head. How could a man do that and still chase after prostitutes?

Ten minutes later my cell rang. It was Michael.

"What I'm about to say didn't come from me. You have to promise me you'll never say who told you this," he said without a greeting.

"I promise, Michael."

Silence.

I waited, imagining him running his hand through his dark, curly hair. Finally, Michael told me.

* * * *

I disconnected, grabbed my purse, and headed out the front door with a clear plan of how to bring the events of the last couple of weeks to an end. The policeman, who'd been glued to my front step most of the day, saluted me as I drove away. He or another cop would follow me, but by now it mattered little. My mind thundered.

"Why would you do this? You of all people?" I said aloud.

I drove west in pursuit of an upscale neighborhood off the main thoroughfare heading in the direction of Atlanta. I, of course, wasn't going that far.

This area had grown up over the last decade, really expanding in the last five years. It had been beautiful woods, full of deer, raccoons, and majestic pines. Woods still surrounded the undeveloped spots, reminding me of its past beauty, sans the large conglomerate stores.

The sun settled high in the sky and glared in my face. Traffic to the mall clogged the streets.

While stopped at a light, I called Detective Watring on my cell. He was unavailable, but I left a message. In all probability my "surveillance" would be on my tail, but not wanting another lecture from the good detective and considering my last experience with police protection, I decided to take precautions.

As I wrapped around the traffic onto Xavier, a curvy, wooded street with sprawling, two-story houses and immaculate lawns, my hold on the steering wheel tightened, and my heart rate accelerated. Could I do this without yelling like a banshee? My foot pressed harder on the gas. Sweat trickled down my neck both from the heat and my internal tension.

After two more turns, a two-story, white brick house with ivy crawling along the outer edges loomed into view. The lawn, fed by summer rains, looked better than a luscious green carpet. Boxwoods of perfect dimensions formed a neat green wall around the edge of the driveway and the front steps. Leafy azaleas mixed with spirea bursting with tiny pink blooms lined the front of the house, and dogwoods sprouted green leaves throughout the yard. A huge magnolia shaded the side porch. The perfect setting for a blissful life.

Right!

A silver Mercedes sports car rested inside the garage, but the other space was mercifully vacant.

If she didn't do it for the money, what possible reason could she give for exploiting young college women? The anger inside me rose to my cheeks, warming them like beams from a sun lamp.

My tennis shoes squeaked on the narrow stone sidewalk flanked with pots of pink and red geraniums. I rang the doorbell. The ding, dong, ding, dong, ding was followed by bark, bark, bark. The door swung open.

The woman's eyebrows rose in surprise upon seeing me. In that instant a memory flashed in my head of a cloudy Sunday afternoon and a woman totally clad in black, her face hidden by sunglasses and a wide-brimmed hat.

"How nice to see you. Niles is not here, but he'll be back any time now. He's finishing up at the hospital."

"It's you I came to see, Mrs. Bingham. May I come in?"

Her smile fell at the corners and her eyes narrowed, but ever the polite Southern belle, she said, "Of course," and stepped aside. "I've got a tennis date in a few minutes, though."

"This won't take long."

She wore a lemon-colored tennis shirt and a matching skirt, both with the distinctive Nike swoosh. In her arms she held a small black dog—some sort of terrier breed, whose tail wagged like a flag in the wind.

Mrs. Bingham put the dog down. The animal jumped at my feet. His black eyes beamed with delight while he untied my tennis shoes.

She did nothing to tame the dog, instead she asked, "How about something to drink? Last night we opened a nice Chardonnay."

"A glass of wine sounds good." I sidestepped away from the canine toward the spacious living room.

Mrs. Bingham's tennis shoes squeaked against the polished wood floors. The dog ran at her heels.

In the five years I'd worked for Dr. Bingham, I'd never been inside his house. I seated myself in one of two matching pink and green Louis XVI chairs. The cushion did not give beneath me, forcing me to shift on the hard surface, uncomfortable both mentally and physically.

My surroundings consisted of a white, fluffy area carpet contrasting with mahogany-colored hardwood floors, a pale green chintz Queen

Anne couch, and a slate fireplace filled with gas logs. Instant fire with the turn of a switch. That figured. Images of Dr. Bingham lugging in logs from the back woods or pampering a smoldering flame like a Boy Scout were as far from reality as his wife's involvement with a ring of prostitutes.

A table next to the couch held a collection of family photographs all framed in silver. Among the smiling faces stood an unsmiling Luke Miller next to a tall stately-looking woman. Luke's first wife, perhaps?

Mrs. Bingham returned with a silver tray. On it sat two thin-stemmed glasses of wine and a basket of Triskets and Wheat Thins. She placed the tray on the coffee table and settled on the chintz couch opposite me. Ever the perfect hostess.

I marveled at the woman's cool beauty—blue eyes icy clear, like a frozen lake in the middle of winter, blond hair brushed away from her small heart-shaped face into a ponytail. A few gray hairs peeked out from the mass of light yellow. Tiny lines framed her eyes and mouth.

She sipped her wine and crossed her shapely legs, looking every bit the model prepared for a photo shoot.

I, too, tasted the wine more for fortification than anything else.

"I'm sorry to barge in on you like this." My voice cracked. All the hot anger that had propelled me out of my house and over here without a second thought had vanished. Now my heart thundered with a cold dread. What if Michael had been wrong?

I cleared my throat to begin again, and peering into the woman's frosty eyes, said, "I know about the ring."

No reaction, not even a blink or a flicker of anger crossed the icy exterior. Nothing. Mrs. Bingham continued to gaze at me as if her eyes controlled my next move.

Sputtering, I continued, "I'm really not interested in why you're doing it. And you don't have to tell me anything, but my concern lies with the young women who've been killed. And, I believe yours does too."

Mrs. Bingham broke her stare long enough to take a child-like sip from her wine glass.

"Whom have you told?" She spoke in a different voice, almost as if the words had been dragged from her throat.

"No one."

"What about Niles?" Three nervous blinks at the mention of her husband's name. Dr. Bingham didn't know. Thank God.

"I said, no one."

The woman's left cheek twitched.

"The police believe one of your clients is murdering these women. The killer is also mixed up with me, somehow. I came here to plead with you to help us find this person before he strikes again."

Or she, a little voice whispered in the back of my head.

My stomach dropped. *No way!*

The woman rose from the couch and walked over to a rather elaborate stereo system nestled in a console under the window. Quietly, she lifted the cover from a CD and placed the small disc in the system. The room exploded with Chopin's "Heroic Polonaise."

I squirmed.

Maybe she really was the killer. I'd convinced myself the murderer was a man. Lines from the e-mails ran through my mind in an effort to determine if anything gave away the writer's gender. Nothing.

Mrs. Bingham stood with her back to me, swaying to the music while I planned a hasty exit, if the need arose.

Finally she returned to her seat.

"What can I do to help?" she said as if volunteering to head the next ladies auxiliary coffee klatch.

My breath whooshed out, unaware I'd been holding it. "I need to see a list of your clients." Pause. "I'll have to share that list with the police. But my guess is they won't insist on my exposing you. It's the list they want." A little white lie wouldn't hurt, now would it? She didn't need to know a police car probably sat somewhere outside her house and my handy-dandy detective knew my whereabouts exactly.

Mrs. Bingham stared at me. "I can't." The two words held complete finality.

My anger and frustration returned with a vengeance equal to the music filling the room. I slammed my fist on the table, shaking the silver tray and spilling wine from our glasses.

"I don't want to sound crass, but you have no choice. You will either cooperate with me and turn over your clients or I'll expose you for the madam you are. My presence here today is out of my loyalty to Dr. Bingham." My voice cracked again when uttering my boss's name. *God, keep me from reaching over and strangling the woman sitting across from me.* "Give me the list and give it to me now."

The eyes that lifted toward mine now contained sparks that matched my anger. "Who do you think you are, marching into my house and making these ridiculous accusations? No one will believe a word you're saying—particularly my husband who will undoubtedly fire you as soon as he hears about this outrageous outburst. Look at me. Do I look like someone who'd . . . who'd do whatever it is you're insinuating?" She stumbled long enough not to incriminate herself.

Proud of her little speech, she chuckled and smoothed back her already perfect hair. Her chuckle was supposed to convey disdain. Instead it revealed anxiety.

"Listen, we can make this easy or hard. It's your choice. People can identify you. How do you think I learned who you are? It's only a matter of time before the police find you in their own way. I'm trying to protect you from all that and from the devastation exposure might do to you and your marriage." *Not to mention saving another young woman from a ghastly death.* "In two minutes I'm going to leave here with or without your cooperation."

I got up. The wine in my glass remained half full, the crackers untouched. The scene looked like a set for an afternoon soap opera.

"Sit down."

She rose.

I remained standing. *Thank God for my height!*

"I don't like your attitude, Jenna. Your threats don't scare me one bit. You're a very small player in this game, and you know nothing about it. But I don't want to jeopardize Niles. True or false the publicity would destroy him. I'll get what you want for his sake, not because of your threats."

If that makes you feel better, whatever. I eased myself onto the uncomfortable chair as she disappeared from the room.

The black dog returned and bounded onto my lap. I scratched it behind the ears while it licked my hand. *The cats will die when they take one whiff of me.*

Mrs. Bingham glided back into the room with the grace of a puma. She handed me several sheets of paper. "I'm only asking that you handle this as discreetly as you can. Some very important people are listed here."

I took the pages without glancing at the names. Before walking out the door, however, I faced my boss's wife and asked the question I vowed to avoid. "Why did you do it?"

She lowered her eyes. Her lip twitched. "I was bored."

God, the little woman with time on her hands became the town's notorious madam. Unbelievable. "How'd you manage to keep all this from Dr. Bingham?"

"That was the easy part." She scoffed and looked away. "He thinks I'm consumed with my public relations business. He's real proud of my work. I have a private telephone line in my office where he rarely goes and my own cell. My calls are at night. He's usually not home until after nine and then he's too exhausted to pay attention to me. On the weekends, well, it's either golf or work. So you see—"

"I hope for Dr. Bingham's sake you'll reconsider what you're doing."

Without waiting for an answer, I hightailed it back to my Honda and cringed, imagining those icy blue eyes following me. But, when I turned, no one was in sight.

Chapter 26

ARRIVING HOME, EXHAUSTED—MY HEAD wound throbbed and my stomach ached—both signaling my extreme tension, I plopped on my bed with my arm across my eyes and listened to my voicemail.

"Jenna, if you're back, pick up," said Detective Watring. "It's important." Pause. "Okay, you're not back. Call as soon as you get this. Please."

I punched in his number. A strange voice, different from earlier, informed me he wasn't there.

"If it's an emergency, you can beep him."

Because I was returning his call, I didn't classify this as an emergency. "Just tell him Jenna called, and he can reach me here all afternoon. Thanks."

After dealing with the cats, who waited with uncharacteristic patience while I replenished their dry food, my curious little self flipped through the pages Mrs. B had given me. If this prize possession was going to lead us to the killer, I couldn't fathom how. Steve's name wasn't on it. Michael and Frank's names appeared, but that was old news. Maybe cross-referencing these people with our patients would uncover someone else. Right now, though, I didn't have the energy. What I wanted more than anything was to get this information to the police and then take a long nap. My head refused to stop reminding me of my recent unsavory run-in with this nut.

My cell rang.

"Thank goodness you answered," Starr said. "Where are you?"

"I'm home. What's the matter?"

She let out a sigh. "Jenna, I'm freaking out about Steve. He's been acting weird. Last night I told him what the police said—you know, all the questions about him and all. He went ballistic. You'd have thought I'd told him his best friend died. He yelled at me, told me to leave him alone, and slammed out the door. He didn't get back till some Godforsaken hour. When you didn't answer your cell and it kept going to voicemail, it occurred to my feeble mind that you'd said something about going home. I figured you were on the road and would eventually answer. Thank my lucky stars you did. I've been worried to death. Tell me what's going on?

"Geez, Starr. I've no idea."

"Steve's not mixed up in all this, is he?" My friend's voice shook.

Well, yeah, Steve might indeed be involved. His angry face when he glowered at me during Starr's party popped into my head. The memory of that look sent my mind reeling.

What I said to her, however, was, "I doubt he's had anything to do with the murders, if that's what you mean."

What I didn't say was that he knew Marty, Fran, and Penny. I'd discounted him because he seemed like such a wimp, but all that remorse could have been an act on the part of a very cold-blooded killer. He knew I was the only one who checked the e-mails at work. He had a key to our office through Starr. Maybe he was angry at me for spurning him. But, why kill the other girls? A distant, fuzzy memory formed in my mind.

"You'd tell me if you thought, well, you know, if you thought he'd done something stupid, wouldn't you?" Starr asked.

Guilt strangled me. "I would. Believe me." Gosh, I hated myself for not telling her about Steve's indiscretions. My promise to him seemed ludicrous now.

"I know that. Thanks, Jen. You've been a good friend to me." Her voice cracked.

"Starr, where is Steve now?"

"He left around eleven this morning, still fuming. I can always tell when he's pouting. Trying to sweet-talk him did no good, though. He looked as if he might haul off, so I shut up."

"Maybe my talking to Steve could help straighten this mess out? What do you think?"

"Would you?"

"Sure. Why don't I come over?"

"He may not be back. He didn't say when he'd be home. The way he slammed out the door, well . . . He's already been gone a long time." Starr's voice said she wanted me there.

"That's okay. I'll take my chances."

When I disconnected, my hand trembled. Feeling as if I were in a dark room with no windows, unable to breathe and no clear way to escape, I inhaled deeply to rid myself of the growing panic inside me. If Steve was the killer, maybe he wasn't after me. Perhaps all these deaths and the focus on me had been part of a deadly, premeditated plan, some sort of ruse. What better way to kill off your wife than to make it seem as if a crazed serial murderer had done it?

I grabbed my car keys and rushed out the door.

That memory tugged harder at me, like an annoying kid who wouldn't let go. It had to do with the night someone attacked me. As hard as I thought, whatever it was wouldn't come into focus. It just gnawed away—close, but not there yet.

I hightailed it to Starr's house, trying to avoid as many red lights as possible. As soon as my car turned onto Starr's street, and I faced her front door, the distant memory suddenly hit me. *Oh, my God!*

Backing up, I turned around, and pulled into a nearby service station. I sat there with eyes closed and imagined myself in Dr. Bingham's office when the lights went out, replaying the footsteps getting closer and closer, step, step, step. My eyes flew open. Just before the smell of onions and the arms grabbed me, there it was. I put my hand to my mouth. The man who'd hit me had limped. I grabbed my cell phone and beeped Detective Watring.

By the time I reached Starr's it was after four o'clock, but the sky was darkening with storm clouds.

I prayed Steve wasn't there. My goal was to get Starr out of the house.

After my knock, Starr opened the door instantly as if she were standing behind the curtain, watching for my approach. "Steve hasn't gotten here yet. Lord only knows where the devil he's gotten to. I'm worried out of my mind."

I followed her through the house to the small den at the back.

"I was watching television to pass the time." She switched off an old rerun. "He's never done anything like this before. I can't imagine what's gotten into him."

Starr wore a faded red blouse, cutoffs, and dingy tennis shoes. She'd gnawed away her anxiety on her newly manicured nails.

"I'm sure he's fine. Don't you want to go get a cup of coffee? We could head out to Jittery Joe's, just the two of us. I'll spring for a latte."

She shook her head. "I want to be here when he gets home. I can't leave, Jenna. But, won't you stay?"

My stomach tightened. "Okay, but tell me everything that has happened. Maybe we can figure all this out."

Starr collapsed on the worn yellow and brown couch that faced the television. *Glamour* magazine rested next to her hand, open to a beautiful female face advertising lip-gloss. Newspapers covered the small coffee table and spilled onto the floor. I perched on the arm of the chair in front of her, facing two windows. Outside, clouds covered the sun, and the wind blew against the pane, threatening a monster storm.

"There's not much more to tell than I told you on the phone." Absently, she picked up the papers and stacked them on the table. "All he said, was 'Leave me be.' Then he slammed out the door. That was last night. This morning he hardly spoke two words to me. I chattered away like my Aunt Glades, non-stop, hoping to sweet-talk him into opening up. But he glared at me. If looks could kill, I'd be one dead chickadee."

I shuddered at the thought. A bolt of lightning flashed, and thunder rumbled.

Starr gnawed at her thumbnail and continued, "When he left, he said, 'See ya later,' and then he took off with me hollering at him to pick up a half gallon of milk on his way home, but I've no idea if he heard me. He caught a major wheel when he pulled away. I spent the afternoon calling around looking for him, but no one has seen him."

Starr began turning the pages of the magazine without looking at them.

"That's been how many hours ago?"

"About six. But, he should've been home by three at the latest 'cause that's when the Braves game starts. He never misses his baseball." She gnawed off more nail polish. "Do you think he's left me?"

Her eyes widened to huge saucers, the pupils dilated. Black mascara smudges outlined the lower eyelids.

Rain pattered against the window.

I took her hand, wondering what she'd do when the truth came out. "Surely he'd tell you before he'd walk out on you like that. Did he take anything with him?"

Starr scowled. "A small box. It looked like a shoe box."

My God! I gasped. He hadn't destroyed the letters.

"What is it, Jenna?"

I gulped hard and took a deep steadying breath while gazing into my friend's worried face. The desire to tell her everything fought inside me like a bull against a cage. I opened my mouth, not sure what might come out, when—before I could say a word—the backdoor slammed closed with a loud bang.

Starr raced toward the kitchen. Me, I stayed glued to the couch, my throat dry, my heart pounding. Seconds later Starr walked in with Steve.

His hair was rumpled and wet, his blue, open-collar shirt drenched.

"If it ain't Jenna," he said, not smiling.

Another bolt of lightning streaked the room.

Steve jerked his head from me to Starr and back as if wondering what Starr knew. His red, splotched face, nervous eyes, and the roll of fat around his belly didn't seem to fit my image of a murderer, whatever that might be.

"Where'd you get to? I've been worrying my fool head off," Starr demanded, her hands on her hips. "Jenna came over to calm me down, you buzzard."

"I had something that needed doing," he said, glancing at me again. He stepped toward the couch.

I stiffened.

"Starr was freaking out." My voice sounded low, almost like a whimper.

Steve took another step toward me and raised his hand as if to strike. My body tensed. But he merely wiped the moisture from his forehead.

A loud knock at the front door diverted our attention.

"Police. Open up!"

Steve edged toward the backdoor as if he might bolt, but Starr moved next to him and took his hand.

Detective Watring bounded through the room with two uniformed officers in tow. All were dripping wet. Steve jumped away from Starr just as one of the policemen took his arm and wrestled it to his back.

"Steve Andrews," Detective Watring said, "you're under arrest."

"For what?" Steve choked out. His face crumpled into a terrified grimace.

"At the moment for assault," the detective said.

I grabbed Starr by the elbow and eased her away from Steve while a policeman placed handcuffs on her husband.

"I'm sorry, Starr. I called the police right before coming here."

Detective Watring recited Steve's rights. Then he asked, "Where were you on Thursday night of last week?"

"I d-do. . .don't know," Steve stammered.

"You were with me, hon, at Jenna's show, remember," Starr responded.

"Where did you go after the show?" the detective asked.

Thunder rolled. A bolt of lightning caused the lights to flicker.

Steve shot a panicked look at me and another at Starr.

"We were together all night, Detective," Starr answered for him.

"Are you willing to testify to that under oath, Mrs. Andrews?"

Starr's face turned a deathly shade of white, looking as if she was about to faint. Tears rolled down her face. She sniffed and confessed, "Steve went out after the show. I came on home by myself."

"But, Detective," Steve whined, "I just went out drinking at Chelsea's with some buddies. Check it out."

The detective glared at him. "Jenna identified you as the man who attacked her Thursday night."

The two other officers took hold of Steve's elbows and marched him out the door.

Before Watring left, I handed him the client list that Mrs. B had given me.

"This may no longer matter. But I'm sure Rosemary would love getting a hold of it."

"I'll deal with you later about where you got this," he said with a sideways smile.

"Is tonight off?"

"I'll let you know, but probably," he said, before exiting. "Looks like we're gonna be pretty busy."

After the house emptied of everyone except Starr and me, she said, "Lord have mercy," and started crying.

I hugged her while listening to the rain beat against the roof.

Once she quieted, I explained what prompted my calling the police. "Right before coming here this afternoon, I finally remembered something about the man who attacked me, and I knew it was Steve. I wish it hadn't been him, but it was. I'm so sorry."

"But, Jenna," she said through new sobs. "I can't believe Steve would have done that. Why would he? It doesn't make sense. Sure enough he acts crazy when he's drunk, but he's never hurt anyone. I've known him since grade school. There's no way he could have done that to you. There must be some mistake." Her eyes pleaded with me.

I pulled her closer but didn't respond.

Later, after rummaging through her meds for a sleeping pill and finally finding an old bottle of *Excedrin PM,* I gave her one and helped her into bed.

Once settling her more or less, I stretched out on the couch in the den. My mind raced. Detective Watring was certain the killer was part of the ring. But as it turned out, he wasn't. The police had also been certain I was the target for the next attack. Now I'm pretty sure it was Starr whom Steve planned to kill all along.

But why? a small voice in the back of my head asked. He seemed so concerned about Starr not finding out about Marty, genuinely panicked at the thought. Surely he'd divorce her rather than kill her. It wasn't as if Starr had a ton of money he'd get his hands on. Motive, Pete Lewis, had said was the hardest part to pin down.

I rolled over on the uncomfortable, makeshift bed, my feet dangling out from the blanket, and tried to push the tangled thoughts out of my mind. But the pieces still didn't quite fit. Steve attacked me, but that didn't necessarily mean he killed those three women. The key had to be in the e-mails and what they said. I needed to reread them in view of everything that had recently come to light.

At 2 a.m. I switched on the television, lost myself in an old Humphrey Bogart movie on the AMC channel and finally drifted off to a restless sleep.

Chapter 27

THE NEXT MORNING, STARR WOKE up with swollen eyes and a red nose, but she'd stopped crying. I fixed cups of tea with lemon and honey—my grandmother's remedy for anything that might ail you—and stayed with her while she drank it.

As we sat at her kitchen table like a couple of zombies, my tangled up thoughts bounced around in my head. Last night—late into the wee hours —I'd turned things around every which way until the pieces slid into place, but my mind kept saying, "Impossible."

"Do you think I ought to call the police station?" Starr asked.

"Detective Watring will contact you. Don't worry."

I didn't tell Starr my theory of who the killer was, and I'd bet my favorite cat it wasn't Steve. Yet, I had to be certain. Maybe it was someone else. *Please God let it be someone else.*

"Why would Steve do that? Why would he attack you, Jenna?"

With hands that wouldn't stop shaking, I put the teacups into the sink on top of the dishes from the previous day.

"I don't know. We'll find out everything when the police contact us."

"Do you think Steve slept in jail last night?" Her lips trembled with the words.

I squirted Palmolive Liquid into the sink and began washing the dishes. "Steve's going to need a lawyer. Do you know anyone?"

"Uncle Monty in Americus is an attorney. Maybe I'd better call him."

I wiped sudsy hands on my jeans. "I'd like to go home, take a shower, and feed the cats. Then I need to run by the office for a sec to check something out. Will you be all right for a while?"

Starr managed a smile. "Yeah. I'll be fine. You go on. I'm real sorry, hon. Sorry for what Steve did."

"I'll be back in about an hour." We hugged. "Then maybe we can go get that latte."

Poor Starr. Maybe when all this ended, Steve would grow up, but that seemed as likely as a white Christmas in Georgia.

I arrived home, exhausted but anxious to get to the office to re-read those e-mails. I fed the cats, cleaned their litter box, but didn't linger with them.

Preparing for my shower, I considered calling Detective Watring with my latest suspicions. Not yet. There was time. I had several hours. Besides I wanted to be sure before saying anything to anyone.

Once under the warm spray of water, I replayed in my mind the events of the last day. Mrs. Bingham responded in much the way I expected. She'd handed over the list of clients as if I'd requested her Aunt Edwina's recipe for apple dumplings. If confronted, the ever cool, confident Beth Bingham could say she'd never seen that list and had no idea where it came from, always a woman looking out for number one. How might Dr. Bingham respond when he discovered what kind of "public" relations his wife really dealt with? No snappy logos and marketing plans for the talented Mrs. B. Surely her less-than-politically-correct business wasn't the best advertisement for a psychiatrist. On the other hand, it wasn't going to be me to tell him.

I'd seen twelve doctors named on that list, including Dr. Coutler, one of Dr. Bingham's colleagues as well as fifteen well-known lawyers. Dr. Bingham's name didn't appear, but if Michael heard about the ring, surely he had too. Mrs. Bingham either blackballed her husband or Dr. B wasn't the kind of man interested in prostitutes—not that such a man existed, in my humble experience. Most of the names meant nothing to me. I lathered my hair and massaged the almond-smelling shampoo into my scalp. Suds fell at my feet.

Poor Starr. All Steve's past indiscretions would surely come out. I'd need to stick by my friend no matter what happened.

My doorbell rang. I quickly ran water through my hair but couldn't get all the soap out before the bell rang again.

Who in the world? Probably Quentin. Undoubtedly he'd missed me again last night and was having one of his fits.

Wrapping the towel around my dripping body, I sprinted to the door, fully expecting to see Quentin or maybe Detective Watring.

"Gosh, Frank. I'm in the shower. Come on in. I'm nearly finished." My heart nearly leapt from my chest as soap dripped from my hair and stung my eyes.

"Oh, sorry," he said as I raced from the door, leaving drops of water and soap in my wake.

My mind flew in forty directions, but I was determined to play it cool. Had the police car been there when I'd come in? I'd grown so accustomed to seeing it, I didn't even notice. Surely it was there. *God, please let it be there.*

"Don't torment the cats," I called to Frank.

I finished my shower and towel-dried my hair when Churchill peeked out from under my bed.

"You and me both, boy."

The cat's green eyes widened with worry, and his ears twitched alert to the sounds coming from the living room. Frank had put on a jazz CD that he must've brought with him.

I braided my hair, slipped into jeans and a T-shirt, and searched under my clothes for my cell phone. Darn, I'd left it in my purse in the living room. I quietly lifted the receiver of the phone in my bedroom. No dial tone. Oh my God! Where was that blasted landline when I needed it?

"Isn't it kinda early for beer?" I said, finding Frank lounging on the couch with his legs crossed, his eyes closed. He held a can of beer in his hand. It was just after 11 a.m. The music on the CD blared. A cigarette dangled from his hand.

Frank shrugged and took a swig from the can with a what-the-hell attitude. He smashed out the cigarette.

"So, what brings you here so early? Don't we have a date tonight?"

"I thought you were out of town." His voice was harsh, his look accusatory.

"My sister was supposed to come back from the Peace Corps, but her plans changed." Lying a little. "Furthermore, Starr had a crisis. I've been over there." Not lying a bit.

I lifted a book from the couch across from him and sat down, holding the book across my chest.

"And you didn't call me."

"I phoned you yesterday, but you never answered."

"You left no message."

"I had a lot going on. What'd you come here to do, cross examine me?"

Frank's Volvo sat in my driveway. The sun beamed off the black surface. Mrs. Sosbee's words flashed in my memory—*The big black shiny car came around again.* What made Frank's car unusual was the shine. It looked as if he'd washed and waxed it every day. Where the devil was my police protection? He seemed to always disappear when things got hot. Geez.

My eyes flew to Frank's face, still hanging onto shreds of hope that I might be wrong. He leapt from the couch and grabbed me by the arm.

"God, Frank, what are you doing? You're hurting me."

But by then it was too late.

"You can't get away with treating me like dirt. You've got a lot of nerve turning your back on me all the time like you do. I'm worth more than a piece of garbage you can toss in the trash. You were supposed to be special." He reeked of beer and tobacco.

Through my constricted throat, I choked out, "Please, tell me it's not true. Not you."

He grinned. His teeth shone like white tusks, and he released a low, guttural laugh. A chill ran down my neck as if a cold hand had touched me.

Frank yanked me toward the bedroom.

The cats scurried deeper under my bed.

Still breathing in my face, he pressed me against the wall and said, "I warned you, Jenna, but you ignored me. You didn't pay any attention to those e-mails."

"Frank," I pleaded, panting like a frightened dog, "how was I supposed to respond without knowing it was you? I got the e-mails and tried to make sense out of them, but—"

"Shut up, you bitch," he said, slapping me hard across the face, causing me to bite my lip and taste blood. Tears pricked my eyes.

Through clenched teeth, he said, "You sound like the other ones. They tried to reason with me. They pretended they cared when they really didn't give a shit. How could they when they had one man after another? Just whores. And you're no better. I thought you were better, but I was wrong. You went in that house Friday night. You're one of them now. Admit it."

He pushed me down on the bed and glowered at me, his face inches from mine. With his right arm across my chest he pinned me down at my throat. Frank was a large man. My strength was no match for his.

I couldn't believe this was happening to me. How could I be so stupid? My whole being denied Frank could be responsible for all those horrible deaths. It was impossible for me to see, exactly like not being able to see Michael for what he was until it was too late.

He withdrew a long thin knife from a holster strapped to his leg and gripped it with his teeth like an Indian warrior. I gasped, but no sound came from my lips. He yanked a cord from the pocket of his jeans, turned me on my stomach, and tied my wrists. Then he flipped me back.

Once he had me tethered, he lifted himself off me and went to my bureau.

My heart thundered in terror, my arms ached and my nose ran, but I held onto one thought. *Get away!* I wiggled toward the end of the bed, my feet draping off the edge.

He opened a drawer. "Ah, you got some more. Good." He lifted my panties from the bureau, smelled and caressed each item, and folded the bras and panties in neat little stacks."It's amazing the different colors the whores had. Red, black, navy blue. Some with frilly lace. I even got a couple of garter belts and thongs." He pulled out a bra and folded it. "My mother had only white delicates and none of these disgusting bikini things."

I wiggled a little farther till my feet touched the floor.

"She made me stop sleeping with her things when I got too old. But her smell stays with me always, a delicate, clean scent." He paused and sighed, and folded a pair of my panties on top of the others.

"Why, Frank?" I lifted myself on my left elbow. One leg fell off the right side of the bed. But I'd stopped moving, afraid he'd pounce on me again.

He turned his pinched face toward mine. He was like another person, a person I'd never seen before. Where was the Frank I thought I might love? *How could I have been such a fool?* His usually neat hair was mussed, and his shirttail dangled from his jeans.

"You're all the same, stupid whores. Disgusting. I meant nothing to you."

He stripped off his shirt and flexed his chest muscles while I eased my other foot down and angled my feet and hips toward the door.

"Frank," I ventured in a small voice, "tell me more about your mother. You've never told me much about her." Even though I'd read her file, Dr. Bingham had dictated nothing of interest, certainly not that she had a lunatic son with murdering potential.

Frank threw down the bra he had at his nose. "Don't talk about my mother. She was the only decent woman who ever lived. I thought you were like her." His voice cracked, and he sounded almost like himself.

"How was I like her, Frank?" *Just keep him talking. Distract him.*

I inched my feet a little closer to the door but not close enough to dash out.

He lunged at me and bent his arm across my throat. I sucked in a breath and winced in pain.

"You're not like her. Never say that." His words sent sprays of spit across my cheek.

Blood trickled down my throat.

"No." I swallowed hard, trying not to gag. "I'm not like her. But you said I used to be like her. In what ways?" *God help me*.

His eyes glistened. He blinked. His pupils didn't look quite so wild. "You were smart and beautiful and tall, like Mama. She loved me a lot, but she only had eyes for my rotten father. Even the day she died, she called for the bastard. He was dead by then, but that didn't matter. My dad was an unfaithful prick of the first order. I would have never treated Mama the way he did, but it didn't matter to her. I told her what a God-awful son of a bitch he was. She slapped me and told me never to utter blasphemy against my father. She loved him completely. But he hurt her." He paused. "It didn't matter in the end because she killed him the same way she did my granddaddy. They deserved to die the way they did. Mama used poison on them both, with me standing in the shadows, watching. My granddaddy fought, but he finally gave up, gagging and screaming in pain. My dad was too drunk to know what hit him."

Frank's eyes turned fierce again. He squinted at me as if remembering he had me pinned under him. He put the knife to my throat. "I like cutting much better than poison."

I winced and turned my face from him.

"You were supposed to love me the way she did. But you couldn't, could you? You're too much like all the rest of the whores." He pushed my feet back under him.

"Why do you say I'm like the others?"

"You lied to me, over and over. I trusted you, but you made a fool of me. No woman makes a fool of Frank Sutter and gets away with it. You do understand that now, don't you?" He spat in my face.

I closed my eyes and tried to turn my head again, but he had me pinned down. Saliva ran down my cheek.

"You make me sick," he said. He took his finger and made an X-mark across my forehead.

A cat yowled from under the bed.

"That damn cat. I'm gonna off it as soon as I'm done with you. Count on that. Why didn't I kill it as soon as I nabbed the disgusting beast? My one mistake. My plan was to torture it. Send you bits of him." That frightening guttural laugh again. "Show you how stupid it is to love animals more than people."

"What happened to Stalin?"

"He tore out of the box when I opened it." Frank lifted slightly and turned sideways revealing the scratch marks along his ribs. Beads of perspiration lined his forehead and glistened on his chest.

My lungs constricted from the weight of his body against mine. "It wasn't you, then, Frank, was it? The one who hit me in the head?"

"What are you talking about, bitch?"

I swallowed. "On Thursday night after the show, someone knocked me out, but it wasn't you, was it?"

"That show was the last straw," he said without answering my question. "I watched all those men leering, calling at you like a cheap stripper. You gave me no choice because you were no better than a whore."

"So you came after all."

"Oh, yeah, I was there all right. It made me puke."

He lifted himself off me and leaned on his elbow while he took the knife and slit open my T-shirt, tearing my skin on the way down. I whimpered. Images of the way he mutilated his previous victims flashed before my eyes. Somewhere in the distance my cell phone rang.

"I'm going to do to you what that cat missed out on. I've looked forward to this moment for days now. The terror on your face is even better than the others 'cause you know what I'm gonna do, don't you. One of those stupid whores laughed at me, dared me to cut her."

If only I could be that brave. Hissing, growling, deep and menacing came from somewhere under the bed, but I barely breathed.

The knife touched the top of my jeans. Frank lifted the deadly instrument to slice through me. I clenched my jaw, held my breath, and braced for the pain.

Suddenly he yelped, leapt away, and dropped the knife on my chest. Stalin hung from Frank's back as if it were a tree. The cat's yellow eyes flashed, his claws tore through Frank's skin.

I dashed out of the room, crashing into Sergeant Pete Lewis. Detective Watring and two other policemen pushed past me as if I wasn't there.

Frank screamed.

Rosemary appeared out of nowhere and embraced me. "Hey, it's okay," she whispered into my hair.

My chest heaved in huge sobs.

"Come on. Let's go sit in my car." Rosemary untied my hands and rubbed my wrists where the cord cut me.

"No." Panting, I pulled away from her. Scuffling sounds came from the bedroom. Rosemary held my wrists too tight to break loose. She wrestled me onto the couch.

When Detective Watring emerged from the bedroom, he addressed Rosemary. "Get her something to put on." He turned to me. "You want us to drive you to Quentin's?"

"Stalin?" I choked out between sobs.

Detective Watring's tired face broke into a smile. "He's fine, a real hero, but right now he's cowering under the bed."

I hiccupped. "Thank God. And Frank?"

"We'll talk later. Go to Quentin's. I'll come there as quickly as possible."

Chapter 28

WRAPPED IN ONE OF QUENTIN'S terrycloth robes, I sipped tea in his living room. Everything inside my head bounced around in dim flashes as if I'd soon wake from a bad dream.

Quentin, Doreen, Lucille, and Alan encircled me while my story unfolded through my sore and constricted throat.

"I never much liked Frank," Quentin said. "He was too moody for my taste."

Lucille shook her head. "Frank seemed like a decent sort to me. He came from a good family and all. His father was a big shot at the bank downtown—president of the Chamber and all that kind of thing. Old Athens—good stock as my mom would say. Just goes to show."

"We may as well admit it," Doreen added. "Frank fooled us all. We were sure you guys'd get married and Quentin'd be the maid of honor. Yep, Frank's sweet-talk and baby face had us all eating out of his hand. Don't you even think about not seeing it, girl. None of us did."

I patted Doreen's arm. "Thanks, Dor."

Alan leaned toward me. "I knew Frank was trouble," he said, with a conspiratorial edge to his voice.

From the looks of things he and Quentin had made up from their little rift.

Quentin gave Alan a friendly push. "Rubbish. You didn't even know Frank."

"That's what you think. I've seen him hanging around the bars. He was a regular. Stuck out 'cause, well, you know." He cocked his head at Quentin.

"Always been a sucker for nice buns," Quentin said, rolling his eyes skyward.

"The boy looked sad," Alan added.

"Sad?" I said.

"He seemed lonely. Never spoke to anyone except when he wanted to cause trouble. You know, complain and stuff."

"But would you have pegged him for a crazed serial killer?" Doreen asked.

Alan shook his head. "Who's to say?"

I, on the other hand, had pegged Alan for a crazed serial killer, along with Steve and Michael and almost everyone I knew.

Quentin pushed my hair off my face. "You look tired, love. Maybe now you'll get some rest."

Rest? What's that?

The doorbell rang. Detective Watring entered. Quentin relinquished his place next to me. Lucille winked at me when she saw the detective.

"Hey, guys, let's go check those burgers we put on the grill," Quentin said.

"What burgers?" Doreen asked.

Alan and Lucille rose on cue. But Quentin had to jar Doreen off the sofa.

"He's the cop?" she whispered to Quentin as they all departed. "No wonder."

The detective's eyelids drooped with exhaustion. "God, what a scare you gave us." He dropped down on the sofa and, without preamble, wrapped his arms around me.

I collapsed in his embrace like a small child who had been lost and savored the strength of his arms and the warmth of his body next to mine. After a few minutes, he pulled away.

"I wouldn't let myself believe it was Frank," I said, sniffing back tears. "Last night I had this feeling about him. Seeing his name on the list struck me. Even though Michael told me about him and the prostitutes, his name on the list caused something to click inside me, like some kind of alarm. Then the e-mails kept floating in my head, how they said I was special and could understand him better than anyone else. Frank always told me stuff like that, but who would think? My own boyfriend, after all." Pause. "Last night, when my intuition kept saying Steve was all wrong, Frank's words floated in my head. Then he showed up at my door, just like that. I didn't know what to do."

"Tell me what happened. Don't leave anything out."

Sighing, I told him about the telephone call to Michael and what he told me—with the exception of Big Mama's identity—and how it took threats before Big Mama gave up the clients' names. "Then later as Frank's behavior kept creeping into my subconscious, well…I should have called you right away, but just couldn't quite believe it. I wanted to take another look at all the e-mails to see if there was a clue that might definitely give Frank away or prove it wasn't him. You know, like maybe the date he sent one or a word he used, anything. Frank wasn't supposed to just show up like that. We'd planned to see each other when I got back in town, but it wasn't definite, and not till later. I thought I had time to check out everything first. No telling what made him decide to come so early."

"Well, Friday night probably pushed him over the edge. He must've thought you were part of the prostitute ring."

"Yeah, he said as much."

I told him what Frank did to me and how he was about to stab me when Stalin leaped on him.

"That cat deserves a medal."

I sipped some very cold tea. "But I'm curious. What brought y'all to the house like a bunch of Navy Seals?"

He touched my hand again and rubbed it with gentle strokes that sent chills up my arm. "When you called about Steve, Pete thought you wouldn't need protection any longer. He took the surveillance off your house. We needed the man for another case. I argued with Pete till I was hoarse. Told him it was too soon, but he was convinced we had our man.

And he kept pointing out we didn't have the manpower to watch you forever.

"Pete and I drilled Steve for hours last night, nearly all night. He seemed like the type who'd break. Lucky for us he didn't have sense enough to demand a lawyer. We used every minute we had, going over and over with him what he'd done. We showed him the crime scene photos of the dead women. That's when he broke down and cried. I thought we had him then. It was after three a.m. Everyone was exhausted. But he still insisted he wasn't a murderer. At nearly four, we gave up. We woke him this morning at six and started over. He admitted attacking you. He wanted you to stop snooping around because if Starr found out about Marty, it'd ruin his marriage. He told us about his affair with Marty and the letters he'd destroyed Saturday morning. But he continued to insist he didn't kill anyone."

"Poor Steve."

"Poor Steve? How can you say that? He gave you a deadly blow on the head. That's assault and it's pretty serious."

"Yeah, but, I can't help but feel sorry for him. He must've been scared to death."

Detective Watring sighed. "By eight o'clock my doubts grew stronger about him murdering those girls. Surely he'd have broken if he was going to. We were on him like gnats on a rotten apple. I urged Pete to cool it. But Pete didn't want to. When we got the report on the prints on that glass you found at Penny's and they matched Frank's, Pete started having doubts too. Ten minutes later Officer Kelley called to say he'd finally got a hold of that Samson guy. You remember?"

"Do I ever!"

"He was hard to locate, never at his place. Anyway, we got the photo you mentioned, and sure enough, Frank Sutter was standing pretty as you please right next to Martha Meeks. By now I'm going crazy. We've linked him to two of the victims and with you." He paused and looked away. "Although still not sure we had enough evidence without any witnesses and no murder weapon, there were too many links to Mr. Sutter to just shrug him off. I had to get in touch with you.

"When I called Starr's to warn you, she told me you went home. Officer Kelley went to Sutter's and found him and his car gone. And you didn't answer you cell. That's when we took off to your place as fast as we could manage. Pete didn't stop me."

We both stared at each other for a few minutes.

"Jenna, I don't want to come on too strong just after you've had such a shock, but you really should have called me as soon as you became suspicious of Frank."

I looked at my bare feet. "You didn't think much of my suspicions of Alan."

He chuckled. "That was different. He'd never been a suspect. Frank was one of our suspects."

"What would I have told you? All I had to go on was a feeling. Frank had changed. He was still loving, but he'd become so persistent, almost obsessed with me. It wasn't until I connected him in my mind with the e-mails that my suspicions mounted, but by then it was too late."

The detective nodded. "You'll need to learn to trust me."

"And Frank? Is he in jail?"

The detective's grip on my hand tightened. "I'm sorry to say this, but he's dead. He stabbed himself in the neck seconds after we barged into the room. I'm really sorry, Jenna."

I stared at him while the words sunk in. "God." Poor Frank. It was still hard for me to believe.

"It's over, Jenna," he said, rubbing my fingers with his thumb.

I looked away. My heart raced. When would it really be over for me? "I suppose it's time to start cracking the books. I've got papers due, Omigod, tomorrow."

"Before you become a student again, there are a couple of things I'd like to ask you so we can close this case."

"Anything."

"Is Big Mama related to a certain good-looking shrink who has eyes for his office manager?"

I used a gesture to zip up my lips.

"Just know, we'll try and handle that matter as discreetly as we can."

"The other thing?"

"Would you call me Rich?"

A warm flutter moved from my stomach to my chest.

"Whatever you say." I paused and then flashed him a big smile. "Rich."

"Come and get it," Quentin yelled from the kitchen.

ABOUT THE AUTHOR

JOAN C. CURTIS is an award-winning writer who has published 6 books and numerous stories. Readers compare her to the great Southern writer, Fanny Flagg. "She writes characters and a story that will stay with you."

Her debut mystery/suspense novel, *The Clock Strikes Midnight*, won the first place Royal Palm Literary Award for literary/mainstream fiction. The *e-Murderer* won the GOLD for mystery, Global e-Book Awards.

Joan has been an avid reader for as long as she can remember. She reads all kinds of books, including women's fiction, mysteries, biography, and nonfiction. Mystery/suspense with a psychological twist is exactly the kind of book Joan loves to read.

"I write about characters who remind me of myself at times and my sister at times, but never fully so. My stories are told from a woman's point of view with a destiny. Characters drive my writing and my reading."

Having grown up in the South with a mother from Westchester County New York, Joan has a unique take on blending the Southern traditions with the eye of a northerner. She spent most of her childhood in North Carolina and now resides in Athens, Georgia.

Did you enjoy e-Murderer?

*If so, please help us spread the word about
Joan C. Curtis and MuseItUp Publishing.*

It's as easy as:

*•Recommend the book to your family and friends
•Post a review
•Tweet and Facebook about it*

*Thank you
MuseItUp Publishing*

MuseItUp
PUBLISHING

Made in the USA
San Bernardino, CA
04 June 2017